THE FAR SIDE OF DESIRE

THE FAR SIDE OF DESIRE

Ralph Glasser

This first world edition published in Great Britain 1994 by
SEVERN HOUSE PUBLISHERS LTD of
9–15 High Street, Sutton, Surrey SM1 1DF.
First published in the USA 1994 by
SEVERN HOUSE PUBLISHERS INC., of
425 Park Avenue, New York, NY 10022.

British Library Cataloguing in Publication Data
Glasser, Ralph
  Far Side of Desire
  I. Title
  823.914 [F]

  ISBN 0-7278-4678-7

Typeset by Hewer Text Composition Services, Edinburgh.
Printed and bound in Great Britain by
Hartnolls Ltd, Bodmin, Cornwall.

Chapter 1

Leo asked himself how he could have been so foolish as to bring his thirteen-year-old son Gideon with him to Rome. This trip had been prescribed as therapy, for him to "relax" – as Moorlock his doctor had put it knowingly – feel completely untrammelled, let fancy take him where it would, forget about London, wife, children, home, business. So why had he brought Gideon along? Quick-witted, sensitive Gideon, who missed nothing?

The trip had come about so suddenly that it seemed to have happened by itself; an act of obscure destiny. At breakfast a few days before, cross with himself for being out of sorts, he had mentioned to Miriam that he had not slept well. At once he regretted the words. In his upbringing, being sorry for yourself had been a sin. And Miriam, brisk and clever and determinedly self-sufficient, had no patience with "things sent to try us", meaning anything that threatened to deflect her mind from the affairs of her law practice or the tidy management of the household, in that order. She replied absently, but sharply, for she was about to rush off to a client meeting, "Darling, if you say that once more I'll scream! For Heaven's sake go and see Moorlock and get him to give you some sleeping pills. Now I *must* fly."

1

He started to say, "I didn't know I *had* said it before . . ." but she was out in the hall giving Estrella, the daily woman, last minute instructions. Then the front door banged shut behind her.

He gulped the black coffee, knuckled his eyes, tried to lift the weight of tiredness. She might be right! It might be something a few nights on sleeping pills would deal with – but knocking yourself out chemically had always seemed barbaric. However, a different thought was forming in his mind – a shadow of a thought as yet – unacceptable but insistent, telling him that his condition was not physical. He tried to face it. He could think of nothing that especially troubled him, no business worries – his business touch was good, and he was rich – nothing out of the ordinary at home. Come on, pull yourself together – when did the broken nights begin? He thought back. They had begun about six months before, or a bit more, some time before Christmas. What had happened then? Nothing special. It had been a busy year, a successful year. Ah yes – something out of the ordinary *had* happened. There had been a great to-do, daily comings and goings, planning, the making of many lists, nice calculations of order, guests, seating, menus – the run-up to Gideon's Barmitzvah celebration. He remembered that he had tried to distance himself from all the bustle and detail, and only partly succeeded. It had been a big affair, far too big for his liking, but he had bowed to pressure, subtle but powerful, from Miriam and her family. The lavish event had vexed him, a world away from his own Barmitzvah, which had been celebrated, if that was the right word, in extreme poverty. His parents had had

2

to struggle to get the few pennies together to mark the event at all. He smiled to himself, a wry, disbelieving smile, for he saw that these reasons for distancing himself could not be the whole truth. The disquieting thought came closer, and became clearer. He saw that the event had shaken him badly, for in celebrating Gideon's progress towards manhood, it had made him face an unpleasant truth, that he did not know how he must treat Gideon from then on – and, inexplicably, he must look for the answer in himself.

Violently he pushed his chair back. Of course it was all rubbish, fantasy. A shadow had come from nowhere and was making him see visions, hear demons. He must be in a bad way. A band of pain gripped his forehead. He glanced at his watch. Nine-thirty! By this time, as a rule, he had been in his Cannon Street office for an hour. He went out into the hall to telephone Moorlock's consulting rooms in Harley Street. Moorlock could see him that afternoon. He would remember, for the rest of his life, how crucial that consultation was.

They had been close friends since Oxford days. Moorlock, a dark, ruddy-faced mountain of a man, had been a distinguished games player and light of Vincent's Club, genial, misleadingly casual in manner, quick-minded, perspicacious. Leo, of compact build, had boxed at middleweight but was no hearty, being also reflective, intellectually curious, and soft-centred, or so he had thought in those days. As sometimes happens with seeming opposites, they had found in each other an answering sympathy, linked by an intense interest in human nature – Moorlock's word for it; Leo had

3

preferred, sentimentally, to call it "the human kaleido-scope", despite Moorlock's reminder that kaleidoscope meant "seeing beautiful forms" while human nature sel-dom lived up to that image. "Medicine insists that you look steadily at the dirty essentials of life, the plumbing! The rest is pretty dirty too, most of the time."

These days they met for dinner about once a month, never, however, with their wives, respecting Moorlock's dictum, "When chaps are in a mood to be themselves, women get in the way." They had also decided, long ago, that Moorlock should not be the family doctor but Leo's alone, so that no "untoward matters" – if ever there were any – could by mischance reach Miriam's ears. Moorlock had observed, "It's as well to keep security tight between *us*. You'd be surprised at the things that can leak out when both husband and wife bend one's ear. I try to avoid it. Apart from anything else it can make the physician's position jolly uncomfortable! Let's face it, *we* know – you and I – where we stand, and we know enough about each other to make it worth our while to keep our mouths shut. Best leave it like that eh?'

Moorlock's wife, Betty, conformed to the specifica-tion he had often talked about in their bachelor days as the ideal wife, "Well-endowed and socially presentable, and of course good for the other, and not too much to say for herself – which above all else makes for an easy life for a chap." Betty was fair, pert yet wary, and had kept her voluptuous figure over the years, and as for her interests, Moorlock was right – they did not go beyond the vogue of the moment in clothes and in most other things too. She was a rare, good woman, Leo had

4

often reflected with a twinge of sympathy – a good heart and great forbearance, and doubtless she needed these gifts, living with Moorlock. When he visited their tall house near Lords, Moorlock paid her little attention beyond essential remarks, or rather commands, "Let's have some more tea, Betts!" or "This toast's gone cold, Betts, how about giving us another lot?" She seemed to expect little else, or if she had any discontents did not show them. Leo sometimes thought back to their courtship, and wondered whether she had sensed, even in those days of wine and roses, that Moorlock would expect no more from her than creature satisfactions, an efficient housekeeper and mother to their children, an acceptable public consort?

When Leo and Moorlock dined together their wives were never mentioned except obliquely, in passing, or when Moorlock indulged in one of his disquisitions on the married state: "The limitations of marriage are with you from the start, though most people pretend they don't exist, or that their partner can be made into a different person. Of course that's impossible, or at any rate you won't live long enough to achieve it. All one can do is find the most comfortable way of tolerating their idiosyncrasies in the long haul of living together. Of course many people simply can't pretend well enough to do even that. Incidentally it's from them I get most of my fees! Though the money's good, it can be dispiriting work."

His consulting rooms were in a late nineteenth-century house with marble front steps and sculptured canopy over the door. Within, heavy leather and mahogany furniture, tall marble fireplace, hunting prints – echoes of Galsworthian opulence and prejudice – proclaimed Moorlock's outward conformity. Doubtless the *mise en scene* was intended to reassure, project the solidity of tradition, and probably it did – but even after all the years he had known Moorlock, Leo often wondered whether his friend really believed in these appearances, or cynically stood back from them.

"A joke in private, against yourself," Moorlock had once said, "is the only joke it's safe to make!" He too, like the house, seemed in masquerade, dressed for the part in black jacket and striped trousers, accoutrements of the days when his father had pursued *his* distinguished medical career in these very rooms.

Entering, Leo saw from the concern on his friend's face that his call for help had come as no surprise.

Moorlock breathed heavily as he sat down behind a leather-topped writing table with gilt floral plaques on the curved legs, leaned his elbows on the edge, great shoulders hunched round broad ruddy features, and studied him from under bushy black brows. Moorlock had never forgotten a lesson his father had dinned into him, that he must peruse a patient's face – however many times he had seen it – as if he beheld it for the very first time. He ran his eye from Leo's high forehead and puckered brows down the thin nose, the deep lines from nostril to mouth, lips dipping at the sides in a suggestion of an ironic smile – all held together in tension. At last he grunted chestily, "This has been building up for some time. I've seen it but kept quiet till you wanted to talk about it." He held up a hand. "Wait! I'll run the rule over you first."

He rose with the little gasp of the overweight. Like

many former athletes who liked the good life, he had let himself go in twenty years. The big frame, once angular, was rounded. A hint of the old poise returned as he moved to the instrument table against the wall beside the fireplace and back again. He measured blood pressure, listened to Leo's chest and back, tested reflexes. He sat down again and said quietly, watching Leo's face, "Well – you *are* a bit tired, which is natural – because you're stressed. I have a feeling it goes back a long way?" Seeing his concern confirmed in Leo's face, and to lighten the tone of things, he relapsed into comradely banter, "Been on any benders lately? No – that's not like you! More to the point, any bits of stuff taking too much out of you?"

Taking the cue, Leo grunted, "No such luck!" Then added, "In fact I'm not sure . . ." He checked himself. He had been about to repeat his words on entering the room, "I'm not sure why I'm here, except for not sleeping well."

Moorlock said gently, "I know. This is not the time to dig deep. That must come later. The fact is you've been on my mind – which is why I was expecting this visit – and I've been thinking about what to do when you did come. I couldn't say anything earlier." He looked over Leo's head at some distant vision of his own, and sighed, "First of all we've got to break the pattern of stress. What I'm going to propose may surprise you!" He grinned and the rubicund cheeks lit up: "You know the old saying, 'A little bit of what you fancy does you good?' Physician's wisdom of olden days, referring to food and drink – and the advice probably did some good emotionally, helping an invalid to find encouragement within *himself* – always the best way – to get himself through a bad time. But I am thinking of the other sense of 'a bit of what you fancy'! I am quite serious. Discreetly of course, with everything under control! A bit of the other – a new one – helps release the tensions of all those doubts and regrets, and guilt – we won't discuss all that just yet – I want you to break the pattern of stress first. Physically you're all right but you won't be for long if this degree of stress continues. There's nothing like a captivating bit of stuff to help a fellow escape from that tight circle of self-questioning, and give him the heart to take a fresh look at himself."

He bent his head and turned the pages of his appointments book, "I see we're dining in a couple of weeks. I want you to get yourself away on a trip right away – cancel your appointments. Not too far away; Rome, Florence, Venice, wherever you like – where you can let yourself unwind. Forget everything.'

Leo had no idea what he had expected, but certainly not this – yet only much later would he feel any surprise. At that moment the prospect of forgetfulness, of peace, so remote an instant before, uplifted him. In that sudden breath of freedom he had room in his mind for a different, startling perception – he saw that Moorlock was beset by a disquiet of his own, so far concealed, that this exchange had brought close to the surface. Then his own cloud descended again, and that awareness vanished.

Moorlock sat silent, a hand shading his eyes as if the light from the chandelier was too strong. He looked up and added, "You must stop feeling guilty about the past! You and I know the score!" He wagged a stubby forefinger and attempted a bluff grin: "Underneath, you and I are sensitive as hell. We have functioned well enough so far only because we have bottled up many things we imagine won't bear examination. It's par for the course. We navigate as best we can, and that's all that can be said for it." He sighed again. "Enough of that. I want you to get the hell out of it and let things happen to you!"

They sat in silence. Leo felt a new, stronger touch of peace – why, where it came from, how long it would last, was not important.

Moorlock was cheered to see the lines of tension on Leo's face soften. It was a beginning. He said, half to himself, "Remember how we used to joke about marriage – sometimes when we had just been to a chap's stag night – that marriage takes the shine off life. The truth is that *life* takes the shine off life! We used to say in the old days that we would never let that happen to us. God, how green we were! Well, we have only one life to live – and we've got to harden our hearts to save *ourselves*. So get yourself out on a flight just as soon you can. And don't worry if nothing does happen to you – that sort of thing's pure chance. I have another prescription in mind for when you get back. I find release in it myself. We'll see."

Moorlock came round the desk and they stood for an instant without speaking. Leo said, "I'll go to Rome. I'll get a flight out to tomorrow if I can, if not, then the day after."

In the taxi to his Cannon Street offices, he leaned back and tried to collect himself. A bizarre image struck him, that of Hoffman looking in the blank mirror in shock at his lost reflection. Yes, that had happened to him too. Could he ever find it again? Was there time for one more try?

The doppelganger's voice startled him; it seemed he had been silent for years. "You have not lost your reflection. It is there before your eyes but you *will* not see it – because it poses questions you cannot bear to answer. Well, this is your last chance."

I have tried to find answers all these years! I want to wipe the slate clean and start again – if I can only find the way. I am not going to give up.

He looked back on his long friendship with Moorlock. How strange that there had never been a communication between them as profound as this one? Though this had been a professional consultation, Moorlock had lowered a few barriers of his own. What had prevented that in the past? Was it the old code of the "stiff upper lip", lampooned in student days, which now, in their middle years, they honoured still? Moorlock's breezy stoicism, the rude contempt for weakness, for sentiment, had never struck him as entirely genuine, but he had always drawn back from probing beneath. Moorlock for his part had never trespassed either. What had Moorlock meant by saying that he himself took that "other prescription"? It seemed so obvious, yet the answer eluded him.

Where was the rose garden, where the Lost Domain? There remained only the prosaic reality of "A bit of what you fancy!" – to be taken and discarded and chosen again as lustreless time drew itself out day by day. That was a grim verdict. Yet for no reason he could think of, he felt confident; a malign influence seemed to have been lifted. Fifteen years of marriage had shrunk away as if they had never been – if this was fantasy, so be it! Movement, of *some* kind, was now inevitable. What it ought to be, where it should lead – or where he wanted it to lead – he had no idea either; but he knew that Rome would show the way.

As for Moorlock's present "prescription", some perversity made him hesitate. Of course a casual affair, if you were discreet, need disturb nothing – or almost nothing. You could pretend to leave well alone, as Moorlock had done in his marriage, find the "bit of what you fancy" and live with the poison of betrayal, concealment, guilt. Or do nothing and stagnate. There must surely be a third way, to start afresh? Ah but where was the youth and strength for that? Where was the innocence and hope! In your forties you were middle aged; an epoch you had joked about when you were young as a time of elegiac fancies and fears of failing powers. Well, maybe not fears but the ghosts of fears – which once you thought you could delay for ever. Most depressing of all he still did not know, any more than he had known long ago, what he wanted from life. How ridiculous to say he needed more time! Time for what? Time to decide what he wanted? If he didn't know now, would he ever know? There was no time left. The demons demanded action *now*, and he could not silence them. A shadowy figure stood beside him – his familiar – whom he had tried not to hear over the years. The doppelganger murmured, "Action without a goal can only be a mistake! Remember what the Cheshire Cat told Alice at the crossroads when she said she did not much care where she got to: 'In that case it doesn't much matter which way you go.' Until you go back along the road and judge what you have done, you have no hope whatever. You have treated women badly, always with some sanctimonious excuse. You cannot go back and confront them all and make your peace, for time and chance and death have dealt with them one way or another. But there is *one* who can stand in for the others. You must go to where it happened and confront yourself honestly. Only then will you be quit of your debt. Not your debt to *her*, mind you – that is never possible – but to yourself. But you must act quickly, or this moment of courage will be lost. That is not all. There is something else you must do, another debt to be redeemed, and you can only do that through Gideon. Do not ask me what it is – or why – you know it in your heart, and you must pluck up the courage to see it."

The familiar's final words prompted an idea about Gideon – though it had nothing to do with a debt; that was absurd. He would take Gideon with him, use him as respectable camouflage.

The doppelganger snorted, "You are being ridiculous – yes and cowardly. You are making it impossible for anything to 'happen' as Moorlock put it. Taking the boy with you is as good as not going at all! You are running away from yourself yet again. Pull yourself together and look at what you are doing!"

Go away. I know what I'm doing. But he did not know. The taut state had returned, and he was being pulled in many directions. One thing was plain but he did not know why – Gideon *must* come with him.

Chapter 2

Rome had always spoken to him with discordant voices: romance, savagery, ruthless power, cruelty – especially cruelty. He could feel that short Roman sword hacking at his own flesh when he thought of the Menorah – Jewish ceremonial candelabrum – carved on the arch in the Forum, reminder of Roman pride in the slaughter of Jews, and of other horrors through the centuries, not Roman but with a similar stamp. None the less, ever since his first days here as an undergraduate he had been fascinated by the glory that was Rome. Was that why he had chosen to come here this time? He was not sure. Whatever the influences at work they were inescapable, and here he was in Rome passing them on to Gideon. He was beginning to suspect that other facets of himself, unacknowledged, were being passed on too.

He sat in a little clearing high in the Farnese Gardens above the Forum, on a stone bench in the shade of a twisted cypress through whose foliage, unmoving in the torrid stillness, thin shafts of gold from the hard June sun struck the sandy ground at his feet. Beyond the clearing shone little points of light where the sun was reflected from shiny leaves poised stiffly in the air as if cast in metal – poplar and cypress and oleander, bay and ilex. From the edges of the clearing a number of green alleys, hedges bedraggled and dusty in the heat, meandered away, interrupted here and there at a stone belvedere. A colony of cats inhabited the clearing, thin and sinewy and purposeful. From time to time, in a mystic ritual, they took turns to glide out from under a stone bench, pause at the edge of its rectangular shadow, then pad across to a bench a few yards off, its stone slab dazzling white in the sunlight like the others. Before entering the new shadow each paused and stared hard into the golden sun in arcane affirmation, then slid under the bench and lay, forepaws outstretched, yellow eyes narrowed, a sphinx stilled in meditation.

Watching them conjured visions of wandering souls relentlessly driven, seeking certainties.

The hard sunlight in the little clearing suited his mood – that and its isolation, for in the fierce mid-afternoon heat the steep flights of steps leading up from the Forum evidently deterred the mass of tourists below. Another feline minuet intermittently passed through, light-footed young women in striped or flowered cotton dresses swinging over bare legs, hair caught at the neck in ponytails or, hanging loose, curtaining faces in mystery, carrying books and drawing blocks and note pads; a holiday study group. Sometimes they passed through singly, more often in twos or threes, faces moist in the heat, noses reddened by the sun, fanning themselves with their drawing blocks. They drew near as if attracted by animal magnetism to his lean, meditative figure, swayed before him in knowing display while they consulted a text book or studiously

14

wrote notes, sauntered to the far side of the clearing to gaze across to the gaunt red remains of Domitian's palace. Turning again reflectively, eyes narrowed against the glare, one of them might point a sandalled foot in his direction, perhaps tempted to share the shade on his bench, then sighed languorously, hearing calls from others in the pathways beyond, and wandered off with undulating step that made the cotton dress cling seductively to thigh and calf, to vanish into one of the green alleys.

Now and then recognition struck him; the poise of a head, the shape of a mouth, a mannerism or tone of voice, an indefinable quality that conjured one of the women in his past – who had stayed her time and passed on in *her* mysterious quest, no longer shared with him. Sometimes the likeness was so exact that he almost called out a name. He chid himself for letting memory play games with him. These girls were not real but shades now demanding to be heard, asking him yet again why love had ended? He was witnessing a parade of his Platonic other halves – their features, their styles, the way they addressed the world, proclaiming the temper and spirit that had called to him over the years. And did so still. Siren songs.

Chiara, he supposed, was among them, and sometimes he thought he saw her flit past. It was she who had led him here on the day of their first meeting all those years before. They had sat on this very bench. He thought of her intense sojourn in his life in the succeeding days, of her soft Roman voice with its quaint English diction returning again and again in the silences after he left her. His thoughts went back through the years – could it really be fifteen years? The time seemed short, not years but days. To tread the past was tempting, feeding fantasies of the might have been, the "if only" of life, poignant with light and shade, Sibylline echoes understood too late.

Here in the Farnesiana, hot whispers of another high Roman summer touched the spirit. He sensed her presence as if she might reappear at any moment from one of the green-walled paths converging on the clearing. Words she had whispered on their last day returned. She had spoken directly to his heart as was her way: "What is it you really want? I know what *I* want. I want to journey with you forever. Let us begin that journey now, and never, ever, stop!" He knew she spoke for him too. Cravenly he had taken flight. Now, he thought he understood why. Chiara, despite one devastating hesitation, had possessed the courage to pursue visions to the limit come what may, and he had recoiled from that courage in fear. Yet he too had once possessed that ardent innocence! When had he lost it? Could he regain it, now, at his age! Hardly. If that was true, then all dreaming was useless. That thought too was unacceptable. There must be something left to life!

Again he asked himself why he had chosen Rome for this trip. Being here was too punishing. The suspicion that there *was* a hidden reason grew stronger. Was it yet another trick of guilt or self-pity? Was it catharsis he had come for, quittance of a debt he owed himself? And had he brought Gideon, also, for an unpalatable motive – to see the place through this youngster's unstained vision – dubious amalgam of parental duty and sloppy sentiment! What new light could the boy's juvenile awareness provide, across the gap of age and time? Nothing could take the place of his own impressions, fixed for ever, of that sojourn here with Chiara. By some tantalising magic of the Furies, every vista in this dream city, every column and decorated corbel and buttress and lofty stone balcony, every hidden piazza, even places never visited with her, conjured *her* image, her voice, husky, eager, resonant with innocence and courage. These things had their place only in his own private world – they must not be revealed to this young, vulnerable spirit.

Gideon had rushed away – it seemed hours ago – to wander the Forum, recreate old Rome, pace the old flagstones in their proper time. He had taken possession of Rome. He had absorbed Georgina Masson's *Companion Guide to Rome* in one great gulp, and carried it now wherever they went, though he seldom needed to refer to it. He had studied the map of the older, inner core of the city so well that he knew the street plan by heart; and though Leo thought he knew Rome, the boy sometimes corrected him, "No, papa, it's *this* way," and was usually right. On this fourth day of their stay, he strode about like a returning wanderer, as if he called up from memory the identity of each stone and pavement and arch and its significance in this palimpsest of a city. Any moment now, he would run up to him, fresh with insight, bubbling with questions which, though drawn from the past, had overtones for the present and future.

He wondered whether Gideon's quick intuition would divine his obsessive preoccupation with the Chiara episode. Unawares he may already have let slip hints of it while trying to talk to the boy about life? Miriam had enjoined him to do that while Gideon was away with him. "It's time you really talked to the boy, darling – about life, you know? Your duty as a father! It'll be a good opportunity while you're both away. In fact that's why I'm glad you're taking him."

Unconsciously he must have evaded that duty? And now he was aware, with a sense of loss, that he had nothing to build on – he had no idea what impression Gideon had formed of him! Why had he never asked himself that question before! He thought of his own father; how much had *he* known his son's mind? Not much, though Father had been disconcertingly perceptive at times. He tried to recall what he had understood of life at Gideon's age, but could remember only that there had been waves of day dreams and fantasies, imagined certainties gleaned from books or older boys at school. What had he understood of adult sensibility? Nothing. He remembered his despair when listening to grown ups talking, when it seemed that their language and responses were hidden in an unbreakable code. Still, if he *had* broken that code, and realised how lost *they* were, his desolation would have been even greater! He must have had his suspicions. Ever since, learning and re-learning life's lessons, trying to re-write events and judgments, he had been trapped in a maze of *esprit de l'escalier* – if only he had understood people, and himself, better? The "if only" of life endlessly repeated.

Thinking of Gideon's darting intuition, it occurred

to him, inexplicably, that these days in Rome would mark a shift in his relations with him, half-welcomed, half-resented – though what form it would take he had no idea. There was no escape however. He must find a way of admitting him to the most secret groves where he himself had walked alone through the years. He had already begun to do that, and part of him resented doing it, and was ashamed. It wasn't Gideon's fault that the future drew him onwards, young as he was, to knock at the door of the adult world! Yes, bringing him had been a mistake. He had other things to think about, so many questions he had come here to answer! The boy was in the way. He could kick himself for bringing him; and yet – Heaven alone knew why – his presence was necessary. The thought angered him.

He thought of Lord Chesterfield – in the dark all cats are grey – the sort of thing one laughed about in student days. It did not seem funny now, for everyone was in the dark! No, he could hardly say that to Gideon. In truth there was too much to talk about; already he must have talked to the boy more than he had ever intended to – though how much of it had been understood he had no idea. He had been aware, however, that every word he had uttered had at the same time been addressed to himself in a different sense, painful, cathartic, opening up vistas within where demons lay in wait. What did he want with catharsis now – or insight, or sensibility? He was a business man! What did these subtleties mean for him now – what had they ever meant?

The doppelganger said: "Years ago you tried to shed your humanity, and I could not stop you. I have cornered you at last! Yes, you are a successful business man – but your humanity is fighting back! So do not pretend that sensibility is useless – or that you deserve nothing better than the spiritual loneliness you have arrived at. You are going to rescue what humanity is left in you. I have brought you back here to fight – and you will do it through Gideon – and only then will you understand why you travelled this blind road for so long. You cannot retreat now. So stop all this self-pity and get on with it."

He answered: Go away. I don't need you. There is nothing to be rescued as you put it. I am too old for so many things. It's all a waste of time.

Leo knew that his familiar did not believe him. He was right too, damn him! He did need to talk to Gideon. In these few days he had tried to talk to him of the meaning of maturity, love and passion and tenderness, values – even though he knew that the distance between them was too great. Values? What an irony – his own record was no shining example! Still, what about the old saying, "The best teacher is the sinner, for he *knows* the cost of taking the wrong road!"

Yet resentment remained. His own father, he reminded himself, had revealed almost nothing. To be fair that was not his fault; a narrow religious tradition, and father's unhappiness, had enchained him to silence. He remembered, now, exactly what his father had done – and at this distance it was comic, a tiny opening of the door with quaint spiritual delicacy. One day when he had been about Gideon's age, father had called him to the kitchen in the tiny tenement flat in the old Gorbals, the windows dark with grime, a sticky flypaper black with dead flies hanging from the ceiling. On the cracked oil-cloth covering the rickety table father had placed a clean piece of newspaper, and on it the Bible lay open, a fat book of yellowish pages with large black print, whose thick covers, when closed, were held together by a hinged hasp and staple of brass, a family heirloom, the only one left. To his child's eye it was a powerful message of tradition. He had often stood before it and imagined the strong broad hands, like father's, that in each generation had undone that brass latch in simple devotion, to draw aside the curtains of time and destiny. On the right hand page father had put a lump of sugar at the beginning and end of a passage. "Read between the lumps," Father said. "Take the first lump and suck it as you read," and went out, braces dangling from the waistband of his trousers, and left him to read alone.

He could see those lumps of sugar now, and the others that had been placed similarly for father himself by *his* father, and so on through the dark past, and felt a surge of tenderness, of compassion – so many years too late. This was the old way, instinct with the sensibility of many generations. The sugar was there to entice the child to read and learn, but it also spoke of the elders' fear that the way ahead for him would be less sweet than they hoped – probably every bit as bitter as their own.

He had sucked a sugar lump and read, and read again – and as he did so he travelled down through layer upon layer of the turning earth, and as he descended a whole world of apocalyptic meaning came within reach, but receded before he could grasp it. The words he read were simple, or seemed so, yet they filled him with fear – for he "understood" them and yet did not! An oracular voice spoke from the page. The printed words ran together into one mighty affirmation, ". . . he went in unto her, and knew her, and she conceived . . ." He tried to reason his way through to the meaning by visualising the life of the "People of the Book" in that distant epoch, in tents in the desert he supposed. The words "went in unto her" surely meant that the man had walked into her tent? In that case, why did the holy book say, "knew her"? The man must already have known her if he walked into that tent? The word "knew" must have another meaning – a terrible one, for otherwise it would have been set down plainly? Years would pass before the truth crept into full awareness, and even then, when in student days he heard the light-hearted words "knowing a woman in the biblical sense", the shame of that timidity and confusion returned. When father came back into the room he feared to ask him to explain, knowing – but not knowing – that the message was about things too terrible to be spoken of. He had often wondered whether he *had* grasped the true meaning at the time, but primeval terror had shut it away. For many months after, lying awake at dead of night, the words resounded in his head, and fiendish voices demanded that he tell them the meaning, and he had answered in fear, "I don't know!" The voices had replied in a mocking sing-song: "Yes you do. Yes you do."

Once more Leo asked himself why he had such distaste for this newly discovered duty to *his* son. He supposed he was resenting his own lost youth. And something else – but he could not put a name to it, not yet.

Gideon had been given the basic information long

22

ago. What the boy now needed – God help him – was preparation for the riddle of the female soul, deadly as that of the Sphinx, the antic dance of desire, lust, fulfilment beyond lust, mysteries that women claimed no man understood! How did one teach the unknowable? He had begun uncertainly with something of Ovid's *Ars Amatoria*. Despite its cynicism it was fair and true as far as it went – awareness of woman, how to achieve your ends by giving *her* desires pride of place and not yours – or pretending to – and never giving too much of yourself lest she enchain you! How ironic these thoughts were, looking back on his own record?

The doppelganger said, "You must dig deeper. Through Gideon you must re-learn many things you once knew about yourself but turned away from – and much more that you refused to see. Through him you have a chance to recapture, like Hoffman, your lost reflection, and learn who you are all over again."

He was probably right – which was why his words were always intolerable – but he would not accept them, not yet.

In spite of himself he did dig deeper. He thought of the pitfalls that had marked his own green progress, days of despair when he had wished his father had told him more about life. When he was older he had seen at last why father had so seldom talked, really talked, because living had made him sick at heart – but by then it was too late to tell him that he understood, too late to give him comfort. It struck him now that he must have begun to sense the reasons for father's sadness earlier than he remembered – about the time of his own Barmitzvah – and the knowledge must have been too

23

chilling and he had retreated from it, for if so strong a man could be crushed by life, what hope was there? Ah yes, Barmitzvah – that day whose *leitmotiv*, "Today I am a man!", at once both uplifting and daunting, pushed you forward ineluctably. Had Gideon guessed as much about *him*, and was he also afraid to speak? Gideon too, with Barmitzvah behind him, must be wondering how to confront the perplexing adult world, yet thrusting forward willy-nilly as he himself had done. Did he fear Gideon's changing vision of him?

He tried to remember how he had met Miriam. At first the memory refused to return. He had been invited to a party on the Cherwell given by Moorlock's younger sister Anne. Miriam, a college friend of hers, had caught his eye there. In the lazy air of an Oxford high summer, with floating white dresses and wide-brimmed hats and champagne, it had been easy to find enchantment. It was a few weeks after he had come back from Rome and Chiara. It had been a classic example, Moorlock had remarked, of the "rebound". He had been given only a hint of the Chiara affair but had guessed the rest.

Why had he married Miriam? It was a question he had never asked before. Miriam had not been his ideal vision of a romantic attachment. He had been drawn to her as to a flame, radiant in youth and passion. Magnetism drew them together, and unthinkingly, inevitably it had seemed, they married. Moorlock with his mischievous remarks about a rebound may have been trying, instinctively, to warn him, but Leo could not – or would not – see what Chiara had to do with the attraction. Leo and Miriam, eager, lustful, clever people, moved without care into a well-conducted marriage; and Miriam's cool, ordered mind organised their lives so skilfully that he hardly noticed, after the first years of desire were over, that they had little to say to each other apart from the daily small talk. Surprisingly, looking back now, he had found the life congenial; it made almost no demands on him, left the past unanswered, freed him for business success. Moorlock, gently teasing, had called it "handing in your chips", but he had shrugged away the thought and buried it deep.

Inexplicably his thoughts turned to Domville his Oxford tutor, daunting savant with the features of a raven and the punctilio of the *grand seigneur*, and the advice he had given him on a day when he had thought his heart was broken for ever – for that morning Myrtle, his first infatuation, had savagely dropped him. Older, harder, she had sought in him proletarian earthiness when all he had to give was innocence; and so she had chosen the very last day of term to tell him she was finished with him. Left standing in the doorway of Fuller's coffee shop, trembling in his desolation, he had realised that he was due to present himself at Domville's rooms to read an essay. He remembered shivering as he climbed the echoing wooden staircase from the cloister, each footfall a passing bell – for him, for hope, for everything. He had hesitated before lifting the brass knocker, miniature replica of the Bocca della Verita – grim reminder of the shock of truth – and unawares brought it down hard. From beyond the heavy oaken door Domville called, "Come!", the voice higher pitched than usual. Domville, knowing the meaning of that violent thud of the knocker, must have prepared himself to deal with yet another end of term sufferer. He sat in shadow on the far side of the square room, his back to the long low mullioned window, a figure in a classic setting, bookshelves lining the walls to the ceiling, gleams of winter sunlight on smooth steel-grey hair. There was something of the dandy about him; he wore a chalk striped double-breasted suit of charcoal grey, cream shirt, blue Shantung silk tie, soft leather slippers decorated with gold thread. He puffed at a stubby cheroot, and through the blue smoke curling about his face studied Leo as he pulled his essay from the folder and began to read. Domville stopped him with a wave of his hand. "Dear boy, I understand perfectly. I am an old campaigner. The pain will pass, it always does." He paused and drew hard on the cheroot.

"I want you to think carefully on what I am about to say – as soon as you can think clearly again!" He smiled, a gleam of light in the long, shadowed features. "Young people at university too often plunge into relationships on intellectual affinities alone – when it is simply blood calling to blood. Desire, lust? The name hardly matters – but this you can depend on, *neither* of these powerful stimuli has any lasting power. It is a fantasy of youth – charming in its way – to pretend it is the higher level of the mind that draws them together! That is rubbish. You cannot be sustained by Voltaire and Madame de Stael all day and every day! Being romantic is splendid and beautiful, but as a daily diet it cannot sustain you. As for desire, it can put you at a woman's mercy, and you must never permit that. When you are young and lusty, desirable women are two a penny, so don't let desire blind you into thinking that the woman of the moment is irreplaceable. You owe it to *yourself* to protect your interests even when you are in love. Women can be immensely cruel. In being cruel they are protecting *their* interests, and you must do that too. The sad truth is that the heart can be cruel, and sometimes the woman cannot help hurting you. I am being blunt with you to save you unnecessary heartache. Choosing a woman sensibly, as opposed to romantically, is simply good sense – there is nothing ignoble in that! Nor does it deny you pleasure! Pleasure, you will find, is quite another matter. You can always have pleasure *en passant*, provided you are discreet . . .".

Domville was silent for what seemed a long time, drawing on the cheroot with emphasis and blowing out long thin cones of smoke. Then he leaned forward with elbows on knees as if to narrow the distance between them, and sighed, "I repeat, the pain *will* fade. At the time, we sometimes imagine that its fading throws doubt upon the quality of our love! That isn't true. We are wonderfully resilient whether we like it or not!" He gave a wolfish grin that vanished at once. "So don't punish yourself and don't feel guilty either. One day you will find a woman who will treat you decently."

The words had startled him. Domville saw his case as run of the mill, in the grand sweep of things unimportant! That was hard to stomach. Domville was right – he did want to wallow in his sorrow. He roused himself and realised that he had read only the first line of the sheaf of papers in his hand. He started to read again, but Domville interrupted gently, "No – you are in no condition to give the subject your full attention! Leave it with me and we will talk about it next term – by which time your youthful resilience will have done its healing task. I can promise you that. Off with you then, have a good vacation, and put all this behind you."

While in the room, Domville's measured tones had kept his grief in check, but when he had closed the door behind him tears flowed, and he was ashamed. Down in the arched stone entrance to the staircase he contemplated the dull green of the lawn in its December sleep. The night before, he had read Donne's poem on St Lucie's Day, "'Tis the yeares midnight . . .". He might have had a premonition, for the words expressed his feelings exactly. After some minutes, shivering in the chill greyness of the cloister, he realised that he was repeating some of Domville's words, recalling their suave worldliness, cynical, even shocking, and saw that they had awakened sensibilities he had not recognised in himself, still to be defined, but mysteriously reassuring. For this service he knew he would honour Domville always – paragon of hedonism, toughened by life but also softened by its balsamic tinctures of compromise and compassion.

Looking back now, it seemed that in marrying Miriam he had tried to follow Domville's counsel. There had been no intellectual affinity. Animal appetite had ruled – for a time – and then care, order, comfort had taken over. Detachment had suited his state. The thought came to him with a *frisson* of guilt. He had preferred a quiet neutrality after the white-hot crucible of those days with Chiara – which had prefigured, he must have realised, the spiritual demands awaiting him if he had

28

stayed with her . . . Miriam was sensible, predictable, made few emotional demands. He had often felt that she preferred not to be aware of her emotions, or those of others, in order to free her fierce energy for her career. He remembered a day, some eight years before, when she had admitted as much. They were finishing breakfast. Out in the hall, Grace the nanny put Judith into the push-chair for her morning outing in the park, and the child was resisting. Grace was fresh from training college, neat and correct in her starched uniform, calm, methodical, punctilious. She had a round open face and peaches and cream complexion, flaxen hair coiled in a glistening crown, good-humoured in an easy, youthful way, given to few words. Something about her irritated Miriam, perhaps the imperturbable manner, or simply her youth! Miriam had been sharp with her for being slow in strapping the child into the chair. He must have made a sign of protest, for while Grace wheeled the push-chair through the front door, still within earshot, Miriam exclaimed, "I simply haven't time for other people's temperament. I need to be firing on all cylinders all the time, and I can't do that if I have to watch out for people's moods. Maybe I should but I can't. That's the way I am."

She had a special gleam in her eyes, challenging, half-joking, but she was not joking. Defending her chosen position was a serious matter. She passed a hand over her cowl of black hair, then touched a cameo brooch at the neck of her white pleated blouse, habitual gestures, especially the talismanic contact with the brooch, the only signs of self-doubt she ever permitted herself.

A bizarre impulse had seized him, to leave the house

then and there and go on a distant journey, not with any direction in mind but simply *away*, to seek some precious thing within himself, lost somewhere along the road. Strange that that thought, dismissed as absurd then, should surface now, here, under a tree in Rome.

Chapter 3

He heard a quick, skipping step in one of the green alleys and Gideon burst into the white glare of the clearing. The boy homed back to him at intervals to announce with shining excitement new discoveries, new dreams, needing to share them, and then, content, went down again to his imaginings in the Forum – as a cat returns from its wanderings to confirm attachment and departs again. Awakened from the brown study he looked at the boy in surprise, for Gideon, at every moment of these days, seemed to have grown taller and broader since the last appearance, the future young man a fraction more emphatic, already beginning to appear, like a superimposed photograph, as a shadow behind the boy still reigning within. He was drenched in sweat, patched blue denim trousers clinging to him, frayed to a hole at one knee, where a flap of cloth hung down; the grey and white football shirt so tight that his jutting shoulders seemed about to burst out of the stretched seams.

Leo had been reviewing "the talk" with Gideon, trying to decide what paradigms from his experience with women were worth passing on, disguised of course. Compared with business, where his judgment was proven, all that sprang to mind was evidence of an unsure, egotistical life, an unscrupulous one as the doppelganger often reminded him. No, unscrupulous was surely too harsh a judgment – mistaken, insecure, no more. His prime mistake had been to meet women more than half-way in eagerness and trust, all defences down, refusing to believe that women were not the tender, unselfish creatures of romance. They too looked after "number one" – as Domville had warned. He had always remembered that warning too late, and each time had broken away – sometimes brutally, blaming the woman instead of himself – wounded and furious. That was no lesson to give the boy! There must be a *right* way to behave, whether it benefited you or not. How was he to explain this without revealing himself as a fool or a scoundrel or both? Yet he must try.

Chiara was in his thoughts as Gideon came near, images of their apocalyptic meeting and the glowing days that followed, faded sepia prints – but there was something more, an almost tangible sense of her. He knew why she took precedence over all the others, as the doppelganger hinted, why she reached beyond him to the boy. Probably the others did so too; mysteriously his whole life was being conveyed to Gideon in demonic whispers. That chorus had been stifled for years. It could never be silenced now. Gideon's needle-sharp intuition must divine its voices in every word he spoke, and he would know the full measure of his guilt soon if he did not know it already, and fear the knowledge. He might even have sensed it long ago. Even now, in the very next moment, he might press him to reveal more, or force him to *evade* more! So the damage would be compounded. Chiara would not go away either. A whisper from her spectral presence might cause the boy to stumble upon that very episode, perhaps the worst of them all, and the knowledge might close the boy's mind to whatever wisdom he had to give him.

Her presence was to be expected. She probably still lived here. The Fates might even make their paths cross! Why, on his many business visits to Rome had it never occurred to him to discover what had happened to her? It would not have been difficult to trace her. There had seemed little point. Perhaps the doppelganger was right – he had buried his feelings too deep and never cared for anyone. If that was so, how could he explain "caring" – love in fact – to Gideon? It would be wrong to present it, with Ovid, as self-interest – you *pretended* to care for a woman only to get what you wanted from her, admiration, emotional and carnal caresses, fidelity? Yes, Ovid had said it all – and what a beguiling masculine conceit it was! If so, what did you live for afterwards, when appetite was jaded and the "long littleness of life" had you in its grip? Of course the boy was too young to know how to question such pragmatism, but his romantic soul would surely demand that there had to be more to "caring" than calculation. No, he must combine Ovid with romantic mythology, the meeting of souls and so forth, conceal the fact that he himself could not believe in it – not now, not for what seemed a lifetime.

No, he had no desire to know Chiara's fate. Lives changed, people moved on, matured further, even if *he* had not! What on earth would he say if he did meet her? What a grisly experience that would be?

33

The doppelganger said, "Guilt is a barren sentiment. But do not turn away from the thought of her. Something did happen to you then. You must go back in time and face it steadily. It may be your last chance to see yourself as you really are. I am sorry for you. You are still a romantic – a romantic checked in your course long ago – long before Chiara by the way! An imprisoned romantic still waiting for a miracle to set you free. You thought you had found that miracle with Chiara. There are no miracles. There are only dreams that *you* endow with power – for a time."

What do you mean by "face it steadily", he asked his familiar, but there was no answer. Here at this spot, where he had halted and gone no further, was there a thread of his life embalmed? Had he returned to retrieve it and follow it as if time had stood still! The idea was absurd.

His thoughts echoed in the clearing so loudly that he wondered whether Gideon heard them. He studied the long shining face, aglow with dreaming, and wished he could divine the boy's vision of the world. He recalled his own, when much younger than Gideon. When mother had died, or rather unaccountably gone away as it had seemed – he was six years old – and father came and went always out of reach, he had imagined that everyone, mother included, was part of an eternal ritual dance in which the dancers converged and swung away and converged again in ever-changing permutations, invisible threads keeping them in mysterious contact however far they might swing away in time or place, a communion which no one, alive or dead, could ever leave. Did Gideon's spirit work as his had done? He *should* know – but he had no idea. How much reality dare he expose him to, or even hint at? The light and shade of life were seldom touched upon at home – the "eternal verities" as he liked to call them, though the irony in the term annoyed Miriam, thinking he mocked her pedestrian logic, which was usually true. They never talked of them now, and when he had once foolishly observed that this poverty of curiosity marked one's passing from youth to middle age she had been furious. She preferred to sweep "life" under the carpet if it could not be ignored completely, especially in the children's presence, her guilt or embarrassment thinly concealed. They should have had the courage to talk more, *really* talk, listen to the children's perplexities in the very moment of formation – and Gideon's mind would not be unknown territory now.

Gideon held out the drawing block he carried everywhere, its stiff brown cover stained with sweat from hands and forearms. He had come to show him a pencil drawing he had done of one of the arches in the Forum below, in fine detail, even to the courses of thin Roman bricks. In front of the arch a stone slab rose above the level of the surrounding remains. Gideon pointed to it. "You know Papa? That platform might be where Mark Antony stood and made his speech! I have just been standing on it, and I made an oration to the members of the Senate gathered round me!"

Leo, relieved that "the talk" was not to be resumed, said, "And did you hear the trumpets sound for you. And did the Senators acclaim you?"

Gideon seemed taken aback by the quick entry into his fantasy, then his face shone again, "Yes I did. And *they* did!" He swung on his toes as if to dart away but turned to face him again, this time hesitantly, and Leo knew that the boy had sensed something after all. Gideon studied him with a deliberation never shown before, "Papa – why did Mark Antony throw himself on his sword when he thought Cleopatra was dead?"

At home Miriam would have interposed briskly with a reply that was not an answer, a form of words to bring enquiry to a stop, "Darling, some people don't know what they are doing when they are upset!" – anything to evade the labyrinthine riddle of love, the light and the dark. And he himself, taking the easy path, would have murmured assent. Now, Gideon's steady scrutiny told him that those days were over. Gideon was forcing the talk to resume after all.

The boy had him trapped. If he answered the surface question only, Gideon would at once find some other route. He decided to give the boy the opening he needed, "Because he loved her of course! People do desperate things when they are in love."

Gideon shook his head solemnly. "Papa that's not a good enough reason! It wasn't worth killing himself for. He could have found somebody else, couldn't he?"

Leo found himself talking about the desolation that struck when you lost a woman you loved. At such a moment the very idea of another taking her place was unthinkable. He felt an unfamiliar freedom and light within as if a door had been opened. Then he saw that Gideon was merely listening politely – what he was saying was too far along the road. He must begin further back, but where?

Gideon hungered for detail. Sensibilities, though he

36

was dimly aware of them, were too insubstantial to deal with. The territory of the spirit was still unmapped. His was the juvenile faith in the alchemy of circumstance, "things" known and measurable, substantial like hunger and cold. He did not know that names, dates, circumstance, would add nothing to the spiritual essence if he could only grasp it. That was in the future, but he did not know that either. And so, looking for supposedly measurable facts, he said, "Did *you* ever lose someone you loved, Papa?"

Leo was held by those large questing eyes, confident, trusting. The boy could only think of "lose" in the sense of one path diverging from another, its course calmly chosen, with no volcanic upset, no sense of tragedy. Still cocooned in childhood, the boy had no means of comprehending the bitterness of deprivation, broken trust, the frozen landscape that remained. Yet behind his question lurked the shadow of future knowledge. He must give him *something*. He decided to give him "facts" in the form of allegory without identifying detail, placing the incidents far in the past – long before the marriage. So he talked about the ways in which you could "lose" someone – strange that the word had such deep and diverse meanings. You might lose someone you loved from many causes, few of them simple. Love itself was not simple. Most people started off by believing that, loving someone, they were automatically loved in return, but that was a mistake, and the most usual cause of "loss". Sometimes love did ignite both hearts at once, but that was a rare miracle, and it was rarer still for it to last. No one wanted to believe that love could fade but it did, and you woke one day and saw with infinite pain that you were *not* loved in return as you had thought, and most painful of all, that you had been mistaken from the start! He thought of Myrtle. Again, as Domville had tried to make him see, people simply changed through no fault of their own, and wisdom came to you only when you accepted that it was so – for accept it you must.

He had been six years older than Gideon when Domville had imparted his stoic conclusions – and still he had not been old enough. What hope of making Gideon understand? There was no retreat now. He must go even further, but still not reveal too much of the truth – for the boy would press him hard with "who, when, where, why?" Those eyes held him! He must protect himself.

Yes, he said, there *had* been times, long ago before he married Mama, where he had lost a woman he had loved. One day that heartache would hit him too; it did everybody, and he must be ready for it. How absurd, he thought even as he said it, to tell a boy of thirteen to be ready for an experience he could not possibly understand! He brushed the thought aside. "You have to grit your teeth and drag yourself out of your sorrow and pain, and you will! Everybody does. 'It's par for the course.'"

How strange that Domville's shade returned again and again; and Domville's *mot*, "It's par for the course." had taken root in his own idiom? So many painful things were par for the course, and his guilt too. Was it right to inflict them so soon on this shining, innocent, trusting boy? It occurred to him that Gideon, even this early, might have sensed his guilt, and knew that it pressed to break free. Perhaps "the talk", and his father's confession embedded in it, was setting the boy free too?

Gideon seemed to shrug it all away with an observation whose maturity evidently startled him. "But Papa, *you* didn't give up? You found someone else. You went on looking and married Mama. So it was all right in the end." His eyes shone with the thrill of taking a step across the frontier into the grown-up world.

There was no honest reply he dared give, not yet, perhaps never. It would mean telling him that he *had* "given up", that he had abandoned the quest for the ideal, as indeed everybody must do. To Gideon at this early stage of the journey, compromise, if it meant anything at all, must surely signify retreat from purity – the coward's way. Worse still, the honest answer would tell him that his father had never loved his mother – she had been a lustful compromise – and he had known it. That she had known it too – he was certain of it – did not lessen his guilt, and the boy must not know that either. Yet the demons insisted on it all spilling out. In retreating from the search he had left himself with no bearings, no truth, no glory, not even hope. How could he even hint at any of it – implying that all his fine talk about love was hollow?

Where was the doppelganger, why was he silent?

Grasping at a straw, he began to explain that another's love could consume you. Gideon's features remained blank. "Consume" obviously meant nothing to him. He told him the story of the shirt that the dying centaur Nessus gave to Deianira, wife of Hercules, telling her that it could reclaim an erring husband. She sent it to

39

Hercules, and when he put it on it burst into flames and killed him.

Gideon looked puzzled: "Did she know it would kill him?"

"No one knows. The point of the story is that love is a blind force, that sometimes it is so strong, so selfish you might say, that it makes you indifferent to the consequences of anything you might do under its influence. It makes you want all or nothing. Hercules had broken his vow to her. If she could not have all his love, then no other woman should have him either. Yes, love can make you do terrible things – to others and to yourself too – that is how it can consume you."

Gideon still looked perplexed. Yes, it *was* asking too much of the boy.

In spite of himself he added, "Of course love can consume you in other ways. It can enchain you, make you a slave of the woman if you are not careful, make you want to please her so much that you become untrue to yourself, turn away from what you really want from life." At once he regretted going this far, but Gideon's next words reassured him – plainly he was still gripped by the story.

"But Papa, what Deianira did wasn't fair! If Hercules didn't love her as much as she wanted him to, then it wasn't his fault! You said that sometimes you just have to swallow the fact that you've made a mistake. She shouldn't have done it!"

It was sad, but wonderful. Gideon was reaching forward with all his imagination but there were too many strands of meaning, too few clues. How could he tell him that love, or rather desire, knew nothing of fairness? Desire and savagery were two sides of the same coin.

He talked on about the "might have beens" of love, mistakes of sensibility, of purpose, and to his relief Gideon showed little curiosity about the identities of the women he had "lost" or of those who had "lost" *him*. Gideon had a question he could not quite put into words. Shifting his feet on the sandy ground, he at last plucked up courage, and spoke with a delicacy that touched the heart. "Papa, was *she* to blame? Or are you not sure now?"

The "she" was Chiara, whom Leo had referred to as "a woman who had been very important to me" – perhaps more important than all the others. The boy could not know how deep the question went. What did blame mean? Had Myrtle been to blame for falling out of love with him – if she *had* been! Was he to blame for running away from Chiara – or Chiara for . . .? Even if he did lay bare the details it would not help matters – Gideon would be thrown into confusion; it was all too strong meat. There were so many ways of being unaware, unfeeling, or merely careless – and the boy was too young to understand such distinctions. How could he make him see that desire was the great falsifier, making you see only what you wanted to? Dare he tell him that love was no talisman, gave you no rights over the one you loved? Love – or was it desire? – promised everything but guaranteed nothing. No, it was too soon for that.

How few certainties there were to pass on? Perhaps Gideon guessed it already? There had been a knowingness in the boy of late that sat strangely with the

41

stripling innocence. He remembered recurrent dreams at Gideon's age – indistinct figures of exquisite gentleness bringing ravishing experience with no beginning or end. Had that dream come to Gideon too? Perhaps in these *louche* days, with so little concealed, there was no need for it?

At that moment Gideon did not feel at all knowing, but full of confusion and wonder, stopped in his tracks by forces demanding comprehension beyond his power. The comfortable childhood world was slipping away, and he was being forced, with a blend of excitement and perplexity, towards images of himself as yet indistinct. He knew that he ought to discern them in the vision of life his father was unfolding, but though he understood the words – or thought he did – their essence eluded him. Papa's picture of the adult world, full of allure and danger, was far from the honeyed whispers of his dreams, but drew him inescapably. As for the questions he was asking Papa, they were not the awesome ones he really wanted to ask, but he did not know how to put words to them. What made him hesitate the more was the intuition that Papa too was shaken by warring forces. But how could that be, with Papa so strong in the world, so wise?

Here on the white stone bench under the tree he saw him inexplicably afresh; he was not the man he knew at home – and yet he *was*. He did not know that his father's inner world was changing, that influences were at work not yet understood – and perhaps never would be – but he was aware of them as a new kind of magic, and that it was working on him too. A shiver ran down his spine. He did not know why this new perception of his father was tremendously important for himself. Here was the familiar figure, the long thoughtful face, high forehead indented above the brows, soft eyes agleam with distant visions, on easy terms with the world. Papa was lean and vigorous with an indefinable gleam of youth, in whom by only a slight shift of the imagination he could see one of the self-assured senior boys high in the school, a prefect or the head of school – youth with the patina of seniority and power. Papa was illuminated by revelations much like those stirring within himself, and he was asking him to accompany him on a wondrous quest, and he wanted to answer, "Yes, oh yes! I shall go with you anywhere you want me to." But he did not know how to say it.

Leo wished he could tell him how to avoid the pitfalls *he* had stumbled into over the years. Where was the heart of the matter to be found, the aim of life itself, by which to test the worth of everything you did? That was what he longed to tell the boy – if only he could distil it for himself.

It was going to be hard, for Gideon would ask for precise co-ordinates to steer for. It would not be enough to say that they existed in that misty territory between desire and love, whose magnetic forces were eternally shifting, desire more insistent but fading quickly, love demanding unremitting pursuit beyond the horizon. Desire was at least unmistakable, while it lasted! Was it not futile to try to tell them apart? Leave well alone, abandon the search, as Moorlock had done. No, that course left you with too many hopeless longings – the gonads had a lot to answer for, nourishing siren visions.

He saw that he was talking over the boy's head and was ashamed. The demons were bringing confession dangerously close. He had wanted to warn Gideon against the romantic belief that the woman you loved was part of you as if she lived within you. You fought to keep her imprisoned, but when you lost her – as sooner or later you did – you felt that you had lost part of yourself, as he had felt when Myrtle dropped him, a kind of death. Gideon had thought the idea comic; you were still the person you had been! He must make him see that the heart had its own logic, and the more you fought it the more you fought yourself. It told you, for instance, that someone who loved you should not *use* you, as Myrtle – and others – had used him. Domville had said that being used was par for the course – and he had not believed him. Gideon too would not believe it.

Though Gideon showed no curiosity about the identity of the women in his past, some reference to them, anonymously, was unavoidable, and he was finding it hard not to lay bare his sense of failure, of guilt – for insensitivity, deceit, cowardice. The truth clamoured to be set free. Of course he had used women – silver-tongued when not telling outright lies, and gone on his way in indifference, even in pride. Who was *he* to say that using people was wrong? Now he saw something in himself that startled him – he had never thought the day would come when he would want to be a model to his son, that fabled wish stretching back through the generations. How absurd? Yet it was there, and so the hope of renewal persisted – of reincarnation without guilt – to make him innocent once more. No, it

44

was not for Gideon's benefit, but his own. No wonder Moorlock was concerned about him. He was in a bad way, caught between incompatible visions of himself.

Where *are* you my familiar, my doppelganger? Why do you say nothing?

There was no answer.

It struck him that Gideon had sensed confession near the surface, and waited for it eagerly. He wished he could tell him that he dared not – that all it would reveal would be unanswered riddles, and not his alone either but of all who had gone before. Well, he must simply invent lessons from the past, *pretend* certainty!

He saw that Gideon had shifted again, intuited less than he had feared, for the boy was firing off questions impatiently as if the answers to life were units of information strung together like multiplication tables, to be placed in memory for casual reference, demanding no adjustment of the emotions. After all, Gideon was still in many ways a child. In recent months he had often seen him swing forward into the speech and manner of a young man, and the next moment back to boyhood, uneasy in each avatar. In the last few weeks his voice had begun to break, changing in one instant to a cracked gruffness reminiscent of a rusty bicycle chain uncertainly engaging the chain-wheel, leaving him confused, then after a few words reverted to the old, piping register. Thin, wiry, with broad, bony shoulders, it seemed that he grew before his eyes, as one imagines a sapling does. The light brown hair, here and there bleached by the sun in streaks of dull gold, overhung grey-blue eyes bright with the quest, the cheeks moist from the heat, glistening with faint down.

The fledgling was already beginning to slip out of reach, and he felt an inexplicable urgency to reach him, to complete "the lesson" while Gideon's soul was still accessible. Complete! When was it ever complete? He tried to recall how long it had taken his own voice to make that shift, but all he remembered was the day it began. He was sitting on the lower floor of a tramcar in the Gorbals and had just asked the conductor for a "penny-half" – a juvenile ticket – and was aware of grown-ups in adjacent seats looking at him curiously, and at the back of his mind, in a delayed reaction, he heard a gruff voice and realised it was his own. They were amazed to hear it from a boy in shorts. He was startled too, and was shaken by regret and doubt. The hand of Destiny had touched him. He was being pulled away from a time that was in a sense already "the past" – familiar, more or less manageable, into a future he knew would not be. He must have been very frightened, for he remembered hoping with all his might that the familiar darkness of his childhood would be replaced by light. What shifts his heart had made in those transitional weeks – or had it been months? – he could not remember, only that it had been a time of anxiety, new attitudes adopted and discarded, hoping that certainty would come; a lonely time too, for father had made no reference to the apocalyptic change. He did not know that father was fighting for survival in those depression days in the Gorbals – he understood father's unhappiness only years afterwards, when it was too late for understanding.

So Gideon must now be malleable as he would never be again. His clay was hardening, and the time for making late impressions was hastening towards its end. A divergent Gideon was forming before his very eyes, and it would not be long before the boy began to declare a new sovereignty and demand that he be dealt with at arm's length – though for a time with juvenile indulgence too. He felt envy at the thought, for he himself had enjoyed no such indulgence, no cushioning. The old Gideon would linger in the shadows, fleetingly glimpsed through the incomplete shell of the new persona, sometimes coming to the fore to voice doubts from an earlier time, unfinished business, but by then he would be unreachable in any language. He felt a premonitory sense of loss – for the many thoughts never shared with the boy, riches of the heart lost for ever through his own sloth, the pursuit of lesser things

The doppelganger spoke. "You are not as sorry as you think. As usual you are not being honest with yourself. You have a deeper motive, as usual a selfish one. Your impatience to form this link with the boy is not what you pretend it is – it is not *his* interest that prompts you. In talking to him you are cleansing your own Augean Stables at last."

But I am not doing it from self-interest. I want him to grow up into a decent person. He stopped. He was talking sanctimonious rubbish. The doppelganger was right, damn him. Anyway I *know* what a decent life should be? I *am* thinking of the boy's good.

The doppelganger made no reply.

His familiar was being unfair. This was a new Gideon – hungry for guidance, suddenly sprung up. He *had* tried to reach him before – and Judith too – but the going had been hard, and he had often given up. The children

47

listened selectively, accepted a morsel of guidance here and there, or made a show of doing so, and rejected the rest – on what criteria he had never fathomed. Or they appeared to obey but made a charade of it, as when Miriam in the past year made a new rule – to be "decent" they must wear dressing gowns when going about naked or in their underwear, which contradicted a previous rule that there should be no prudery, bedroom and bathroom doors open, respect for the body divine more important than stuffy convention. One day she had woken up to the problems that puberty would bring, and decided to amend the basic principle "for the sake of what people might think" – a distinction too subtle for the children. Judith followed the new rule for the sake of peace, but Gideon either dourly "forgot", or carried the dressing gown over his arm while going about naked, as if its mere presence, not its use, was enough – behaviour that Leo's company sergeant major would have entered in the Charge Sheet as "dumb insolence". Leo had never favoured the previous "permissiveness" but had chosen – from indifference he supposed – to let Miriam have her way. Dumb insolence now and then became open defiance. When Gideon was in what Miriam called his "bolshie" mood he rejected all advice with the surly response, "Leave me alone to do things *my* way!" Leo had no patience with these outbursts, when talk was useless and toleration would be seen as surrender; and was tempted to give Gideon a good hiding, to hold the line against further revolt. But Miriam said that would be barbarous, and he stayed his hand, and tight-lipped hours followed.

At such times Miriam said, "Don't upset yourself. It's the age! They are all talking like that these days – what can we do?"

"My father knew what to do – give me a belting. That soon put a stop to any nonsense!" Her defeatist words fed his anger, especially when spoken in the children's hearing – as they usually were – in effect telling them that their leaders were divided. They quarrelled over that, for she would not accept that divided leadership was worse than none. Often, seeing a crisis approach he signalled to her that they should deal with their disagreement in private, but she ignored the appeal, and then, if he could not evade the quarrel he roughly cut it short, which at least meant less wear and tear on his nerves. Thinking about it in calmer moments, trying to be fair to her, he reminded himself that Miriam, in *her* childhood, had absorbed the dogma of "progressive" education – her family had had some connexion with A. S. Neill – including the conviction that quarrels and temper should be allowed to run their course in the open. He suspected another motive too, so deeply hidden that she might not be aware of it. Knowing that he would never fight to a finish in front of the children but would leave her in possession of the field, a quarrel that ended in his apparent retreat was a way of showing the children that *her* view of life, not his, was in the ascendant.

The doppelganger said gently, 'You chose her for her flesh alone – an immature choice and you knew it. Of course it brought no sympathy in matters you cared about – a classic case of self-punishment! The examples of that lack of sympathy may seem trivial

49

now, but they were *not*, for you remember them still. You saw the rough steel in her and pretended not to. When the gonads are in command, wisdom goes out of the window. In the years that followed, you pretended to care about nothing; in effect you cauterised your emotions, and turned away and made money. I am glad you have allowed awareness to return. It hurts of course, but that is par for the course too. As for cleansing your Augean Stables, there is plenty to be done. Think back to the rug-making episode. You saw the signs clearly then, did you not?'

The doppelganger was hitting hard. The incident returned with astonishing freshness – and sourness. On the day they became engaged Miriam had said, as if the words were long prepared and she assumed instant agreement, "I'm going to buy rug-making materials and we will sit by the fire and make a rug together! Won't that be fun?" In her progressive middle-class set there was a conceit he had cynically dubbed "romantic slumming", the fantasy of sharing perspectives with the proletariat – a pint of bitter at the local, or doing manual work which conjured a craft culture that had faded long ago. It was chic for a young couple to make a rug. The conceit was perhaps consistent with the mental state of post-war days, austerity and "making do", but it also reflected the lingering influence of pre-war "sandals and socialism". To him it was repellent, for it mimicked the life of the world he had come from, and to which in spirit he still belonged, the lower depths, people for whom manual labour was not an elective pleasure but a killing burden. For the "romantic slumming" was a display of grotesque insensitivity – and he felt hurt on their behalf.

He had tried to make her understand but she could not, or would not. He had sensed, too, that that example of emotional blindness indicated much else of a like kind beneath. Yet he was complaisant, and answered her facetiously, trying not to hurt her feelings, hoping she would take the hint and let the matter drop. "No, thanks! It sounds too much like hard work!"

"Oh but it's so good for you! There is spiritual healing in working with your hands. Our trouble is that we have lost that contact with *real* things!" She held him with that steadfast hazel gaze, the Cupid lips parted, confident, intent only on victory.

"*Your* lot may have lost contact! I haven't. I spent five years knocking my guts out in a factory, to say nothing of burning my eyes out in night school before I had God's own luck and got to Oxford. I've still got the calluses on my hands – look!" He guided her index finger over the hard patches on the inner surfaces of fingers and thumbs and along the top of the palms. She bent her head, appearing to look. "I see. Yes I do see." Then she took heart again. "Still, maybe you'll change your mind. It really is quite fun! I am going to buy the rug-making outfit anyway."

The doppelganger was right of course. That absurd exchange should have been warning enough. He had compromised, ignored the rug-making and other attempts at romantic slumming.

When he talked of compromise to Gideon, the boy had replied with the impatient certainty of youth, "But Papa, if you have to compromise, you shouldn't be married to the woman at all – isn't that right?"

Out of the mouth of babes and sucklings!

Why had he ignored the warnings? The doppelganger had a neat answer, too neat – lust had blinded him. That was letting him off lightly. He had not *wanted* to see! Why had he waited all these years to see her clearly? He supposed he must have loved her, in some fashion – that qualification said it all! Desire had lost its fire; but that was not a fair way of looking at it either. You got used to a woman. The appetite ceased to be tested to the full as it was with someone new, and you could never know again the immediacy that gripped you when you were young and eager and romantic, and careless – and stupid! Yes, stupid, for in youth every conquest was an intoxicating victory – but in time you learned that it was not all you imagined – as he must somehow tell Gideon. In those far off days *getting* the woman at all was a wonder that clouded all perception, made all questioning irrelevant, but for that moment only! In a few years – in these headlong days who could say when that would be – Gideon would discover the wonder for himself, but sadly something else too, that it could never be repeated, for each was unique, and none could be weighed against another – a truth that could not be taught but learned from many disappointments. He must tell him, somehow, that *every* moment in life was unique, never to be found again.

Cleansing the Augean Stables! What a damning image? Trust the doppelganger to drive a point home! Yes it was accurate enough. You forgot so many of your mistakes, but *they* never forgot you! You never thought of them lying in wait for just the right moment when your guard was down. But why now? And here? That he must cleanse them through Gideon was probably right too – excoriating every single nerve – and there was no escape. He must enter Gideon's heart for the very first time – and his own too – whatever the consequences.

The demons, questions deafened him, but they were too late even if he dared answer! Gideon, in his fashion, would voice them too, but of course he could never tell him the truth. The boy would be devastated. Besides, through him, the truth would find its way back to Miriam, though surely she must already suspect some of it – if she had ever stopped to think at all?

The doppelganger said sternly, "The questions are not too late. Unless you answer them, you will remain enchained – tortured with impossible dreams. Look at these girls!"

Two more of the dreaming girls entered the clearing and paused in the torrid air, swung on tiptoe in automatic coquetry, skirts swirling and rising on supple, softly tanned legs. A surge of lust burned through him. Sweat rose in his face. He wanted to forget that Gideon stood beside him, move over to speak to them, make some approach – what did anything matter! It seemed to him that the rage of his blood roared out loud for all the world to hear. Was it his fancy or had the girls' attention quickened? He dared not look at the boy. He gripped the edge of the bench to stop himself getting to his feet and traversing the few metres of white sand to where the girls stood – it did not matter which one! – certain that the fiery run of his blood would work its magic on one of them. He wondered if he was losing his reason.

The doppelganger said, "You torture yourself with impossible desires. I am not saying that these girls are unattainable – but in your locked up state you can do nothing. You must break free. And Gideon, in his innocence, will show you the way."

Why do you tempt me? I see, and I don't want to see! Yet I must.

"I know. You have no choice."

If only, by some sorcery Gideon were suddenly older, and he himself nearer his age, and they could be free – comrades in the chase, share their feelings about these two "targets", as in the old days he and Moorlock compared impressions of girls giving them knowing glances – "show out" – as these girls were doing, willing quarry?

He thought he saw in Gideon's face a hint of a like curiosity, not yet full knowingness, shyly glancing across at the girls, their shaded faces half-turned away, pretending to study Domitian's palace – exchanging remarks softly, glancing round at them.

Chapter 4

The first signs of this new Gideon had appeared about three months before, on a day of emotional turmoil, a landmark day for them all, though none realised it at the time. They were seated at a late Sunday lunch, and Frances was with them, close friend of Miriam's from schooldays who often stayed with them, almost a member of the family. She was the catalyst that day, and made them see themselves, and each other, differently.

When had Frances become an honorary member of the household? She seemed to have been one of them always. He traced its beginnings to a day when Miriam was heavily pregnant with Gideon, and he had come home and found her on the chaise longue in the sitting room weeping, and feared that something was physically wrong. There she lay, the great mound of her draped in a blue mohair rug, face stained with tears, the telephone on its long lead on a little marquetry table at her side. She had started her maternity leave from the practice a few weeks before, and had begun to spend the late afternoons resting like this, and listening, as she often said, to her insides, or rather feeling "him" bumping inside her – she had decided that she was going to have a boy. "No it's all right – it's not *me*! It's poor Frances."

She had just finished one of her long telephone talks with Frances, hearing about her tormented love life.

"You gave me a fright," he said. "Coming in the door just now I thought it was something serious!"

"It *is* serious," she said sharply.

He marvelled again that Miriam, so robust in her treatment of life, so hard-headed, could be in tears about a woman's bad luck with men. He mentally dismissed the matter.

Miriam stretched her back under the bulge. "Frances is so unlucky. Men are so heartless. She seems to attract the wrong sort – happy to have a bit on the side and then, when she really needs him, running for cover. Anyway I want to get her away from her flat, and especially her phone, for a little while. Give her some peace here, and give her moral support – help her over this bad patch. Do you mind if she stays here? It might be the saving of her. Actually I've got a selfish reason too. It's maybe my 'delicate state'! But I want to have her with me here for that reason too."

The little while lasted for many weeks. He saw a new relationship between the two women – or new to *him*. They were locked in a total feminine intimacy, thirsty drinkers at each other's spring. Each word, gesture, sigh, was full of meaning for themselves alone. He thought of little girls at play in the park, moving in a secret dance among the flowers, in full converse but making no sound intelligible to anyone else – and this was happening between two grown women, an eloquent and necessary celebration of their gender. Gradually the convention of Frances coming and going in honorary family membership was established – Frances perennially unlucky in love, Miriam the comforter.

In other respects the two women were equally matched. In her world of television and advertising Frances was as successful as Miriam in the law. Shrewd and hard in her business life, however, part of her had remained innocent. She was voluptuous, more conscious of herself physically than Miriam, with a knowingness that sat oddly with that girlish innocence. Gideon admired her because she was chic and glamorous and warm, and at the same time a figure of mystery and power. Judith worshipped her in a different way; for although Frances was Miriam's age she seemed much younger, young enough to see in her one of the clever, poised, sixth form girls at her school, regarded with awe and envy from afar, whose total competence she longed to possess.

Frances was slender-waisted, with hour-glass figure, silky Titian hair falling to below the shoulders, finely moulded features, soft brown eyes, attractive in a dreamy pre-Raphaelite fashion. Sometimes Leo saw her as a nymph in a Brotherhood painting, in flowing white, pensive among reeds beside a dark pool in a mysterious grove. He could imagine her white-hot in love, reaching out to encompass the whole of life in a single moment, hungry for certainty. That was part of the revelation on that day of the Sunday lunch.

Miriam had picked daffodils in the garden and put them in a crystal vase in the centre of the long mahogany dining table; he remembered them, symbols of new born purity and hope, as an ironic feature in view of what followed. She had put place mats on the polished table instead of on a cloth, and the cool colouring of the flowers was reflected as warm highlights in the reddish timber, matching the scarlet in the children's cheeks. They had just run home from Sunday school, their effervescence heightened at seeing Frances. All should have been set for a spring celebration of innocence.

Frances had not been expected that day, but it was accepted that she could telephone at any time – often with virtually no notice – to say she wanted to visit; when she did so on a Sunday morning Miriam knew she wanted to have a heart-to-heart talk to "sort herself out". These talks punctuated their relationship every few weeks, sometimes more often, whenever Frances – and sometimes, he suspected, Miriam too – felt the need "to be girls together". Lunch cleared away, the two women closed the dining room doors behind them and settled in armchairs before the french windows, a tray of coffee on a low table between them, and talked till tea time.

When Frances telephoned after breakfast that morning to say she wanted to come for lunch, Miriam was disconcerted, for she had arranged to take the children to her parents for the afternoon. Miriam's tidy mind disliked seeing her plans disturbed. Then a premonition sent fear through her – *this* heart-to-heart talk would be no ordinary one. She thought of putting her parents off, but filial guilt stopped her. She could hardly reveal that duty to her friend took precedence; and she hated giving a false reason because "lies always found you out!" To put Frances off, however, was also unthinkable. She proposed the first alternative that came to mind: if Frances would stay the night they could have their talk after dinner instead? Her friend sounded cast down at the thought of even a few hours' postponement, but quickly changed course. "My dear, of course it can wait – unlike . . ." She halted, sounding confused, then added breathlessly, "It's all right! It really is! But I may whisper something to you in the kitchen if I get the chance."

The melancholy in Frances's voice made Miriam long to take her in her arms and give her love and sympathy. But there could be no changing the plan now – her sense of discipline detested retreat from a decision; and so, breathless now too, anxious to make a gesture of solidarity and warmth, she said something she instantly knew was absurdly out of place. "Listen darling – while I'm out with the children, why don't you and Leo go into the park – it's a gorgeous day!" She was ashamed. The words were inane, the sort of thing you said "when you were not quite yourself". Thinking about it later she knew why she had said it. In her fear for Frances she wanted to hold her fast, if only vicariously through Leo.

Miriam craved normality. You must never let events knock you out of control. You must pull others back to the normal too. Wildly seeking a straw to hold out to Frances, going into the park to walk off your Sunday lunch was a sturdily normal thing to do, affirming solidity and self-control at a crucial time. She would ask Leo to be especially gentle to Frances, to offer emotional strength for her to lean on. He could be wonderfully sympathetic when in the right mood. Simply by being with Frances and talking – keeping her talking! – he could hold her steady till she returned.

Miriam tried not to show her fears as she busied herself getting the children off to Sunday school. When the front door banged behind them she strove to hold the echoes of their cries and laughter in her mind, talismans against chaos. Leo, passing the open door of the kitchen on the way to his study, saw her bustling about abstractedly, lips compressed, and knew that Frances was the cause. It was not difficult to guess what Miriam had divined from the telephone call. Frances had been "in trouble" before and must have come through it unharmed, so why not this time? He was on the point of saying so but thought better of it. Miriam must be thinking of the tragedy of Janet a year earlier, one of the little group of school friends who had kept their links close over the years. He had never really known Janet, having met her only briefly from time to time when she was in London on leave from her British Council work overseas. Tall, spare, with no figure to speak of, straight fair hair worn in a tight plait round her head, she had struck him as a colourless middlebrow keeping life at arm's length, whom he could not imagine ever getting near enough to passion to be swept out of control. He had been wrong. In depression after an abortion, alone in a hotel room in Rome, she took an overdose of barbiturates and was discovered too late. Miriam had gone about in a fever of pain and anger – angry with life, with men for "using" women, with Janet for denying her friends the chance to help her through her despair.

If *he* ever reached despair so deep, he had asked

60

himself, would he too make it impossible for friends to save him? He thought he would. He would be possessed by one aim only, flight – from the storm of regret and anger within, from the implacable Fates. He would crawl away alone and know no more – feeling only disgust, with life, with himself for falling so far. It was easy to understand how Janet must have felt. Miriam could not, or would not.

She and Frances had clung together for many days, the house a temple of grief, homage, soul-searching. Gideon and Judith had crept about half in fear, half in perplexity at the atmosphere of world-destroying magic, while the women told the beads of darkness. They had tried to reach towards the women in sympathy, to understand, but did not know where to begin. Had they sensed that a similar burden would descend on them too some day, and that there was no way of preparing for it? He had begun to tell them how disappointment and defeat could crush the spirit, and had seen in their eyes, behind the perplexity, many questions they did not know how to ask – how do you know this, Papa? Why, why, why? – and decided he dare not take the explanation further, not yet.

Miriam now feared, therefore, that Frances – this time – might be brought down as Janet had been. He had no feelings about Frances and her predicament – if one could still call it that in these indifferent days – except that he did not want a repetition of those grim days after Janet died. He thought it unlikely. Frances was tough and practical – but evidently not practical enough if Miriam's fears were well founded. He supposed he ought to give Miriam a word of comfort, but what could he say? He was not even sure that Frances *was* in trouble, and neither was Miriam or she would have told him by now. When Frances arrived, the two women would have their usual hurried whispering session in the kitchen, and there might then be some hard news. He went on his way.

Over the years he had been distantly aware of Frances' turbulent but unfulfilled love life, mainly at second hand from Miriam, but also from Frances herself, in hints let slip in conversation of an evening after the children had gone to bed – which he should perhaps have encouraged her to enlarge upon but had never mustered enough interest. He knew he ought to feel sympathy, and sometimes he fleetingly did, but the feeling was instantly overlaid by temptation. He had never noticed any reciprocal sign; she and Miriam were special "pals" and he, simply because he was there, she treated as a pal too, but a lesser one. When she was in the house, however, he was too much aware of her. He sometimes imagined the soft centre of her as a wondrous, predatory marine flower, tendrils waving in beguiling rhythms, ready to enfold and hold tight for ever, or try to – in her case foolishly, for it seemed she chose married men. Why did women behave so stupidly! Moorlock said, "If women were sensible would we get so much fun out of them, 'playing' them, humouring them!" Still, how could they let themselves be *caught*, again and again, by the demands of their in-folding flesh?

Frances and the children arrived at the same time, and even through the thick study door he heard the excited cries of the children and the richer voices of the two women pitched higher than usual. Had the children sensed Miriam's anxiety? They would now be especially clinging, eager to discover more. He heard Miriam say, "Now children, coats off and hands washed ready for lunch. Off with you! Aunt Frances wants to talk business with me, so you must leave her to me just for the minute."

Frances chimed in, taking the cue, "Yes, my darlings, it's some boring grown-up business I must talk to Mama about. So run along!"

Just before lunch, as he passed through the hall, Miriam hurried out of the kitchen and with a nod beckoned him to follow her into the sitting room. He saw Gideon and Judith at the dining room french windows, heads together. In case one of the children followed, Miriam pretended to point out something in the front garden, and said in an urgent whisper, "She's had another abortion. This time she didn't tell me she was caught – I don't know why. I am so upset for her, much more than the time before – well, you can guess why!"

"For God's sake, not *another*?" He whispered back – he had almost added: "the silly bitch!" but stopped himself, saying instead: "These days it's surely avoidable! It passes belief."

Miriam turned to go. She must get back to Frances in the kitchen before the children rushed in and pestered her for clues to the obvious upset. Ignoring his words – it had all been said before – she whispered, "Promise you'll be with her all the time I'm out. Every single minute! I'm so afraid this time. I'll be back as soon as I can and take over."

So Frances *had* whispered the news in the kitchen, doubtless transparently disguised. One of the children must have picked up the exchange – they were expert eavesdroppers – and promptly decoded it, hence their heads together in the dining room.

She was hot with worry for Frances, as well as fury on her behalf – fury for being a loser because she was a woman! How well he knew Miriam's cry of "woman as loser". How tired of it he was! He did not know that she wept for herself too, that in her friend's pain she herself was necessarily joined. From habit when deeply moved she put her hands to her brow and swept the smooth black hair back from the widow's peak, then pressed her palms to her ears. "I wish I could *do* something!" She searched his face. If only he would say one word to show that he understood?

All he could think of was his anger at her trying to draw him into it. She never gave up! She can't help it, he told himself, but to hell with it all the same.

Sensing the thought, she whispered hotly, "When will you see that it's not simple? Women are *driven*! Driven by our accursed biology, by our *womanness*." She bit the word off. "By a sort of glory in it too, fools that we are! By a need to proclaim it, partly to ourselves it's true, something a man can *never* understand!" She sighed and repeated his question, "Why again?" She shook her head, and some of her fury faded – at least he was taking *some* interest! "Ask her yourself. God knows it might do her good to talk to a man about it, a man who's not involved with her, that is."

Miriam sometimes remarked that she was glad Frances was not his type. The statement, teasing, provocative,

64

always amazed him. Did she really not see how aware he was of Frances, that figure, the warm creamy odour of her flesh, the sense of her impatient blood, and a provocative shrewdness that could reach out unerringly to his mood of the moment? Her position as honorary member of the household was delicately poised between the casual closeness of family, and personal intimacy. Sometimes the balance mysteriously shifted and she came near to treating him as if she were indeed the third force in a *ménage à trois*, and temptation was great. At those moments, as an unthinking protection, he reminded himself of a quality in her just beneath the surface, an impatience not unlike Miriam's, a will to dominate, and that was enough to quench the fire. Long ago Miriam must have sensed this aversion without examining it too closely, and felt safe.

Her suggestion that he have a heart-to-heart with Frances startled him. His question about the abortion had been an idle one. Still it would be interesting to hear how Frances would talk about the promptings of her viscera. He wondered if Miriam had ever said to herself, thinking of Frances, "There but for the grace of God . . .!" Why had he never bothered to ask her? In truth he *had*, in many different ways over the years, usually when they had cracked a bottle at dinner *tête à tête* when the children were tucked up for the night, the wine encouraging vacant curiosity. With characteristic bluntness she had said, "Yes I *have*, often! God must have it in for women! Giving us this accursed biology and the damned emotions that go with it – yes and chains too, the need for supports that imprison us – love and marriage and husbands!"

That had been in the early days, before he had given up. At first he had thought, "She can't mean this. It's an intellectual conceit!" Then he saw she did mean it, that her anger and resentment were real. Impatience getting the better of him he cried: "You can't turn nature upside down – you can't re-make what you are!"

"You're right! It's not worth talking about! Men *have* been dealt a better hand than we have and that's a fact! Women can't live at ease with our biology and the wear and tear that goes with it and that's a fact too! If only we could live life like men, have babies without the unbreakable attachment they bring and go on our way as men do! But something inside us pulls another way, into the old pattern!" She shrugged with that teasing smile and added, "Maybe that's why I'm in the matrimonial side of the legal profession acting for women – trying to correct women's raw deal by just a fraction? There's futility for you!"

The bottle finished, they sat in silence, each pursuing secret thoughts of "if only . . .". She never failed to add, "Darling I'm a little drunk! None of this makes any sense! How could it? Our viscera and all the tangled emotions that live there make us petty and jealous and possessive and dependent all at once – and that's a terrible combination to live with, especially the dependence we hate most of all. Never mind – this is the wine talking. We don't do too badly, you and I when all's said and done, do we now!"

That question, though lightly put, was searching. Both knew it was not meant to be answered and never could be, but they nodded and smiled and were glad to leave the subject behind. In the after-dinner ritual

66

– she stocking the dishwasher, he snuffing the candles and clearing the table, they followed an old detached discipline of putting discontents back into their hiding places.

The code in which Frances gave Miriam the news was "a friend has had a little operation" – relic of the arch talk of the school dormitory. The children, meeting Frances on the flagstoned path to the front door, must have intuited the tensions in her, and so were primed, and circled shrewdly in the hall, listening with intense care to the two women greeting one another, and seized on the change of tone in the kitchen that signalled the coded message.

Then, heads together at the dining-room window, Gideon and Judith knew and did not know. Gideon shrank from thinking of it in detail, instinctively drawing back from an area of labyrinthine darkness still too close for comfort. Something deterred him from telling Judith what he knew, an unfamiliar sense of responsibility, an inexplicable conviction that he must protect her from frightening thoughts. Here was a new, arresting awareness – knowing that there was a time, a season, when it was right to glean mysterious knowledge from across the frontier of the grown-up world. For Judith that season had not yet come. She must be allowed to have her world of magic still. For him, that world was fading.

She whispered, "But an operation's got to mean cutting her open – it *must* mean that! You must tell me." She gripped his sleeve and gazed up into his eyes with something of their mother's intensity: "After all she looks the same. People die from operations don't they? Do you think she might die? Why won't you tell me!"

Once more he thought of the words, "Today I am a man." From now on there would be many times when he must be silent. How strange that Judith was suddenly too young to talk to about some things? She was only a little girl after all! And he was – what? He was not sure, except that he was changed. "Today I am a man" sounded so natural, as if he had heard the words for years! Where was the boy who had inhabited his body before? He was still there – it was silly to think he wasn't. But he was far away.

"Don't talk rubbish!" he whispered, impatient but trying to be gentle. "It's not like that. I mean – well, it's not really a proper baby you see – it's sort of like a tadpole – well, not exactly. Anyhow you don't feel anything. It's hard to explain. Wait till you do biology. You're a bit too young. But you mustn't say *anything* now – it will upset them all."

The adults should not have been taken by surprise. Miriam and Frances were drawn into themselves, questioning the past and the future. Their inward concentration must have infected Leo. He tried to understand what abortion meant to a woman – not *any* woman – to Frances. Where should the man's feelings be focused now – *her* man, whoever he was? He was being naive. Of course the man had backed away! He thought of the brutal talk of youth long ago, when one had spoken of "stamping the girl's card" and moving indifferently on, and it was weakness to admit that you cared. The demons mocked him – what thoughts were these for a middle-aged man? He studied

68

Frances, trying to imagine the whispers she had lately heard within her, now desperately banished. Or did she still hear them? Where was the outward sign, a tremor of the lip or eye, evidence of the journey retraced to its beginning and now cancelled? She was as poised as always.

Even if the adults had sensed the children's imaginings they could not have foreseen the form of the attack.

In the dining room a slight breeze moved the long net curtains behind him, whisper of spring and the turning year adding to the children's excitement. Frances sat on Leo's left, and Miriam beyond her with the serving trolley to hand, and Judith sat on his right facing Frances, and Gideon beyond her opposite Miriam. Between gleams of pale sunlight filtering through the overhanging foliage in the garden, it seemed to Leo that the broad-shouldered boy was changing before his eyes, drawn far beyond his years by the news that hung in the air among them. Gideon sat gravely erect in his grey and white football shirt and tight denim trousers, head inclined as if a weight bore down on the bony shoulders. That vision of a new avatar in the boy awaiting its time should have come as no surprise, but it did. He was shaken by envy, by regret for his own lost years, bewildered to see Gideon the fledgling silently pursuing, narrowing the gap. He was angry with himself too. Why should envy hit him now? No, it was not *now!* He had chosen not to see it before.

"I fled Him, down the labyrinthine ways,
Of my own mind . . ."

It was not fair to think of him in that fashion. The pursuer was his own unappeased spirit, and Gideon the innocent messenger telling him not to forget! These regrets, these longings were his concern alone, locked away forever long ago – or so he had imagined. Had Frances been a catalyst for this too? That was immaterial. He would have given anything to be away from them all, with no need to respond or pretend to be in control when God help him he was not!

Did Gideon know, he wondered, that a new persona was taking possession inside him, the clay reshaping itself crucially, the spirit becoming sensitive in a new way. Gideon was usually the more vocal of the two children, enquiring, commenting, ceaselessly testing them all, while Judith watched, noted, waited her moment, as if Gideon did the ground work for her and she quietly sifted the evidence and made the telling conclusions. Now it was Gideon who was silent and Judith who girded herself to speak. In her long-sleeved navy blue dress with dark blue silk cravat hanging down beneath the points of the broad lace collar, hair caught back behind her ears with a dark blue velvet band, she could be mistaken for thirteen instead of her ten years – alert, implacably persistent, a force to be reckoned with.

She leaned forward and held Frances with a dark questioning stare and Leo knew that a shot was being prepared and tried to think of something to say that would stop her, but no words came. Judith knew she had everyone's attention. She lifted her soup spoon to her lips but changed her mind and put it down with care, her face white, and shifted her intense stare to

70

Miriam, and the effort to hold her voice steady brought the words out in a low monotone: "Mama, when I'm going to have a baby will they cut *me* up as well?"

Miriam blushed, partly in embarrassment, partly in annoyance, but swiftly recovered. Leo always marvelled at the intuitive umbilical cord that told her of shifts in the children's ceaseless guerilla campaign, how ready she was to feint and parry, dissemble, slyly outflank the attack and seize the initiative. How did you even begin to answer such a question? As always it was not one question but many, a jungle of wrong assumptions with no beginning or end in sense. Miriam's way was to cut through the tangle and choose one simple question to answer, or rather pretend it was simple, and in any case that it was unimportant.

"Oh no, darling, of course they don't cut you up! The doctors and nurses at the nursing home are there to make it easy for the mother's body to do all the work by itself – as they did when you were born, and Gideon. You'll understand all that when you are older. It's all very natural and healthy, nothing nasty about it at all darling, nothing at all!"

Frances had gone as pale as Judith. The girl turned to her, great hazel eyes burning. "Oh Frances, *you* tell me – do they get over the operation?" She spoke as if they shared a secret.

Miriam had been about to close the door on the matter by adding, "So you see it's not really an operation at all – it's simply helping Mother Nature do her work!" Judith's first question had been a feint. She had moved to a different meaning of the word operation, the true one. Since she had now addressed herself to

71

Frances, to interpose now might strengthen the girl's suspicions.

Frances, shaken by the precision of the attack, could only follow Miriam's lead and avoid the real question. Her spoon poised on its way to her lips, she answered as casually as she could, but she knew her voice was not as steady as it should have been. She must have intuited what Miriam had been about to say, "You see – having a baby isn't really an operation at all. It's helping Nature do her work!" She was about to add, "Of course you get over it," but could not face the words, and said instead, "And then you are so happy afterwards, as Mama was when Gideon came and then you – and – and . . ."

Her discomfiture impelled her to continue – to block further enquiry – but her feelings were too taut now, and she could find no words; and unthinkingly, perhaps to create a pause and collect herself, she put her spoon down, still looking at Judith, and missed her aim and hit the spoon on the edge of the bowl, rocking it, and for a second the contents seemed about to splash into her lap. Leo reached over and steadied the bowl in time. In the little flurry of confusion Frances and Miriam gave exaggerated exclamations of relief, magnifying the incident. "Thank goodness you were quick!" Frances turned to Leo. "This is a new skirt! My first day out in it!" She passed her hand over her lap, looking down, then turned to Judith again, "Now what was I saying? Oh I know – but what on *earth* has got into you today, talking about babies and everything! Have they been talking about it this morning at religion school? I can't think what bit of the Bible that comes into!"

Leo heard other-worldly voices shriek above their heads, the Furies in tumult.

Judith had seen through their attempts to deflect her. Characteristically she dug her heels in. Close to tears of frustration, perhaps of fear too, she strove to form the incisive, inescapable question – and lost her way. "Mama please! Please tell me – do they give the baby back to you after the operation if – if – ?" Something stopped her and she gulped a deep breath. "Oh Mama there are so many things I want to ask and I don't know how to." She looked from Miriam to Frances and back again. They *must* help her. They must.

Gideon blushed. He knew the technical facts, or so he thought, but little more. Inexplicably in recent days he had begun to prefer gradualness to Judith's shock tactics. Fascinated, waiting for more clues, he spooned his soup and said nothing.

Leo tried to imagine the little girl's thoughts, logical enough in their fantastical terms. How "simple", in the child's magical mind, it all should be? The child demanded an equal magic from the grown-ups, all answers complete, with no uncertainty. How unlike real life! He remembered what must have been comparable visions when he was about her age, when he had imagined that birth happened in a hell's kitchen lit by leaping yellow flames from great torches, where the kernel of life was opened up, rearranged, and with terrifying sorcery quickened and sent on its way into the world. He wanted to say something calm and logical to put the girl's feverish speculation at rest, but Miriam gave him a look that told him to stay out of it. This was, he could almost hear her say, "women's business".

Mother and daughter must find the right moment to cleave together in the primitive communion of blood and gender.

Where did you begin to understand the mystery of the hidden female world – fragile yet powerful, with its incomprehensible laws – dormant within this alert child, awaiting its day?

Judith had shot an arrow at a venture and knew that it had found its mark, but she did not know how to exploit her victory, how to force the grown-up to spread out the unknown map for her. She was not even sure what knowledge she wanted – and unaccountably she feared it, yet hungered for it. Alas the grown-up world would not open its gates any further – not yet. One day – oh yes, one day! – she would find the spell to open them.

Could one ever explain to the girl, Leo wondered, what she really wanted to know – as yet too mysterious to be given a name – the hidden minuet of the viscera and the emotions entwined in them, their implacable rules, the burdens of obedience and the penalties of defiance, the true meaning of choice, of responsibility? She demanded simple answers – as if such things existed! That too she was not yet ready to be told. Perhaps Gideon was? Yes, that challenge was imminent.

At last Miriam persuaded Judith to wait, Mama would find time soon to sit down and tell her all she wanted to know. Miriam sent him another warning glance, "Say nothing! Whatever is said will not be enough – it is too soon to tell her all she wants to know."

Obscurely, Judith knew that the matter was not as

simple as Miriam pretended, and this frightened her the more; for if a special discussion was needed her unease was well-founded.

Trying to see life as these young eyes saw it, Leo had the startling illusion that he was re-living his own adolescent uncertainties. It seemed that all the old questions were still unanswered, and never would be, at least in any fashion that disposed of doubt. They were part of the given, what you started with, and what remained with you – however hard you tried. If Gideon and Judith were to intuit that Miriam and he and Frances were no further forward than *that*, they would be defeated before they started, as doubtless he himself had been at their ages? And for all he knew, so had Miriam and Frances. If he and Miriam had already passed on to Gideon and Judith their own uncertain comprehension of life the effects could not be cancelled now but merely influenced, and probably in small degree only, towards an unknowable good. Even that hope was probably groundless. He could not recall anything they had given the children by way of good example! How could you tell them that every choice they made was almost certain to fall short of expectations – in the things of the spirit, that is, the only ones worth anything – and that increasingly the future would consist of confronting the "if only" riddles of life, deeds and words and hopes regretted, but nearly always too late to erase or change? Here sitting with them was yet another example – Frances!

Chapter 5

Frances flung the question to Leo over her shoulder, "I suppose you're going to ask me why do I put myself through it like this?"

She was sitting on her heels before the open dishwasher while he handed her little piles of crockery from the long kitchen table. The question had burst from her in desperate defiance, as if she said, "I am talking to you like this because I know what you are thinking and resent it and don't know why! Somehow it must all be said out loud!"

Nothing was happening normally. Miriam, contrary to her usual orderly custom, was about to leave with the children without seeing to the clearing up after lunch, anxious to get the visit to her parents over as soon as she decently could. Leo, unusually for him, followed her to the front door. A wave of sadness had swept over him – not for Frances but for himself. In the doorway he held Miriam by the waist from behind and whispered, so that the youngsters waiting impatiently at the front gate should not hear, hardly knowing what he wanted to say, "Don't worry. I'll hold her steady."

Miriam leaned back against him, half-facing the children, and whispered, "Be gentle with her. This is worse than the other time, much worse. I feel it in my bones."

He hugged her, not too closely, not too casually, for nothing must strike the youngsters as out of the ordinary, and kissed her ear and whispered, "It's all right. I'll be like a brother."

Making his way back to the kitchen behind the stairs he felt that all the winds of the world had been let loose – in the house, in *him*. Was Frances the catalyst? No, it was more than that. Something within him had been ready to break free – no wonder his normal disciplined calm had gone. Why had it happened? *What* had happened? Why now? He knew the answer, and did not want to know. He was a blown runner with no wind left. He had no room in his heart for anyone else's troubles. He wished he did not have to go back to the kitchen and be responsible for Frances.

In the silence after the front door had closed, each feared to utter a word lest everything spill out, undigested feelings, spiritual baggage put together perfunctorily over the years and now demanding acknowledgment.

They moved stiffly between dining room and kitchen carrying little piles of serving dishes, crockery, cutlery, stepping aside to make way for each other, automatically apportioning the tasks. Each waited for the other to begin.

For Frances the compulsion to speak was becoming unbearable. If only she could keep it all locked up till Miriam came through that door again. No, she would burst! Silence was now impossible. Small talk would be even worse. Yet how could she "unload" to Leo?

They had never really talked. She would have to begin so far back – but where? There was so much pain to be proclaimed, remorse, fury – yes, fury – as well as that thin voice in her belly, now gone. Yet not gone! All the same, Leo was a decent man. She reminded herself that something had very nearly happened between them – so long ago! – but Miriam had got to him first. Look where she might have been now, in this serene house, with such children, her own realm to govern! Life was so cruel. Still, precisely because of that lost turn of the wheel with him, perhaps she *could* talk to him after all? There was no choice.

So her question *had* been a challenge, to make it possible for her to say so many things racing round inside her head. And she was not sure, now, whether she had indeed said them. "I don't know how to say it all. I want – I am not sure *what* I want any more! I want to know what I *should* want. If I did I wouldn't be in this mess, and I am angry and sorry for myself, and ashamed. I can't go on behaving like this! Help me if you can. Help me if you dare!"

Within his tumult he sensed these cries and pitied her; and it seemed simplest to agree with her. He said, "I suppose I *was* going to ask you that question. But I can't even begin to imagine how you must feel about . . ." He could not bring himself to say "the abortion" and said, ". . . your decision."

"I didn't mean the abortion!" She snapped, and wanted to say more but could not, and looked at him for help. When he said nothing, she went white and stood up. "I thought I could talk to you." She bit her lip, and swayed a little.

He reached out to catch her, and she tried at first to push him away, then the next moment clung to him and let him hold her. She had misunderstood his silence and was angry – he was obviously retreating behind a man's predatory judgments on women and therefore on *her*. A woman "asked for" what she got. That was how they thought. Then a quality in his silence made her lift her head to look at him. The long contemplative face was looking far away, with an other-worldly stillness she had never seen in him before; and for no reason at all she was comforted and stood away a little, and the anger faded. Here was a decent, considerate man who had always stood a little aloof, whom she had known only in Miriam's shadow – well, not quite that either, for she had always sensed a voice within him that spoke to her condition but timidly retreated, a link of sympathy, a lonely echo in his heart. Yes, she could talk to him after all.

She sensed his disquiet but thought it was on her account, that his heart was moved for her but he was not sure what to do. She should not have snapped at him like that! Strange that after all these years he was an unknown quantity? Of course he was not a loving friend as Miriam was – well, how could he be, being a man! – but, yes, he was surely a *safe* friend. She was entitled to trust him, ask him to listen, share her burden, give her detachment – oh yes she needed a detached man at this of all times! – and sympathy, yes honest sympathy. Next to Miriam what safer confidant could she have?

She knew she was going to pour out everything and in doing so question herself more deeply than she had ever done. Perhaps it was best that Leo was here instead of

Miriam, for she would be forced to explain herself the more, suppressing nothing.

"I'm sorry," he said, thinking his reference to the abortion had shaken her. "I shouldn't have mentioned it – not that way."

"I didn't mean that. It's – I am going to sound so stupid, so weak, so immature, so helpless. I'm sure you think I'm tough! Everybody thinks that. God I wish I were." She turned away from him to hide her face.

She waited for a blessed word from him to steady her, to assure her that he really wanted to hear everything. His silence wore her down and she spoke out wildly again. "You've no idea how alike we are, Miriam and me – I suppose that's why we've been so close all these years! I may seem hard – well, a woman has to be, hasn't she? Oh but I need tenderness! And some men don't understand – at least – at least – well we've never really talked, you and I, have we? Leo, I don't know what it is I want from you except for you to understand! I want – I need . . ." She wished she could stop talking but was afraid that if she did she would collapse altogether – speech provided a slender semblance of control. "God I don't know what I'm saying – but please . . ." She put a hand over her eyes and gave a little sob, and turned to face him. "I must have a shoulder to weep on! Please – it sounds so . . ."

What he now said would afterwards seem to him unimaginably cold, but it was all he could muster. "Never mind what it sounds like. Pretend I'm your brother if you like. I won't tell anyone."

She leaned into his arms again and wept noisily on his shoulder.

80

He held her as one holds an invalid, solely to transmit comfort and hope, while he tried to keep his mind free, distance himself from his own concerns, quieten the voices within – but her grief held him fast and it seemed that *her* voices were joined to his and cried within him too.

Her lamentations stirred him, telling him that the calm he had thought he possessed till now had been a sham, a deadening of his spirit – and her arrival that day, once more defeated, had unaccountably recalled him to life. By some awesome magic she wept for him too.

Trembling in his arms she intoned the catalogue of her stumbling progress, images of hope and exaltation and downfall, wounds of disenchantment, wrong commitments, wrong lovers – as if his arms were a confessional and not a single shaft of remorse or guilt must be withheld. Gradually his detachment left him, and it seemed that she spoke for him too. How could the catalogue be the same? Then he saw that the facts were unimportant – it was the ache of the heart that was the same. The quest differed only in superficial particulars. He did see one crucial difference. She *knew* what she had failed to find and he did not – or would not! He envied her the knowledge. She at least had the courage to look into her heart and confront the reckoning, and these tears amounted to far more than simple lamentation. In this confession she had not spared herself; it was a fierce cleansing, and even the pressure of her body upon him as she spoke, letting her weight down heavily on him, was part of that submission too. Where could *he* go to weep – who could *he* lean on? No, that would not do at all. A man did not weep, and did not lean on anyone either.

Distantly he had been aware of this pain for a very long time. He had stood away from it, pretended that as long as it remained unidentified he could childishly wish it out of existence. As for his "mistakes", to see them as his alone was surely taking self-punishment too far? Some of them were not really his at all – things his women had done or the ways in which they had done them, or pathways in the labyrinth he had omitted to explore – or simply his bad luck. Shabby excuses.

He began to listen to her carefully, now and then agreeing or adding something of his own, his words sounding remote, as when profound truths are uttered in the grey mists of a dream, to fade on waking. They stood closely embraced but not in the way of lovers, rather as survivors of a storm supporting one another while they gathered strength to continue along the road. Murmuring together, listening to echoes in each other, gradually their pain lost its sharp edge.

He wanted to remain in this other-worldly madness, the fugitive illusion of safety – removed from time – with her leaning into him, his shirt drenched with her tears, her arms reaching upwards, childlike, round his neck. They might indeed have been children, safe in innocence.

She returned to her original question again and again. "Why do I put myself through it like this?" Back and forth she coursed over the ground. For the most part it was a keening, ringing with sadness, resentment, self-pity, and that recurrent cry of, "If only . . .!" But when she touched on the continual dicing with pregnancy, her voice became charged with a feverish flippancy that shocked him, "After all I suppose I've been lucky. I've only been 'landed' twice!"

That brought him awake, and for no reason he could think of he was angry with her, "You call that lucky? *Only* twice! Why *at all* for Heaven's sake?"

He realised he had spoken too sharply and stroked her back in contrition. To himself he said, "How could she be so crass as to put a pistol to a man's head that way – or try to! These days – at her age! She could have achieved the same result by simply *pretending* to be pregnant? She wouldn't be the first! But why should I bother? I don't give a damn anyway."

She must have sensed his thoughts, for she began to deny ever trying to pressure a man, not with her *insides*! The thought fascinated her and she returned to elaborate the denial.

The lady doth protest too much . . . She must know the real answer – or answers, for there must be more than one.

"Men don't understand!" she cried. "A woman isn't properly alive until her insides are awakened and tell her so. It's no use trying to explain it – there are no words for it – a sort of magical whisper in the silence of the night! Oh yes, that's true all right. It really is! I know it – and oh how I longed to go on hearing it!"

The intense pre-Raphaelite visions held him in spite of himself, the quest for the authentic experience, for purity, for spiritual fusion beyond passion, beyond ecstasy. And something else, a gleam, a force mysteriously familiar that sounded a warning – but he could not identify it, or did not want to.

That thought wakened him. The sunbeams piercing the venetian blind had shifted on the tiled walls. The lunch-time heat and odours of cooking and food had faded. She stirred too and looked round in confusion as if the disorder surrounding them reflected her own state, and moved away a fraction and touched her hair. "I don't know *what* I've been saying," she breathed, her eyes misty. "But there's so much more!" She was silent for a few seconds, then seemed to draw herself together and said with sudden vigour, but still whispering, though there was no one else to hear, "Let's get this mess cleared up quickly and get out into the park? Do us both good."

In silence they made short work of what remained, the dishwasher packed and started on its programme, everything put away, the table and work surfaces wiped clean. She ran up the stairs to the spare bedroom – Aunt Frances's room the children called it. He went to the hallstand and took down a thin wind-cheater jacket and shrugged it on, and waited among beams of weak sunlight touching the dark wood. Time and memory and dreams were broken into fragments whose edges hurt, and he wished she was far away. He wanted to discover what it was she had made him see and what he must do. He did not want to listen to her any more, but he must let her talk herself out and sympathise. He would listen with part of himself only.

He looked up and saw her pause in the doorway of her room, her figure outlined in diffused sunlight. She had draped a white cardigan over her shoulders that emphasised the tightness of her black sweater. She came down the stairs with a swinging step in what seemed a switch of mood, as if the febrile flippancy with which she had referred to being "landed" had taken hold of her again. He did not know why he resented it.

They walked into Regents Park and crossed the open meadows towards the rose gardens. There was a hesitant warmth in the air, the sky dotted with flecks of high cloud; a fitful breeze ruffled the giant powder puffs of pink and white blossom. He thought about her renewed self-possession, a brave show of that outer strength that had misled him over the years. So it was a hollow shell? Not really, simply the ability to function in two separate compartments – the outer one for the world, business, the public persona, the inner one for the emotions. If only he could do that. Long ago he had given up trying, suppressed the inner life in order to function at all. Perhaps her way was no better after all, considering the mess she was in! The thought brought back some of the wildness of the confessional in the kitchen, but he could remember little of the revelations – only her turbulence, and a great loneliness that was his too. He wished the doppelganger would speak. He needed his help, the first time he had ever admitted it. No word came.

As they walked, her wild talk returned. He heard it as from a distance – punishing talk, searching for causes, reasons for each crisis, each wrong step, each misplaced trust. Again and again she returned to her mother's primitive warnings from a different epoch, perhaps from many epochs before, hard to believe now – "Do not give yourself cheaply!" They had sapped her confidence, leading her to seek an unknown perfection, innocently, foolishly, with passion, a safe haven in certainty. From time to time she paused and waited for him to say something, be involved in her self-inquiry, prompting him with a dry laugh that was not a laugh at all. Please share the waste of sad time with me! Help me to break free.

He did not want to share her wasted time. He had too much of his own to digest, newly realised through her. She talked on.

They reached the broad walk leading to the Goetze fountain and its mythic greenish-grey figures, which had drawn him so often in the early years of the marriage, a hermetic refuge among square trimmed hedges where he had sat alone and dreamed that his quest continued – though to be there at all meant that he had abandoned it. The doppelganger spoke at last. "I told you so at the time. You had stopped trying to find out who you are, and without a clear vision of yourself you cannot be at peace, and will seek the wrong things always. You are angry with this woman because she has made you see that at last. Unless you can hear your own voices you cannot find an answering one in anyone else! Long ago you *did* find one – in Chiara – but the commitment she demanded frightened you, and you fled from her. In fact you fled from yourself! You settled for something infinitely less demanding, with Miriam, thinking it was safer – whatever 'safe' means! As for this woman, you can do nothing for her. Your business is with yourself – you must discover yourself while there is still time. And time is short."

On the long rows of benches lining the walk, middle-aged couples dressed in greens and browns, composed, comfortable, sunned themselves in silence, looking straight ahead, stilled in their Sunday places like figures in a Seurat painting. She was drawn to them in their fixity but also repelled; she was angry for wanting to be like them, searching no more. She glanced at Leo; the long sallow features were tense. Timidly she said, "It's hard not to envy them, though they look so ordinary." Ashamed, she added quickly, "I suppose I shouldn't say ordinary – but it's not as if they – I don't know how to say it!" She meant, "They do not look as if they have sublime visions." She was not quite herself. Every now and then she was gripped by the hysteria that had swept through her in the taxi after the "little operation" – only forty-eight hours ago! – delirium of longing, of defeat, of remorse for the life expelled. These comfortable faces on the benches mocked her, and pitied her too. "Be as we are! Stop looking any further. There is nothing better to be found!"

He was too sick at heart to respond. He thought of the doppelganger's words, unsparing as always. Of course he had known – and not known – what he did! Denial of knowledge had been a childish game. He thought of that other childhood game: Who could hold his breath longest? You tightened your lips and were bursting, and your head swam and you half-wished you *could* fade away into that other, unknown world and discover what it felt like to be "there"! You gave up and were back where you started and wondered why you had attempted the journey at all. This game of hers was grimly different; you never could return to where you started. Had *he* been holding his breath through the years of marriage – living in expectancy, waiting for a wondrous shift to send his spirit forward again? No.

The time of experiment was over. There was, after all, no way forward!

And Frances? She was spinning into absurdity with girlish fantasies of perfection. He forced himself to answer, "You mean it's easier for *them* to be happy than for us! You mean they expect less! What *is* less? And who are *we* to say what is less or more? Maybe they don't know what they should be looking for, any more than we do?"

He raged at himself – why did I say "us" and "we" and let her see how things are with me?

She gave no sign that she had noted the slip. She walked patiently beside him trying not to see the comfortable faces, looking ahead to the fountain and its greenish wet figures and the dark trees beyond. She saw that he was no longer calm and solid and at ease with himself, and was afraid. Once more, a solid support had weakened under her touch. There was so much more to be confessed, examined, judged afresh. Perhaps he was right after all – there was no such thing as less or more, but something that rang a true note in the heart. What was it? Where was she to look for it? How would she know it?

At the fountain's perimeter the few benches were unoccupied, evidently because light gusts sent spray over the basin's rim on to the surrounding asphalt. They found one on a dry patch facing the afternoon sun, and sat and felt the hypnotic spell of the rise and fall of the water and its rainbow gleams. She did not know that this quiet corner had been his place of retreat long ago, but she sensed a release of tension in him as he surveyed the flat green hedges that moved in the April breeze, and the bronze figures in the basin stilled yet moving. She felt release too. Here it was safe to think without boundaries, let the last defences fall. She arched her back against the worn wooden rail incised with many initials, and moved her upturned face slowly from side to side, nudging the sun, listening to the rustle of falling water. She spoke softly, "That time I got landed before, I was so tempted to have it. How strange to say 'It'? But I couldn't bear the thought that every time I looked at the child I would think of – of *him* – the father who should have been there beside me. Alone with the child, I would never be complete. It is unfair but it's true. I can rage at that, as I often do when I am on my own but it's the way we are made. Was I right not to have it? I still ask myself that, especially sometimes when I look at Judith – my child would have been her age now, and I have missed all that – all the closeness, the tenderness, the warmth flowing between, and myself reflected through the child – *my* child! – and out into the world. But where would I have been now – I mean making my way in the world as a woman, with the child always reminding me of failure at the very heart of me? All the bitterness and disappointment. And the thought of that man walking about there free as air – not giving a damn. All the logic in the wide world cannot cancel *that* out! With that dragging me down I don't think I could have fought my way through to the top of the agency. I wouldn't have been tough enough to carry both burdens by myself and that's the truth. I didn't think of that as the choice at the time, but I can see it now. How lucky Judith and Gideon are, with you and Miriam so solid, so balanced together?" She saw his lips tighten and caught her breath, remembering his admission – the words "us" and "we" that had said so much. Impulsively she touched his hand. "It's all right – whatever you say to me is between *us* and nobody else. Nobody! Not Miriam, nobody. Trust me. I swear it."

He nodded without expression and she was not sure if she had been right to give him that assurance – which was itself an intrusion. She moved away at a tangent to talk about Judith's questions at lunch. "Could she have overheard what I said to Miriam in the kitchen and put two and two together? How quick she is? I could see Gideon was thinking about it too but keeping his thoughts to himself. What a fine boy he is turning out to be – well, he'll soon be a fine young man! Leo, it *is* strange the way I care about them – as if they were my own children! It feels, sometimes . . ." Her eyes filled with tears and she could not continue. She had been about to say, "It feels, sometimes, that they are all I've got for the future! Isn't that strange – and sad?"

He had not understood. What could the children's opinion matter to her – at this of all times? He wanted to be bitter, dismissive, but the doppelganger's words stopped him. "Do not be harsh with her." He curbed his anger; she was expressing a kind of envy. Wrong-headed she was, but at least she had feelings – more than *he* had! He returned to the original question – why put herself through all this. "You could prevent it," he said. "Isn't that where the guilt is?"

Before she could stop herself a voice within her spoke out loud. "It's not that. Part of me says I'm not guilty at all. I need to give myself completely – an act of faith I suppose."

He was tempted to ask, "Why with married men, with the dice loaded against you?" It would not be fair. When the chips were down, something within must invite rejection. Who was he to ask such questions – with *his* record?

She might have intuited his thoughts, for she gave a dry, joyless laugh, blinking hard. "Why with married men – I can *feel* you thinking that! Some cry for perfection in me, I suppose. I can't explain it any other way." She shrugged heavily. "Now I feel a door has banged shut inside me, and my heart turns over when I look at Judith and Gideon. I love them so, I want to give them so much of myself. I've lost too much time. It's getting late for me to start having children – and living on my own, well it's out of the question now. I know what I've done can never be repeated – that is I mustn't let it! And I've got to turn and – yes, turn and look at myself again, *hard*. And do you know? – I find myself doing that through Gideon and Judith. I can't explain it."

She wanted to disown the words but part of her was glad. She had never admitted to these thoughts except as dream voices cancelled on waking, but now, having spoken them out loud, she felt a shiver of triumph. She had broken through a barrier – but *what* barrier, and where it had brought her, she must still discover.

Chapter 6

A ghostly touch on Leo's brow brought him back from
the fountain. A drop of sweat slid down his forehead
and absently he wiped it away with the back of his hand,
which was itself moist from the hot, damp Roman air
– a dreamer opening his eyes disorientated. He looked
about the little clearing with the unpleasant impression
that many things had changed. The pale stone benches
still blazed in the brazen sun, the cats lay in the hard-
edged black shadows beneath them in much the same
positions as before, and from somewhere in the maze of
green alleys there floated the languorous female voices.
The last waking vision had been of Gideon's lanky form
racing away into one of the alleys to return to the Forum
below. That seemed hours ago. In the stippled shade of
the cypress the breathless air hung heavier than before;
the afternoon was surely well advanced. He looked up
through the dappled ceiling of stilled foliage. The sun
seemed as high as before. He glanced at his wrist
watch, turning the strap to free the leather from his
sweaty skin. It was his habit to make a mental note
of the time, wherever they might be, when Gideon or
Judith or Miriam went off on their own. Gideon had
been gone ten minutes.

In the dreamer's compression of time he had travelled back through the years beyond the marriage to earlier lives, old loves, old doubts, and failures not understood at the time, emotional debts unpaid. He began to see why he was aware of disagreeable change. Many of the debts were owed to himself – *by* himself! More disturbing, he saw what the doppelganger had meant when he had talked of seeing himself anew through Gideon. So quittance of those debts might come by that route – but at what price? Talking to the boy was now no longer a matter of simple duty but a quite different imperative – to open a forbidden door in himself. Why had it been forbidden? The question was irrelevant, and besides the answer would come only when the door was opened.

The doppelganger had said "dig deeper" – meaning not simply lecture the boy in the abstract but talk of real life, real passions, real jealousies, real disillusion – how you treated people, well, yes, women! What irony for *him* to pontificate on that! In any case how did you reach such depths with a boy of thirteen, even one as eager and clever and intuitive as Gideon, trying so hard to reach out far beyond experience, too far along the road for him even to know any landmarks in the distance, or have any idea what it was he wanted to know? You thought you were taking him a step forward and then the boy's next question demanded that you start again even further back.

As if to emphasise that point Gideon burst into the clearing, hair on end, with the familiar look of expectancy and doubt. "Papa, you talked about Antony *loving* Cleopatra, but I can't picture love? Is it the same as —" He flushed. "Well, I can't say it — I mean the things the older boys talk about — with girls?" He flushed deeper. "The songs are all about love but do they mean *that*? Is that what you meant? I don't think so somehow — I think you meant something else . . ."

He rocked on his toes while his father pondered. He liked to feel that his questions were not easy to answer, for that meant he was testing Papa with nearly grown up thoughts, some of them indefinable, fleeting visions that he could only express in half-formed imagery. He sensed, too, that Papa knew he was testing him, and so these exchanges were becoming an accepted game, not yet between equals but reaching forward to the day when that would be true.

While Leo cudgelled his mind for a better way to convey the ineffable, the doppelganger spoke. "He *knows* only the visions stirred by the blood, yet he also knows that there must be more. He does want you to go deep, but is fearful too. He knows and does not know that these depths are mysterious and dangerous, shadows as yet out of reach, whispers in his soul like yours at his age. Of course most of it cannot be made articulate, and in any case you yourself are still in doubt, but you have no choice but to try. You will be surprised how much he will seize upon, though in a language far beyond *your* reach, for he will transmute it into *his* magic. Be careful. Though in talking to him you will be exploring yourself, choose your words. Stop your obsession with how women treated *you*. Think of how *you* treated them! And remember that what *you* tell him, *he* will put to the test by asking what *you* did in a like situation. A lot of what you did will not bear examination!"

That's not fair, he answered him, most of it was not as bad as you think and even the bad bits were not all my fault.

The doppelganger did not reply.

Still, the doppelganger was probably right to some extent, inconveniently so as always. He would have to swallow his scepticism, his bitterness. Every word, every example, however disguised for the boy's ears, would recall too much. Besides, how could he avoid the unwary hint, the ironic turn of phrase or tone of voice, that said more than he intended, and laid him open to the boy's keen interrogation?

Apart from that, he asked himself, why should I help him succeed where I failed?

Words of his father's returned, the hard grey granite voice reincarnated, and he felt his presence. "Children arrive. You feed them and clothe them and teach them as best you can to be decent people, and then they must go into the world to fend for themselves. There's nothing more you can do."

It was the day of mother's funeral, when as a little boy of six quickening his step to match father's long, heavy stride, reaching up to hold his hand, he had walked with him away from the large men in blue collarless shirts and braces shovelling brown earth on to the coffin in the hole on the windy hill, down an avenue of bare trees towards tall wrought iron gates patterned in intertwined foliage.

"You will not understand what I say now but you will when you are older. It hurts me to speak now, but young as you are I cannot help trying to tell you what is in my heart. It has to do with duty – my duty now but *your* duty when your time comes. A child is sent as a test from God – to test one's faith, to test one as a person, at least that is what we are told – though why we need to be tested by that as well as everything else I have never understood, as if all the bitterness of living isn't test enough! When you are a bit older you will read in the Bible how God told Abraham to take his little son Isaac to offer him up as a sacrifice? That is one way of putting it. We suffer and we *never* find out why, as Abraham never found out why. Maybe we are not supposed to find out? Maybe there *is* no reason?

"You will go into the world knowing none of the answers just as we did, your mother and me, and do your best as we did, that's all. People talk about parents expecting satisfaction from what their children achieve in life, but it's all dreams to stop us giving up the struggle! But if a child has a hard life, it hurts us, for it means we did our job badly, a job *our* fathers and mothers couldn't explain to us, as *their* fathers and mothers couldn't, and so on all the way back. And nobody understands it now either, though everybody pretends to. Expect nothing from life and you won't be disappointed. If life does throw you a few crumbs from the table, be thankful and make the best of them for you might not get any more. One thing is sure, God is without pity. I should not say that. It is a sin to speak of the Almighty like that – but He must know that my heart is broken. So be careful."

Those words sounded a sombre descant in his heart ever after, a *leitmotiv* of chronic cynicism.

Father had judged himself too harshly, which had made him sound so hopeless on that day – and on many other days afterwards. Father too had been a dreamer, and perhaps he too had lost his reflection and never found it again. Could father have been trying to rediscover it that day, by talking to a boy of six – forced to do so, as he himself was now forced to talk to Gideon?

> *"The fathers have eaten sour grapes,*
> *and the children's teeth are set on edge."*

Most of the damage may already have been done by then. He remembered shivering as father spoke, feeling the bite of sadness in his words. Had he passed it on to Gideon long ago, and had Gideon recognised it unawares, as he himself must have done? Gideon's children in their turn would have *their* teeth set on edge at the appointed time. There was no escape and no cure! The ritual stretched back through the generations and implacably into the future – the substance inexplicable, but the emotions awesome in their power. It seemed, indeed, that in questioning him Gideon wanted his own ordained forebodings confirmed. Could their talk achieve no more than that?

He saw now how father had prepared him for rejecting happiness when it seemed within his grasp. The message had been clear – fearing that life's promise would inescapably fade, you designed its destruction in advance! Though father had treated mother badly, by his gambling, and perhaps worst of all the profound discontent that had darkened his days, he had truly loved her. That was the dreadful paradox. There could be no doubt of it – as another lapidary statement had revealed years later, not long after his thirteenth birthday.

It had been an evening when father had shown more than usual bitterness and tension, coming back to the little tenement flat from the factory with drawn face and tight lips, bringing food in little brown paper bags, and setting himself to prepare the evening meal and cook it at the coal range in the tiny cobwebbed kitchen. Having eaten in silence and washed up the few chipped dishes and pots at the shallow earthernware sink, father sat down at the kitchen table to darn socks; and then, characteristically, a thought had burst from him as if the pressure within had mounted beyond control. What other thoughts, too awesome to be spoken, were caught behind that lofty brow and lean hard features? Many more years were to pass before he understood what father had meant when he spoke of a broken heart, and that his severity – punishing himself first and foremost – had been an attempt to conceal the relentless pain of it.

"Listen my son," he had said through gritted teeth, head bent to his darning, the long thick needle flashing to and fro, over and under the crossed strands of grey wool, closing the torn heel. "I want you to know this. I have gone on loving your mother all these years of her death. That is why I could never marry again, even though it might have made things easier in some ways – for you especially perhaps. I wanted to go on seeing her as she used to be, even though she was not here any more, even though I wept every time I thought of her

98

standing here in this kitchen. I have had enough. I wish I could say, 'God bless you' as you go into the world – as you will soon, but I am afraid to hope – that is the truth. Hope hurts. My heart was broken long ago. All I can tell you is do the best you can with your life. Only *you* can say what 'best' is. I cannot say what that is any more."

He heard that gritty voice now, and felt the emotion that had shaken it, and now he knew – and the thought threatened to burst out – why he had turned away from Chiara, and not only Chiara, but others who had gone before. She had been the last attempt to find his Hoffmanesque reflection, and now the poignant memory of her, of what might have been, was almost unbearable. He had feared hope, as father had feared it. How could he tell Gideon *that*, even if he could find words? It had never occurred to him till now that father, fighting a losing battle with his bitterness, had planted it in his son. Father must have known he was doing it but could not stop himself. How could he blame him? And yet he did. He understood him now, at last. He must keep father's guilt locked up inside him. Yet he must warn Gideon, somehow. He would find ways of saying it all, but keep father out of it. He would paint pictures to show what love was, what it could do to you, how it hypnotised you, made you believe in a vision of perfection even though you knew, somewhere at the bottom of your heart, that it could never be true, and that the vision itself – the mirage you had invented – was all you would ever possess. Dare he tell Gideon that in spite of that the pain was worth it?

The doppelganger muttered, "Say it if you like, but

he will not believe you, even if he understands what you are trying to tell him – but you must try, for your own sake!"

As he began to speak he felt a fugitive lightness of heart in the midst of a weight of remorse he had not felt for years, and he tried to hide the tremor in his voice with a cough to clear his throat from time to time, knowing that Gideon would not be deceived.

Chapter 7

Chiara had come into Leo's life fifteen years before, in a moment when Death hung close. It was during a storm of Olympian ferocity, in a Dakota flying over waters where Odysseus had fought his fate, over Scylla and Charybdis and the Siren rocks.

At noon on a hot summer's day they had taken off from Reggio for Rome and climbed into a cloudless sky. The other passengers, solid business men in dark suits, had settled down into normal quiescence in the cocoon of the little cabin. Suddenly – or so it seemed, but the grappa he had drunk before take-off might have dimmed the passage of time – the sky was dark as night. Hard rain battered the little window beside him with the drumbeat of hail. Titan hands tossed the plane about the sky. Soon they were flying low over the sea, close to mountainous black waves whose curving white edges reached up high as if they would at any moment drag them down. Above the drone of the engines came crash upon crash of thunder like salvoes of heavy artillery. Forked lightning threw saturnine brilliance across the sky. Leaden cloud hung low like a wrinkled roof, threatening to press them down towards the leaping black waves. The aircraft shuddered and lurched as the wind gusted in the turbulent air compressed between cloud and sea.

He contemplated the faces in nearby seats and wondered if his own features showed as much fear. He was very frightened. Sitting there unable to change events, he simply wished the whole experience to end quickly, one way or the other.

They hugged the coastline. He peered down through the rain-flecked window at little towns nestling in coves at the foot of saw-toothed cliffs – which in the unholy twilight resembled children's stage sets, the houses little cubes of chalk topped with terra-cotta, lit by glow-worms. Tiny harbours stretched out their arms like crab claws curving one within another; over which the sea crashed in white foam, squat fishing boats within rearing high at their moorings. If only he were down there at a quayside bar watching the plane lurch by, idly imagining its passengers' thoughts!

Soon he saw a great carpet of lights ahead – surely this was too soon to be Rome? The pilot took them down fast, the plane veering and tilting. They hit the ground hard and Leo watched frozen as the right wing tip seemed certain to touch the dark Tarmac; but the plane rocked back to tilt the other way, rocked again, then levelled and rolled along unsteadily and slowed to taxi-ing speed.

The young stewardess in tight beige uniform stood halfway along the short gangway and announced, first in crisp northern Italian and then in hesitant English, that Rome airport was closed because of the storm, and Flight Control had ordered the pilot to land here at Naples and wait for conditions to improve. As if to emphasise her words a mighty gust seemed about to lift the plane off the ground. The statement about Rome airport was odd. A storm of this magnitude must affect the whole region – and reading between the lines, even this landing had been "marginal" but there had been no choice! The authorities must have ordered *all* aircraft to land where they possibly could; and rather than upset passengers on this flight by revealing their alarm, chose to refer only to Rome as being closed! Though the statement was true it was not the whole truth.

The pilot swung on to a narrower runway and taxied through the streaming greyness to the dead end of it, turned the aircraft to face the way they had come and switched off the engines. There were no other aircraft in sight, no airport buildings, and no people. Had the control tower directed them to this remote spot so that if the gale did blow them over, only the plane would be damaged, and its occupants? In the sheeting rain all he could see was an expanse of dull green meadow and in the distance a few lonely trees; beyond was a grey emptiness that must be the sea. The syncopated clamour of the elements battered the soul. Now and then the wind eased slightly and a wall of mist drifted in from the sea and shut out the world completely. They were prisoners at the edge of the world.

The only link with it was the stewardess, ardent sprite in close-fitting tunic and tight skirt. Fluffy bronze hair framed round olive features, high cheekbones, large brown eyes, slender nose, full lips. A tempered, disciplined quality behind the innocence took his mind away, and there came to him a potent memory of long ago, Suora Achiropita, the young nun in charge of the dining room at the convent of Santa Prisca where, with other students in Rome, he had often eaten an evening meal. Achiropita! Classic Botticelli beauty, contemplative, shining within – how he had longed for her in those green days! How often he had gone to Santa Prisca and sat at one of the long tables in the low whitewashed refectory simply to gaze at her in wonder and desire? Had she sensed his passion and secretly, in spirit, accepted it? He never knew. Why did the stewardess bring her back to mind now, with that fury of desire?

Yes, the stewardess did possess a nun-like quality, perhaps suggested by the uniform, a similar barrier – the same air of being detached yet involved, of composure, of spiritual strength. In her closely buttoned tunic of vaguely military cut, her compact figure was taut and balanced, as enclosed in serenity as Achiropita had seemed to be in those far-off days of innocence.

That dedicated composure must have been sensed by other passengers, who now turned to her for support in the suddenly menacing world – posing questions for which answers were either unnecessary or beyond her competence. Had she been in such a storm before? How dangerous was it to fly through? How long did "they" – the pilot, the control tower, the authorities – expect it to last? Slender straws.

With a soft smile she confined herself to giving comfort. All would be well: *pazienza*! She went forward to the flight cabin and closed its narrow grey door behind her. In a few minutes she returned with a careful message from the pilot; the company, recognising the inconvenience to passengers, due to circumstances

104

obviously beyond its control, offered free drinks, as many as they wished, subject to availability. The twenty or so passengers gave a collective grunt, perhaps of resignation, or simply relief that *something* was being done for them, however irrelevant. She went aft to the narrow tail section where a shelf and a cupboard served as bar, and soon passed along the gangway dispensing whisky, brandy, grappa, Campari, even small bottles of champagne, whatever the plane's small stock offered. They were accepted with the automatic obedience of patients in a hospital ward. Glasses were quickly emptied and held out to be refilled – many times. Sweat gleamed on foreheads and cheeks. Features became dulled as if blinds were drawn. A few passengers opened document cases and rustled papers. Some sank deeper into the narrow grey seats and stared blankly ahead. Others dozed off.

She retreated aft again and sat on a pull-down seat near the little bar, hands clasped in her lap, contemplating her flock.

After nearly an hour, during which she had passed along the gangway several times with drinks, she stopped half-way along the aisle and announced that the control tower had given the pilot permission to continue the flight. A quality in her voice, a stiffness in her full lips, betrayed a shadow – something withheld. The storm seemed undiminished; the sky was still black. Later he would marvel how fatalism dulled the judgment. He could have insisted on leaving the plane, walked to the airport buildings and taken a taxi to the station and continued his journey by train!

The engines started up again, their roar muffled

beneath the buffeting of the tempest. Shakily the plane rumbled along through attenuated curtains of mist. Now and then an especially heavy gust threw the plane sideways and he expected to feel the undercarriage plough into the sodden grass alongside, but each time the pilot corrected the swing in time. If only he would change his mind and let them all remain on *terra firma*! Whirlpools of storm water danced on the black tarmac. Soon they were low over the angry black waves again.

He looked back and watched the stewardess unfasten the seat belt in her take-off seat in the tail section and rise to her feet. Indefinably she was changed. Rigidity had replaced the supple ease. She caught his eye and was stilled, features frozen as if a secret discourse had been overheard; then she nodded to herself, absorbed. In a few minutes, keeping her balance by holding on to seat backs, she passed along the aisle again with little chrome trays of drinks. At the row of two seats where he sat she reached across to him – the man in the aisle seat beside him was sprawled asleep – with a fresh glass of grappa. He had not asked for one but took it gratefully. She hesitated, then bent closer and whispered in his ear, "It is understood that Rome will give admittance this time." He had made no enquiry. Something in the statement worried him; the word "understood" hinted at doubt! The control tower had surely not allowed the pilot to take off without knowing whether Rome would let him land? It occurred to him that "understood" might have no special significance, but was simply her imprecise use of English! Then he saw the truth in her eyes. Fear had conquered discipline. Her words were an excuse, a cry from her darkness. Nothing had

106

passed between them to prepare for this, only laconic exchanges when accepting a drink. Some quality in him had spoken to her condition, given her the confidence to make this timid link.

Now that she had confessed her fear, his own was reinforced. Death was beside them. That was certain. He tried not to show it. He saw the tension in her face soften, and then a look of perplexity. A rush of blood inflamed her features and she seemed about to retreat. Then he saw her doubt fade. Unawares he must have silently answered her appeal, and reassured her too, and the link was made fast. It did not occur to him that there was anything strange in this communion born of the presence of Death. Normality was gone. There was nothing left but primordial essence, language of the blood. She turned away with an indefinably eloquent movement, bending backwards a little from the hips while still her great eyes held him, a statement of trust. A secret had been confessed and was safe. She went back to her post.

In the eerie greyness the plane buffeted its way up the coast. The 200 kilometre flight from Naples took longer than usual. Nearing Rome the plane did not dip to begin the landing approach. Instead it circled wide over the sea, and again, and yet again, and he could not bring himself to count further. At last the plane turned away in a still wider sweep and headed south again. Rome had instructed the pilot to head back to Naples and put down there and sit out the storm. Its force had seemed to slacken on their way north, but now its gusts shook the aircraft as violently as before.

When they were nearing Rome there had been a

107

stirring in the cabin, not the normal confident resumption of worldly awareness as a flight neared its end, but cautious, qualified, as if hope were dangerous. With this announcement a cry rose up that was more than disappointment or anger; it had the sharp edge of fear.

They flew from Rome to Naples twice. Leo thought of the Flying Dutchman seeking mercy from the land. Over Naples the control tower told the pilot to circle for a while, presumably hoping for a lull just long enough to set the plane down. They wheeled low beside that gothic coast menacing in the steely grey light, over Ischia and Capri and the Siren Isles, swung back under jagged crags that plunged sheer into the white-crested waves, and far out over the sea again.

On their last attempt to land at Naples, they circled while permission hung in the balance. Then the judgement came – landing was refused; they must turn north again for Rome. Surely this would have to be their last attempt to land *anywhere*! Fuel must be low. Outside the window he saw a black shadow. Death flew beside them.

Before he knew what he was doing, aware only of the apocalypse possessing him, he had risen from his seat and stepped over the legs of the sleeper next to him, and moved hypnotically towards her, standing at her post in fragile semblance of composure, hands clasped low before her, great eyes upon him as in a trance, drawing him to her. In defiance he brushed Death aside. He took her in his arms.

It would be years before he understood what he had done. The answer came to him when he read Axel

Munthe's account of the moment during the cholera epidemic in Naples, in a room in the convent of the Sepolte Vive where the Abbess had just died, when, overborne by the sight and smell of the massed ranks of the dead, certain that Death was advancing in final triumph, an uncontrollable force threw him into the arms of the young nun standing near, an embrace of desperation and defiance which she returned with equal violence, ". . . mad with lust in the very face of Death!"

Thinking with recurring guilt of what he had done, Munthe wrote of the power that had compelled it, ". . . an immutable law of equilibrium between Life and Death. Wherever this equilibrium is upset . . . vigilant Nature sets to work at once to readjust the balance . . . Compelled by the irresistible force of a natural law, men and women fall in each other's arms, blindfolded by lust, unaware that it is Death who presides over their mating, his aphrodisiac in one hand, his narcotic in the other." Of course Munthe's experience was not an exact parallel. The stewardess was not a nun, the feature that had shocked Munthe more than any other – taking wrongful advantage of the young nun's fear as she stood alone with him contemplating the Abbess's corpse, her discipline no longer protecting her. In substance, however, it was parallel enough.

An immeasurable time later, daylight restored in an opalescent sky, she gave a muffled gasp and drew away and feverishly smoothed her tight skirt down, looking in fear over his shoulder down the length of the cabin. Dazed, he followed her glance. No one had stirred.

Some were sunk in drunken indifference or sleep – and the others, their minds concentrated on the fine balance of Life and Death, had no room for meaner things.

They looked into each other's eyes with a feeling of returning from afar – but they did not want to awaken fully. The signs of mercy were not to be trusted. The tempest gusted and the plane shook and rocked, faltered, dropped, recovered and struggled on again. Death was standing his ground.

He saw a brilliance in her eyes, exaltation and perplexity in conflict – and horror and despair. What had happened? What had driven him – driven them both – into this surge of the blood as if the last day of the world had come and nothing mattered any more!

For her all was beyond belief, but with no escape from the truth of it – not yet distancing herself from what she had done, for she was powerless to dispel the glory. Could this lustful fury speak of her true self, at last released? She could not disown what she had done, for that would cheapen it, and herself too. They had been strangers with no reason to be closely aware of each other, and in truth were strangers still. Yet when he had taken her in his arms it had been heaven-sent, a benediction. Immediately before, she had been a hollow shell with a wind of fear howling through her. She had fought the impulse to sink down on her knees and beseech the Holy Virgin to intercede, as she had seen her mother do at times of extreme anxiety during the war. She had even whispered a prayer for help to resist that very impulse. The next moment she had seen him rise in his seat and knew he would come to her and she had been ready for him

110

– or rather not *she* but that someone else inside her –
and had felt no surprise.

She was still near enough in years to the Magistrale
days and the nuns to imagine what they would say if
they knew. The nuns would surely say that what she
had done in terror was a venial sin, for Death was
near. That was no comfort. What she had done with
this stranger, all control abandoned, was wanton and
wicked, and she would never be free of that knowledge.
The thought left her incomplete. She needed to know
more about herself and what she had done – and what
it meant – but now, in this slim segment of time between
life and death, that was impossible. She was caught in
a single swing of the pendulum between rejecting the
event and the need to cling to it still, for Death was a
passenger on this doomed flight.

Her cheek touched his again, a whisper of impetuous
contact, then drew away. He fancied she searched his
face for guilt to equal her own. Till that instant he had
felt only blind lust and forgetfulness, and then confusion
as the senses relaxed. He thought he understood why
she looked for guilt in him, to comfort herself for her
own loss of control – for if *he* felt guilt too, some decency
was left! No – he could not accept guilt, not yet.

The telephone on the bulkhead buzzed. She leaned
her upper body away from him and took the handset
from its rest and listened. Replacing it she whispered,
her breath quick and hot, "Rome has consented to
let us attempt to land. They do not want to do so.
The tempest is too strong and there is debris on the
runway, but we have not sufficient fuel to continue
in the air." Her slim shoulders lifted and dropped,

and she searched his eyes again and said softly, "I do not know what to say. But there is not time to speak. I have much to do now. We have only few minutes left."

She meant she must see to the pre-landing procedures; but the words, "only few minutes left", had another meaning. Rome had agreed to an attempted landing only because fuel was nearly exhausted. The landing would be a gamble, but it could not be evaded or postponed. Yet all must be done as if normality ruled. He saw discipline return to her, telling her to behave as if she really believed that these landing procedures were no more significant than on any other day, that life was not about to end, but would return to her as it had been before the storm – in every sense.

With a twist of her hips she began to release herself from his embrace, but not unkindly. A new resolve seized him. The spell must not slip away. He whispered, "I must see you after landing. I do not understand either but I know that what has happened is important – and good. It is not just – *this*! There is so much more. You must believe me."

She must tell him there could be no sequel. If only there was time to think, wait, measure! There was no time at all. The pilot was about to start the desperate landing run – he had said in his breezy way: "I'm going to put her down fast! It's all right – I've done it before. There's no other way."

What had happened remained beautiful, dreamlike, though tinctured with the inexplicable, with danger. A voice within insisted that she had been driven by innocence alone – innocence and fear. She wanted to

112

believe that. In the whirlwind of her mind she searched for a still point. One thing was wondrously plain, but awesome too; she wanted the magic to remain with her, half-real, half-fancy, in a secret world where everything was possible and nothing "counted". Here he was so close – her flesh still sang with the dizzying heat and pressure of him – demanding that the dream *should* "count", that they must allow it to take them further. She must give her answer now, this minute.

Like a gambler unable to resist "plunging" on an unseen card, she knew that the risk she was about to take was inevitable, as was the imminent landing attempt. If she did meet him later in the day and behaved with complete propriety, then the benediction, and the innocence, would be redeemed.

She nodded agreement and could not resist touching his hand.

As he turned and went back along the aisle towards his seat, something in the set of his tall, slender frame with its dark head of unruly hair told her that he too was shaken by warring voices, and she was perversely comforted. Her cheeks burned again.

Going about her tasks automatically, she thought back to the instant that had taken her over the brink, when the pilot had said over the telephone in his brisk professional tones, "We have a bit of a fuel problem." She had seen through to his true meaning when he had added quickly, "Don't worry! We'll get down all right." That had said it all.

Her distraught self-questioning took her mind off Death, but fitfully. She looked into the little elliptical mirror above the bar shelf and settled her beige forage cap on her head at the correct tilt to the right, trim and jaunty with its knife-edge crease, and secured it with a tiny gold clip that would lie hidden in her hair. She put powder on her flushed cheeks to dull the sheen. Drawing on her white gloves she realised her hands were trembling, and a scene returned from the distant past, incongruous yet mysteriously linked to her wild state. She was standing before the mirror in the door of the great mahogany wardrobe in her parents' bedroom while her mother dressed her for her first Communion, and childhood guilt brought a tear as she wondered whether she would ever achieve the innocence the white dress proclaimed, let alone sustain it for all time. Where was that innocence now? Where had it ever been?

She knew nothing of this man, only the contact and heat and the enfolding sweetness and strength. What did knowledge or logic matter, in these few minutes that might be her last? What place was there for "normal" thoughts? She tried to cancel them, but they persisted. They belonged to the assessments the old tradition schooled one to make, the kind her mother made, and the mothers of her friends, match-making thoughts ranging over possible choices among the families in the milieu, as *their* mothers had done before them, and so on back through the generations. That tradition insisted that no meeting with a man was ever unimportant, and therefore each must be rigorously judged from the very first with the future in mind lest the demon strike you too soon and honour was lost. And now it had happened! Nothing fitted, nothing was in its right place – in this moment when there was a void where the future should be. She straightened herself and ran her hands down her sides, and shifted in her clammy clothes.

Like her friends she was pulled between divergent worlds. At twenty-two she understood in her bones the inherited propriety in which her parents and other elders of her family had grown up, the old Italy – even to feel a secret sympathy with it; but she also felt an eager response to a new awakening in these post-liberation years. Her traditional family recoiled from the reckless modernism of the young women of her age, the more uncompromisingly because, belonging to the minor landowning class, they shared its slower, cautious approach to life. Her father, a prosperous lawyer, was a natural conservative. Her mother was a traditional materfamilias who still wore the characteristic shiny black garb, her hair in a tight bun. They had instilled in Chiara a strong sense of duty that often made her subdue her new woman beliefs to spare them anxiety. However, in her tight circle of friends drawn from similar families also rooted in the land, the effervescent talk returned again and again to a longing to be free of the old view of right behaviour, to make up their own minds on all things afresh, to possess *liberta* – though with secret reservations. Another credo for the times was on their lips, more momentous still but even less understood, *realizzarsi* – self-realisation.

Each knew its meaning for herself, her own special one. There was little logic in the talk, only a wild coursing of the spirit. Self-realisation demanded that the shibboleths of the old Italy be disowned together with the emotional debris left behind by the war. However, a nice delicacy was observed, a hedging of bets. Outwardly they conformed, as she herself did, to the old code, while in secret they went their own ways, within limits. The code said that you must not arrange to meet a man whom your parents had not already received in the family home, and you must not be alone with *any* man unless an adult brother or other suitable relative was with you *all the time*.

A girl's honour hung upon that. And honour was important. Claretta, a cousin recently married, had for more than a year before the ceremony broken that rule and kept assignations with her betrothed *alone*, with the connivance of young relatives who lied to conceal the fact that the chaperone had not been with the couple every moment of their time together – sometimes not even in the vicinity! Chiara had been part of that conspiracy, and it had been on her conscience ever since. If her parents ever discovered that she had lied to them, if only by her silence, they would be deeply hurt and would never trust her again, and that thought was upsetting, for where would she be – *what* would she be – without that trust?

Chiara was given to slow, measured reflection in the instinctive way of her country relatives, ruminant like their beasts. Sometimes, these days, she had been consumed by capricious anxiety. Things were moving too fast within her. She needed to pause, her soul needed stillness to catch its breath. Her friends scoffed, "Stillness of the soul? Only the old ones want that!" Even so she fancied, sometimes, that they felt as she did but dared not admit it. Perhaps the elders' view of life, matured through the generations, was not such a bad guide after all?

For Chiara and her friends the confusion of war, and of the liberation only a few years behind them, might have been a lifetime away, remembered if at all as transient turbulence in the crucible of adolescence. As for the world before the war, that was as distant as pre-history. Chiara had been fifteen when American and British troops drove in victory through the streets, and she had watched in astonishment as girls of her own age and older – and some even younger – climbed on to the dusty chariots of war to be lewdly fondled by those muscular soldiers in their glowing manhood. She had been breathless with excitement and envy, and guilt for thinking such thoughts. How anxiously her parents had tried to shield her from contamination! Those girls, her father had said, were behaving like whores. Her mother had wept for them, for throwing away their honour.

She still felt twinges of guilt for her defiance in taking the airline job, which her parents regarded with almost the same dismay, especially because she sometimes had to spend a night in another town on a stop-over, when she might consort with heaven alone knew whom.

Her friends saw the job as a badge of freedom as a new woman, and that pleased her. She used the freedom prudently, partly because word of what she did might find its way back in gossip to her parents, but mainly – she sometimes reminded herself in surprise – because of a care for her integrity not very different from her mother's strait view of what a woman owed herself. When in another city on a stop-over she kept the company of female staff only, in restaurant or café or out shopping. When she was not away with the airline, her social life followed family regime, a closed circle of visits to relations or family friends in the city, or to the country to stay with them on their properties. group sorties to theatre or cinema. Talk of *"realizzarsi"* was uplifting, but in real life every step took you into the unknown; you had to be sure. She was "keeping herself" for the right man. Ah yes, that was the crux where the values of her set diverged from those of another age, at least on the surface. Her mother had married the man chosen for her; that was the way they had mapped out a girl's life. And so it continued to be, in the milieu to which her parents were joined by blood and marriage and "links of interest" generations old. Claretta's husband had been chosen for her, and her cousin had been content with her parents' choice, for Claretta had known and liked him from the infinite crossings of their paths in the milieu as she grew up. So perhaps the old system – the elders shrewdly observing the rising generation over the years, refining choices for each budding adult – had something to be said for it after all? Still, she had often told herself, *she* would be different; she would know – really know – the moment she saw "him" for the first time. The thought that she was keeping herself for him always brought a secret smile of wonder and of comfort.

The certainties of the nuns at the Magistrale returned. They had been easy to accept in girlhood days when life was so clearly spread out before them, so simple. Sin was natural, they had taught, only too natural, but

118

when you sinned you must reject the deed at once lest its meretricious allure ensnared you totally. After today – Oh God let us got down safely! – sin would never again be as self-evident, so easy to evade, as the nuns had said it was.

Back in his seat, the shadow of Death returned, but he thought of him fleetingly, a companion on the journey – and that was settled. In the moments left, what was he to think? He was dumbfounded by what he had done. He did not even know her name! Memories of the war returned – brutal and licentious soldiery, Death forever close, and that sardonic soldier's thought, "I shall never pass this way again!" Ah, but that had been different, not better or worse but different, a world with no horizon, only desperate compulsions, no questions asked or answered. You took what you could for tomorrow was – *never*! There must be no comparison with those days. There behind him, only a few feet away, where she busied herself putting everything in order – everything! – there had been kindness, innocence, a true fusion. He needed to believe that. Above all there had been a quest for purity, something he thought had died in him long ago. Were these thoughts, or something like them, in her mind too? *She* might crave absolution, but he could think of no equivalent to fit his own condition. So he tried to silence doubt with reasoning that was really irrelevant.

He agonised over whether she would keep her promise. The doppelganger broke in, "How absurd you are to be concerned about that! The truth is you are guilty because you used her. You have used many other women, so the guilt is not new. You are trying to convince yourself that you are "serious" about her and therefore no guilt is possible! You have played the same game of self-deception many times before. She could have been *anyone*. She really *is* anyone! You made her promise to meet you again because you cannot tolerate the guilt of dropping her as indifferently as you used her, which is how it would seem if you got off the plane and walked away – though that would be the honest thing to do, and the best thing too."

You are wrong. There *is* a purity here. There *is* something magical. You are so damnably prosaic. Why won't you believe that a miracle can happen?

The other said calmly, "I am not blaming you for a bit of fleshly indulgence – a moment of lust, the blood driving you, perfectly understandable! But will it look any better if you take her out a few times and pretend to be in love with her and have your oats and then go on your way as you have often done before? The truth is you are ashamed of what you did. And I must say I am surprised at the risk you took. It would have gone badly with the girl if someone had looked round and caught you. She is lucky to have had time now to – well, need I go into details? That apart, I am worried about your need to invent honourable excuses for your selfish actions. Not that I object to your deceiving people if it suits you – if you can get away with it. But in heaven's name do not deceive *yourself*! No man in his senses believes his own lies."

You always see the bad side. I need to see her again. It's got nothing to do with guilt.

120

"Don't complain," the other said severely, "when I have to say, 'I told you so.'"

Stubbornly he asked himself again if she would honour her promise? As always he looked for portents. Where was he to find them, knowing nothing about her but the physical memory, the quiver of her pressing close, the hot vapour of her flesh, her touch, but above all the intoxicating innocence! He tried to imagine her feelings now. The old proprieties in Italy were powerful still. Yes, she might well draw back.

The plane tilted sharply forward and all speculation was swept away. Soon they sped over trees bent under the gale, leaves blown flat on the branches. He thought of the pilot, the fallen fuel gauge staring him in the face, deciding that he had no choice but to put the plane down fast and steeply. With the tempest shaking the aircraft it was risky, especially if storm-borne debris was scattered in his way, but the alternative, the usual slow preliminary circuit and then a normal glide path, might mean an empty fuel tank while still airborne! A runway rose up to meet them, swirling with storm water. They hit the ground hard and bounced and struck hard again, the impacts jarring the spine, tilted and righted shakily and raced on, the water parting in a wide foamy wake in which storm wreckage tumbled and made separate wakes, some of the pieces quite large, broken doors, window frames, tree branches. The undercarriage had only to hit one of the heavier pieces at this speed and . . .! He held his breath.

They slowed to taxi-ing speed, and then there were indeed a few jolts as the wheels hit small pieces of wreckage, but their luck held. Haggard passengers sat up and yawned and stretched and feigned unconcern, glancing round warily as if daring anyone to hint at the fear now suddenly cancelled.

Arrived at the stopping point, the pilot signalled for the rear door to be opened. Chiara tried hard to turn the heavy locking lever, usually easy enough for her to move, but this time she had no strength – body and soul were still in conflict. She flung her whole weight against it and the bolts moved and the door opened and the cold wet wind struck her face and the shock was blessed.

Chapter 8

How innocent she had been, she marvelled at the end of that day, to think she could re-create distance between them? The spell held her, no longer madness but possession. They moved in measure. Thoughts were answered without speech. "*Think each in each, immediately wise . . .*" Warning voices were stilled. There was an inevitability in their being together and she knew, before the evening was far advanced, that she would be with him in the coming days – he planned to spend a week in Rome. Prudently, for that evening, she had recruited the chaperonage of the secret network among the younger members of the extended family. It would protect her for the rest of the time too. She would switch rosters so as to do ground duties for that week at the airline's office in the centre of town, leaving her free at about four in the afternoon. Besides, and here her breath came even faster, that week of his stay in Rome would place a limit on her commitment; she could then retreat if need be, and no one would dare reveal her secret – every member of the network had something to hide!

Yet amid this intoxicating sense of possession, never before experienced, there was a shadow – she had so far been a rebel on the surface only, and the young women in her circle knew it, sometimes referring to her in wonder as "too faithful to be true". What she was doing must somehow be made respectable, first of all in her own eyes – and secondly, though she would not have admitted that it was in second place, as viewed by the family; how she could reconcile the two, she did not pause to think – but she knew she would do it, somehow. She *was* faithful to the code, as her friends said, and wanted to remain so if at all possible. The compromise between fidelity in the letter as opposed to the spirit – represented by the network's "protection" did not disturb her greatly, though she would have preferred to do without it. One day – ah that was looking too far ahead! – she must contrive to be seen with Leo without that conspiratorial device. Whatever happened she must be at peace with herself. As the evening passed in quiet felicity, that thought assumed increasing importance; Leo's existence must somehow be legitimised. If it was not, then the miracle would slip away, and she would forever be incomplete.

On that first evening she did run some risk of discovery, though probably not great. They dined at the Galleassi in the Piazza Santa Maria in Trastevere, at one of the array of tables that slanted outwards from under the blue and white canopy towards the fountain in the middle of the expanse of old grey stone. Since the Galleassi was on the main tourist circuit it was unlikely that any of her family or friends would go there. If they *had* been seen, her medical student cousin Mario, who according to the scenario was out with her in a threesome with his sister, had an excuse ready – his sister had felt faint in the heat and he had walked with her to the river bank to take the air and back again. The unknown man seen at the table with Chiara during their absence was an English friend who happened to be passing and had sat down for a few minutes of polite conversation – and after all it was a public place so Chiara had been quite safe! The flimsiness of the excuse, in the unlikely event of its being used, would probably be passed over, to be entered into the family reckoning of credits and debits.

All trace of the storm had gone. In the still, sultry air, flocks of swifts swung out from lichened walls, their delicate pointed shapes wheeling against the fading cerulean sky in massed rustle of wings, a susurration of dreams. They spoke little. Thoughts drifted between them, visions, intuitions seeking confirmation, bridges of sympathy. Perhaps some were made explicit, but they could not be sure. Afterwards they strolled hand in hand in the clinging night air through alleys compressed between mysterious walls of wrinkled stone, crossed the Tiber by the bridges linking the island to the banks, and at length reached the Spanish Steps. They ascended to the stone balustrade in front of Santa Trinita dei Monte and stood pressed together and looked across velvet roof-tops under the stars and down to narrow avenues of lights leading to the Corso, where late evening strollers lingered. Innocence and purity renewed themselves, the terror and the lust on the plane not forgotten but recollected now as a necessary, potent prelude, but left unexamined. That would come later.

The doppelganger said in his ear, "What do you think you are doing? This is adolescent nonsense! If you are determined to play out your pretence of love take her to your hotel. You did not stint yourself on the plane, so why waste time now!"

I want to be sure that this is real, that it is not, as you say, self-deception?

"Standing here like moonstruck virgins will not prove anything. I suppose it *might* make her believe you're serious and not just wanting to get your end in. Which is all you do want if you are honest with yourself. So get on and be done with it!"

You are often right but not this time. But anyway I can't – her alibi for the evening only gives us till eleven o'clock and I couldn't simply rush through dinner and get her to the hotel – even if she was willing! – that would have been brutal!

"That scruple never bothered you in the past! You have had so much experience of women and yet you refuse to learn from it! Of course she is ready, *now*! You hesitate because you are afraid of letting your desire bind you to her! That fear of woman has been with you since childhood. When your mother died all you knew was that she had unaccountably left you, as presumably all women would sooner or later, leaving you with nowhere safe to plant your love. So a woman entraps you and leaves you – that was the pattern of life! Therefore to escape that fate, *you* entrap the woman and leave *her* before she can leave you! It is time you freed yourself from that fear. One day you will tire of the search for the dream woman who will be bound to you irrevocably. She does not exist! Or you will find, if you are very lucky, some other link with a woman, some other communion, beyond desire, and will forget your fear at last. But I am beginning to doubt it. Or the gonads will tire, and you will tire too – and one experiment more, or one less, will then make no difference."

I am not such a fool as you think. I know what I want. Leave me alone. But he was uneasy. The doppelganger knew him too well.

"I am glad to hear it, but show me – *show me*! But do not contrive to make it fall apart in your hands as you have often done before. You are very skilful at doing that, but the cruelty is as great, if not greater, than simply dropping her. You must not do it. But I am afraid you will."

She had told him of the alibi plan with excitement and innocence. The conspiracy was part of the social game in the milieu, and all must understand it so that all could be protected by it. Even as she spoke she was surprised at herself; she was taking him into her confidence too soon, in effect making him part of the family conspiracy. She wanted him to know that meeting him like this was loaded with responsibility, that it needed the foresight and protection of others, with *their* honour also at risk. In telling him, therefore, she was testing him too.

Her explanation conjured images of the *commedia dell'arte*, masked figures changing identities and roles in the shadows, deceivers and deceived in a common understanding, each furthering other, private designs. Here was an ancient tradition of enlightened self-interest, with all in the younger generation of the milieu committed to keeping a chain of mutual support strong. Did the parental generation not remember it from *their* youth and see through it? Or perhaps, preferring to forget, they implicitly sustained it? Honour was thus selective, conditional. This evening her cousin Mario, supposedly dining with Chiara and his sister, was with a girl in a rented room near the Termini, and his sister in a room in another part of that quarter with a medical student friend of his; *their* illicit assignations in turn protected by yet other fictions, a delicate web of interdependence presumably stretching even further! At the end of the evening everyone must return to the respective family house, each young woman accompanied by her alleged chaperone.

The doppelganger saw too much, and always at inconvenient times! He did fear being trapped by desire. Desire distorted your vision, made you lose your way. Was that the convoluted lesson Father had tried to give his little boy of six? Nothing good lasted, nothing precious was safe. Love, purity, trust were illusions? Woman the enchantress always let you down – not always her fault but one way or another it happened. No! Father had surely had in mind his own destructive impulses, his own lack of vision, but an ancient sense of honour had prevented him opening his heart to the little boy. Or perhaps he *had* tried, and the boy, unable to comprehend Death, seeing mother's shade hover near yet inexplicably failing to come to him despite his tears, had misunderstood everything Father had said – except the pain behind the words.

The doppelganger was silent.

In that stillness together at the balustrade Chiara sensed the disturbance in him and was perplexed. Was he not sure, as she was now, that there was no turning back? Here was an unfolding of the spirit mysteriously anticipated as if it had waited for her all her life. A voice within said: with him I shall find myself at last, and what it will tell me I do not know, but I feel that he speaks directly to my soul. And now I know. Now I am sure.

She woke from the reverie and glanced down at the luminous dial of her wristwatch. Something about her action disturbed him, not the movement itself but the incongruous feeling of reprieve it gave him. Reprieve from what? From the doubts the doppelganger had stirred once more?

She kissed him. "We must now go. It is necessary to be punctual."

"Wait," he said. "We must meet tomorrow and then . . ." He wanted to say more but the words would not come, and she said it for him, or some of it: "I know! I know now. And I will. I am certain. I still do not know why it is so. But I think you understand me, and that means everything."

They hurried hand in hand down the ample curve of the Steps, the stone underfoot milky white in the moonlight, and reached the bottom just as a taxi set down a middle-aged American couple at the orange-lit glass door of the English Tea Room. In the taxi, her mind now incisive, she told him it would be safer for her to come to his hotel the next day rather than meet him "in the open" again – they had met at the Galleassi. Though that statement was marginally true, it was a fine touch of self-deception and she knew it. She was joining the other young women of the milieu who had crossed the crucial frontier of honour and went to a man's room. They might even see it in her face, as she saw it in theirs. She was not the woman who had taken off from Reggio that morning – that was a whole epoch away.

Suddenly they were settled together, but not in the manner he had known with any other woman. Desire was at ease with itself now that its immediate aim was assured. Nothing more needed to be said. Some of the tension had left him; but he still felt it in *her*, in the racing pulse in her hand, in the eager pressure of her body as the old vehicle rattled and swayed.

When they arrived at a shabby grey palazzo in a narrow street beyond the Termini, bells in a nearby church began to strike eleven. He told the driver to wait. They went in through the wicket in the massive wooden doors and found Mario and his girl, Lucrezia, waiting in the shadows in the dark archway within. Mario was dapper, with dark bushy brows and keen eyes that gleamed in the faint moonlight reflected from the grey stonework, and had a dandyish air despite the sober navy blue suit and white shirt and plain blue tie, perhaps the effect of the wide-brimmed straw hat tilted rakishly to one side and pulled low over his brow. Was that an extra stroke of camouflage, Leo wondered, or a mischievous bohemian touch? Lucrezia, slim, with rounded cheeks and puckered lips that gave her a surprised look, and dark shoulder-length hair, stood behind him in deeper shadow, his left hand clasped in both of hers. She gave Chiara the knowing look she had expected, which said, "So you have gone our way at last!" – and dropped her eyes. Mario nodded, absorbed; he was thinking of what he would do if the other couple in this phase of the concealment plan, Carlo and Teresa, were late – there was always an alternative move in readiness for such an eventuality, and since the timing of each rendezvous was narrowly critical, he would have to make the decision quickly. The next moment, as the bell finished booming the hour, Carlo and Teresa scuttled in through the wicket, breathless. Mario gave a happy grin, showing large jutting teeth.

The small inner quadrangle, where the edges of old, uneven flagstones were caught in moonbeams, was still. No one came in or out. In a few upper windows in the sombre stone, dim light shone at the edges of heavy red curtains, but no sound came from them. Nearby in the side wall of the archway, the *portiere's* window also showed a weak electric light but no one came out to see who had met in the archway to change partners, doubtless not an infrequent ceremony, and discretion well rewarded. Here was yet another black market, the discreet provision of an important service, respectable accommodation for the breaking of family rules, vulnerable too, but in nearly everyone's interests to leave undisturbed. In this quarter there must be many *hôtels de passe*, but the apartments in this decayed palazzo were doubtless still socially superior, where people left in reduced circumstances by the war maintained standards by letting rooms for a few hours of privacy to recommended people. Mario and his friends were unlikely to be known here by their true names.

Superficially these two couples were astonishingly alike. Carlo was much the same build as Mario if perhaps a trifle heavier in the shoulders, and also wore a dark blue suit, white shirt and plain blue tie, and an almost identical straw hat – in the obscurity they could be mistaken one for the other. Teresa, much the same

131

proportions as Lucrezia, also held herself with slightly bowed head and had rounded, surprised features – they too were cousins – and dark shoulder-length hair, and wore a similar white high-waisted dress with dark belt. At a passing glance in the shadows she could have been mistaken for her kinswoman. The choice of players and costume for the evening's enactments had been shrewd.

The four of them, with that ineffable cohesion of people who know each other well, acknowledged Leo with just enough warmth – owing it to Chiara – reserving judgment. Then they briskly turned to the rest of the night's adventure. Carlo and Teresa departed with Lucrezia to take her back to her parents' house. Mario decently retreated a few paces towards the wicket and turned his back, to allow Chiara to say a secret farewell to the stranger.

She whispered, "Good night, *mio caro*, till tomorrow?" In the shadows her features gleamed with happiness.

"Yes," he answered with a sigh. "Till tomorrow. I wish you did not have to go – but – well, till tomorrow then."

"I know," she said with a wistful tilt of the head. "I wish it too, but you see how it must be? Till tomorrow."

She turned slowly away and went to the door and Mario looked out first and glanced up and down the street then took her hand and she followed him out. They must first collect Mario's sister from her assignation, whence both would take Chiara to her parents' house in Parioli, and continue on to their own parental home not far away.

He stood in the cool shadows of the archway till the throaty roar of Mario's old Alfa faded completely, then went out to find the taxi. The driver, a sharp-eyed little man with a patient, knowing smile, had discreetly parked some fifty yards away, outside a similar grey building whose door had a name plate in the style of ecclesiastical establishments, gold lettering on a black ground: *Seminario Ponteficio del* . . ., and switched off his engine and lights.

Leaning back on the cracked leatherette upholstery as the battered vehicle trundled its way to the Piazza Montecitorio, Chiara's hectic whisper lingered in his ears. The old excitement at the approach of full conquest returned. Would possession bring certainty this time? Certainty of what? He was no longer sure. No woman had ever been "his", not completely – to hope for it, as the doppelganger said, was simply one more youthful fiction. The reason for wanting possession was irrelevant. He wanted more than the fleeting dream of it, ending as it always did with that feeling of losing the woman who had been his a moment before – as she rose from the wrinkled sheets and stepped away in every sense, enclosed in her undulating, contemplative secrecy, complete in herself once more. Not his – not his at all! Well, not until she had a mind to enclose him again. But the next time, and the next, and all the other times till the journey with her ended, he still did not know what moved her, what whispers of eternity she listened to, what visions lifted her heart when she contained him, the convoluted riddle of her existence forever out of reach; and that little cry from her, seemingly from far away in the depths of her heart,

133

was only the echo of his own exploding lust. He had hoped, each time, that it would mean something lasting, riches he could cherish and meditate upon for ever, but it never did.

What was that "something more" he sought? There had been fragments of time, brief as lightning flashes, when he thought he did know, when he seemed to reach into the heart of the woman – when she *had* opened the shutter a little but instantly changed her mind and locked herself in once more. If only he could hold that revelation fast! Would he find it in Chiara? He was ashamed to be asking that question once more, recalling days of clumsy youth all over again, pursuit and experiment and hope, and so many disappointments. He had fought the doppelganger's counsel and was no further forward. But wait – something *had* changed. This time he would not retreat. However, if he did not find it in Chiara – if his instinct was wrong this time too – he would give up the quest for ever.

The doppelganger said, "I am sorry to see you open old wounds again. You know a lot about yourself but refuse to accept much of that knowledge. You say you have fought me? You are being unfair to yourself. Understanding is painful. I am not against you enjoying yourself. I have never wanted you to abandon experiment, but you must be ready to accept its spiritual demands, which of course you can never know beforehand. You cannot expect the road to be marked out for you in advance. No one can, and if one could, few would dare face life at all. I have warned you against this adventure because you are drunk with desire and determined to believe it is love. It is far too late for you to be doing that. Have her by all means! But it will not be the possession you dream of. Not with her. Not with any woman! The crude truth is this – by possession you mean freedom to give nothing of yourself. If you continue to want that, you will get no further along the road."

You are telling me that I will never grow up? for God's sake I'm thirty!

"If you can ask me that question, there is hope for you. But remember that this woman Chiara will demand *everything*. Nothing less will do. I think you already know it. Which is why your old doubts return. You can draw back from this affair now – or enjoy her first. In some ways it will make no difference."

You disturb me. Whenever I think I am certain of something, you show me the side of it I don't want to see! I will not draw back from her. I will do as I always have done with a woman, or tried to, explore myself through her, delight in giving her delight, and hope to feel that surge of wonder coursing through her and into me that I have been waiting for all these years – and then I will know, really know, that I can entrust myself to her. So go away with your maxims and homilies. They don't help. They don't help at all.

"Entrust yourself! I am sorry to hear you talk like that. You do not *entrust* yourself to a woman! You take her with you along the road. And you will not reach that decision by mingling the sweat of your lust with hers but in far more subtle ways. As for telling me to go away I cannot do that because you need me. I am the only one you can trust to tell you the truth!"

Chapter 9

As Mario drove with Roman panache through the narrow back streets, he said little to Chiara, partly the exercise of a nice discretion, partly because he still lingered in the evening's communion with Lucrezia. After some time his mind drifted to Chiara, and he wondered how this unknown Englishman had entered her life and sent her, hitherto so correct, whirling to join the rest of them. There would be a great upset in the family if she got serious about someone nobody knew anything about. Rebellion, at least for the girls, was usually with people "known", of your own kind. For men it was different, except at the end when you had had your fling; and then you married within the network, into a known family, with useful linkages within reach. What was Chiara doing, breaking out like this with an unknown fellow? He thought he knew her. She had always been so correct. Perhaps not correct but simply afraid? Now of course it was their duty to stand by her when she needed the usual closing of ranks – whatever their doubts were. All the same, if she went on like this, going with strangers – behaving like a man in effect! – when the time came for her to settle down, people might discreetly edge away from her lest *they* be contaminated in the eyes of the family networks – cruel but true! He would be sorry to see that happen to her. Perhaps, in a little while, he ought to have a quiet word with her, remind her to watch her step and not spoil her chances. She was his favourite girl cousin.

Chiara was glad not to have to talk. She liked Mario, though his medical worldliness – he would be qualified next year – especially the low jokes from the hospital, often upset her; but he was good, though hard. No, hard was too harsh a judgment, practical rather, and shrewd, and she could talk to him as she might have done to the older brother she often wished she had. It occurred to her that he disapproved and was too considerate to show it. She shrugged the thought away. She would think about it some other time.

She thought of the knowing scrutiny of Lucrezia and Teresa, a trifle superior as from seasoned campaigners, and contemplative too, with a hint of envy – yes envy! – as if they said, "If only *we* could know once more that first tremor of excitement and expectation, and fear and impatience too, that we see in you this minute – but knowing what we now know!"

She had sensed too that they looked to her for assurance that all was well, as children do when watching one of their number face a "dare". Would Chiara's "investment" of herself in this unknown man turn out well? She said to herself, "Can I trust my instincts? Could one ever know a man?" The question would not go away. In all her tomorrows how would she answer it? She thought of the coarse exchanges heard over the years between Mario and Carlo and their male friends, that had shocked her with its absence of feeling, its seeming pride in affirming contempt for women – and yet the next moment they could be so sweet and protective and dependable? Was it all pretence? And if so, why did men need to take refuge in that ignoble posturing? She did not know that she was already thinking in a more self-possessed way – she had been close to the fire that day and knew what it could do. Women's feelings were so much more balanced. There was a certainty buried in the depths of her where new life would one day begin. Men veered so violently from confidence to doubt. How sad, how unfair, that divergence was?

Oh God in heaven how quickly everything had changed? Unfamiliar calculations must now be made, new contingencies foreseen and planned for – shameful in some lights but necessary. Would he have thought of that? She felt sure he would. A woman had to protect herself. In a single day a new lifetime had begun, and the old one was already out of reach.

Thinking of the two girls sinning but doing so in a sense under the family roof, it struck her again, but this time with greater force than before, that *their* liaisons could be made "honourable" with no embarrassment. Their companions were known to the families, and were "respectable". She, however, faced an unnerving obstacle. She must somehow bring *her* man into the open – she blushed to find herself thinking of him as her man! She must find a way of making him known to her family and thence to the milieu at large – respectably. Oh it was early days to be thinking of that! No, it was not. A woman was so vulnerable and the network could be cruel. She must think far ahead.

Even if, heaven forbid, this *was* going to prove a passing affair – and there were plenty of *them* going on, though some of the girls might not realise it judging from talk overheard among the carefree bachelors! – to legitimise Leo would still be important; it might even ensure that it *did* last! Soon she must think of a convincing story, how and where and with whom she had met him. In that too she would need the conspirators' help – so that there would be a natural reason for him to visit her parents' house. That is if all went as she wanted it to. That shadow would not go away. Silently she prayed to the Holy Virgin. "Please let it be so! I do not mean to sin, but I am driven – and there is so little time. Please forgive my weakness. I *will* confess. I *will* do penance. I will make this honourable as soon as I can. It *will* be blessed one day – I am sure of it!"

Mario would surely help her think of a good plan. Among her male cousins he was the closest to her. He was clever; he could be trusted.

The next afternoon, at the end of her shift at the information desk in the Via Barberini, Chiara went into the women's staff room at the rear and changed out of uniform into a day suit she had brought with her that morning. It was light beige, not unlike the colour of the uniform. She felt the colour flattered her, bringing out highlights in her creamy skin and the bronze tints in her hair. That it recalled the uniform must have been important too. It too fitted tightly but without the crisp, military line; the jacket with puffed sleeves, nipped-in waist, and flared over the hips, the skirt narrowed to mid-calf.

The room was peaceful, separated by a little lobby from the bustle of the outer office. In an armchair nearby sat a woman in uniform, in her mid-thirties, with short peroxided hair in tight waves close to her head. Her voluptuous figure sagged a little, the long ruddy features hardening. Carmina had been a cabin stewardess and now did ground duty as "mother hen" to the young female staff. Her husband, a former pilot with the airline, had deserted her; and now, with two children to bring up, she worked all the hours she could. Instead of taking holiday leave she persuaded the management to let her do relief duties for extra pay, and sometimes worked double shifts. She was resting from the clamour "out front".

She drew hard on a cigarette as she studied Chiara. After some minutes of silence she took the cigarette from her lips, blew smoke from the side of her mouth, and said quietly, "Go with care. He may not be all you think."

Is it really so plain? Chiara asked herself. She liked Carmina, shrewd, kind, who could be comradely one moment and motherly the next. She was sorry for her – her life a cruel sequel to the first happy days of lustful youth and limitless hope. She tried to sound unconcerned, "What are you thinking of! I am going shopping with a cousin in the Via Condotti."

Carmina gave a husky laugh, "You go to such trouble to meet a cousin! Listen. I know the road you are about to take. I can see your heart is high in the air, far away. That first time is once in a lifetime – and you give the man more than you think. How foolish we are – we women who think we are free! I say these things for

140

your sake. I know what men can do to you. I wish I did not know." She looked away at the blank grey wall dividing them from the outer office, from the world. She sighed and got up stiffly. "Ah well, I have tried. But in God's name go slowly. Keep it as long as you can! Do not fear for it – it will stay fresh!"

She stubbed out the half-smoked cigarette in a heavy glass ash-tray in front of the dressing table mirror, then got up and put an arm round Chiara's waist in a gentle hug, a sad salute, then turned heavily away, to return to her post in the outer office.

Chiara was shaken by the older woman's harsh vision of life. She was also angry with herself for being so ready to tell a lie. One should be able to live without lies. She did not want to see that the web of protective alibis maintained by the younger members of the milieu, which she too now depended upon, was a much bigger lie, indeed a tapestry of lies constantly elaborated. When the nuns at the Magistrale had talked of life opening out into putrescence unless you fought hard to sustain innocence, she had only half-believed them. Now the corruption was already at work inside her, insidious, inescapable. Carmina too must once have been innocent, and believed that good intentions were protection enough, when all around her the opposite was true. So everyone conspired in that blindness, knowing and refusing to know.

With sudden impatience she snatched up a white parasol she had brought with her that morning. It was an heirloom her mother had passed on to her, occasionally carried on formal family occasions, betrothals, weddings, christenings. Perhaps, unawares, she had brought it as a symbol of refinement, to bolster confidence, but there was irony too, for its dated elegance, with long ivory handle topped with a silver horse's head, was also a tie with tradition, with correctness! She stood with it before the long mirror in the door of the clothes locker, hand outstretched on the horse's head in a pose straight out of an old sepia fashion plate. She noted with approval her high colour and parted lips, and nodded to her image.

She went out by a side door to an alleyway where the taxi she had summoned was waiting, and told the driver to go to the Pantheon. From there it would be a short step through narrow back streets to Leo's hotel. Her visits to the Pantheon obeyed an inner voice, unpredictable, imperious. She did not understand the Pantheon's importance for her and perhaps never would. There, despite the crowds surging across the vast arena like waves in the sea, the spot under the centre of the gigantic coffered dome remained her private shrine, a celebrant with her own singular sacrament, hearing whispers of eternity she did not hear in church, intimations from the furthest reaches of creation. She sensed a brooding presence looking down through the round hole in the top of the dome – the *oculus*, the huge eye – probing deeply into her, the awesome touch of divine power. As a girl at the Magistrale she had even dreamed that the great dome was an upturned enlargement of her own loins where her hermetic certainty lay in wait, and felt a turbulence, an exaltation. Once, the turbulence persisting long after such a fancy, she had spoken of it timidly to Father Umberto in confession and he had said, evidently shocked, that such thoughts were sinful, pagan, and she must cleanse her mind in penitence. She must remember that the Pantheon had been a pagan place to begin with, implying that in his opinion it still *was*, but such talk had been far above her head. Perversely his words had strengthened her attachment to that secret communion under the dome. To her relief he never again referred to her pagan thoughts about it.

On this day she stood there for some minutes and the whispers and shufflings of the crowd were silenced. Some certainty returned, but as always not enough. She waited for a sign as in the Magistrale days, some change in the air or in the echoes syncopated high up in the potent dome, but no new voice spoke to her, only that distant tremor, a breath from the original genius of the place, a whisper enigmatic as ever. Then it seemed that something touched her cheek, light as a falling petal, and she turned quickly but there was nothing, no petal floated down to the gleaming stone floor, and no one was near enough to have touched her. It *must* be a sign! She threaded her way through the crowd and out into the heavy humidity of the bustling Piazza. She could not question herself further. Fate had decided.

Chapter 10

For the first part of that day Leo had worked with his usual discipline, sitting at the writing table in the dove-grey room, beneath tall windows opening on to an inner courtyard. The shadows cast by the brazen sun moved imperceptibly on the yellowish masonry reflecting its heat into the room, the hum and rumble of Rome only slightly muted, insistent in the background. On other such days, awaiting the first private assignation, he would have worked fitfully, decoyed into sensual dreams, casting his mind forward to that first scent of her when she entered the room, plagued by doubts, impatiently dismissing them, pushing time away. Today he had been undisturbed. He bent his mind to his notes, projections of investment and capital efficiency, infrastructure needs, labour, distribution, product mix. At midday, the sun burning straight into the room, he reached out of the window and disengaged the slatted shutters from the hinged clips on the wall and swung them closed, the slim beams of golden light illuminating his papers perfectly well, and worked on till nearly two o'clock when hunger finally halted him. He locked his papers in his attache case and went out.

It was too hot, the wrong time of day for a walk, but

as a matter of discipline – mad dogs and Englishmen! – he forced himself to take a turn round the Piazza, but the sun beat hard on his head from the cloudless sky and the heavy air wrapped itself round him like a damp blanket, and he sought the cooler shadows of the narrow flagstoned lane flanking the hotel, where round tables under Campari umbrellas were ranged against the wall. The last in the line was unoccupied. At the others, English holiday-makers ate and drank in noisy delight, with exultant references to the "poor sods" at home unable to escape post-war austerity. He wondered how they could confront the heaped plates of pasta and veal in this heat – and quantities of heavy red wine. Temporary escapers, perhaps they felt duty-bound to be greedy! A trifle self-righteously he confined himself to a roll with provolone cheese and a glass of cold beer. The line of tables left little room for the hurrying throng, shop-girls with dark cowls of hair and pert faces and quick tight hips almost brushing past, sober-suited business men with baggy leather brief cases, the younger men in shirt sleeves, jackets neatly folded over an arm with the lining facing outwards. The stream thinned and was gone. The harsh rattle of metal shutters being pulled down on shops echoed in the little street. The blank heat of the Roman afternoon took hold. He wondered at his composure. In the past when he had felt as calm as this, it had been a sign that he did not really care! Was the doppelganger right? His familiar was silent.

The gourmands at nearby tables, now tipsy, found a new excitement. Lean Roman youths in tight flared trousers and American-style short-sleeved shirts sidled up to them conspiratorially, selling what must have been fake Parker pens for the equivalent of one pound sterling, not in the familiar branded boxes but wrapped in crinkly cellophane. "Real Parrkerr! Little money! Black market!" they said with downward movements of the palms pretending secrecy. The fuddled revellers bought eagerly. Habits of mind died hard, to beat postwar scarcity. Or was it to steal another march on the "poor sods" at home? Should he tell them, in a spirit of British solidarity, that they would find the real black market in the shadow of the parliament building close by? It was none of his business. He finished his beer before the youths reached his table and went back to his room and his work.

Nearing four-thirty, the appointed trysting time, he locked his papers away once more. He was suddenly restive. He thought of taking another turn round the Piazza. That would not do – she might arrive while he was out. He sat down again at the writing table and stared at the shafts of sunlight, now angled a little more to one side of the room, streaming through the shutters. He tried to think of nothing, and must have succeeded, for suddenly the sunlight was slanted further to the side. She was nearly an hour late! The demons plagued him with doubt. Was this another of those blows women delivered with such cruel finesse precisely timed at the very moment of expected renewal? Then came fury. Being late was a show of indifference. How often had he meekly tolerated it, sometimes besotted enough – no, stupid enough – to humour the woman? He thought he heard a tap on the door, soft, timid, but was not sure. He decided to challenge Fate and wait for a second knock, even a third. The third did come, a hard, desperate thud of knuckles. He called out – some obstinacy made him remain seated at the writing table – and she opened the door and stood hesitantly in the doorway. He was struck by the beige colour she had chosen, and understood the signal and was glad and rose to go to her.

When she had first tapped on the door, her head dizzy with the dream and with the "sign" at the Pantheon, she did not know she was late. The exchange with Carmina and the meditation at the mirror and the final reassurance in the Pantheon had seemed to occupy only a fraction of time. Her mind held only one thought, the transformation awaiting her beyond the door. Hearing no answer she at first felt no alarm. She knocked again. Despite the sultry air she was cold. She looked at her watch. Heavens! So late? Even so, this silence could not be true! Surely he would have waited? Something might have happened that had not been her fault? Then fear struck her; had something happened to *him*? Her heart beat as loud as a drum. She knocked again, hard, and her knuckles hurt. She heard his voice and in her confusion told herself that he *had* answered before and she had not heard. She turned the handle and paused in the doorway, and thought it odd that he remained seated at a writing table with no papers on it, and sat so stiffly. Then he looked her up and down and something he saw in her – she was sure of it – changed him, and she saw the same illumination in him that had captured her on the plane, and her heart lifted and she wanted to rush to him but something held her fast, and she looked at him with an equal intentness, making sure, and was happy. She stepped over the threshold and closed the door, and with new self-possession rotated the little locking knob. As she faced him, he was enfolding her in movements completed almost before they began yet each lasting an eternity, interwoven with hers, precisely directed, and nothing was said.

The feeling that *she* was possessing *him* was every bit as strong as she had dreamed it would be. She knew that she would feel this certainty with him always, that life was changed forever, and no exaltation could equal what she now felt.

In no time at all the evening had gone. The reception desk telephoned to say that a gentleman and a lady had arrived. The conspirators must not be kept waiting.

She proposed a later trysting time for the next day, an hour later. She did not tell him why, and he did not ask. She already knew that she would visit the Pantheon before seeing him again. Perhaps there would be another "sign", more explicit?

She was to go to the Pantheon every day that week before going to his room – she had never visited the sanctuary on successive days before. She was breathless each time she reached her halting point at the centre of the arena beneath the dome.

One evening, lying beside him in the other world between sleep and arousal, she found herself telling him of that compulsive sacrament, and was amazed, and a little frightened, but she could not stop – she dearly wanted him to understand. He said nothing, but leaned over her and caressed her with his lips in a communication that reached down into the depths of her.

Can he possibly know the inexpressible things happening to me? For even I do not know what they are doing to me? I only know that it is heaven sent.

Next afternoon, as she moved dreamily through the cooler air of the Pantheon towards her place under the dome, she was startled to see him standing on the very spot. He turned, having recognised her firm step among all the shuffling ones. She blushed and trembled.

"I won't stay," he said close to her ear to make himself heard above the voices and echoes. "I came here on impulse. Don't ask me why! I'll go now and wait for you in the room."

She could not utter a word. It seemed that his presence in this private sanctuary of hers had changed everything. Was the precious communion broken? She was not sure. Before she could form any words in reply he had slipped away into the crowd, and tears were in her eyes. She looked up at the sky through the great hole and slowly the turmoil subsided. Once again she felt the ethereal touch of that brooding presence. "It *is* all true? It must be? I *am* changed. He has changed me. Why do I not feel sinful? I feel whole. I feel that what I am doing is pure, for my heart is pure. Tell me it is true." Stillness spread through her.

When she turned away she had moved on; but in what direction she did not know. She had stood there longer than she had ever done before. She went out and something made her stand still under the great black portico, the serene influence of the interior still enfolding her, separating her from the indifferent ambience of the Piazza below. Reluctantly she pulled herself away. As she made her way through the steamy bustle of the resurgent afternoon she wondered if his caprice in being there waiting for her had been another "sign". She was aware of something new to be confronted, its nature hidden yet crucial, that she must understand and accept wholly. This new demand hung oppressively over her till she reached the narrow street that opened out into the Piazza Montecitorio beside the hotel entrance, then her head cleared, as it always did when in her practical country fashion she faced a new test. Whatever it was, she would find a way through.

On his way back to the hotel, half-closing his eyes to the dazzling afternoon light, he puzzled over his caprice in going to the Pantheon. He had not intended to be there before her. He had wanted to catch sight of her standing under the dome, to see what her demeanour revealed of the mystical experience that was so compelling. Did religious experience reveal outward signs? He was not even sure what it was. He had never felt it himself, or rather he was not sure if he would know it if he had, though he had often longed for it. Yes he did believe in the God of the Old Testament, the Almighty of the Torah, but not as someone you could *communicate* with. If she claimed to communicate with *her* God he must believe her, though the Pantheon, a pagan conception, seemed an odd place for it. Belief, he supposed, could cancel all discordances.

He began to see his visit in a new light. He had wanted to see if she was as innocent as she seemed. He had wanted certainty. The doppelganger said: "No! You are looking for an excuse to punish her for what she is! You punish all your women, sooner or later. Why do you punish them for giving you happiness? Your fear of the enigma in woman is simply an excuse, part of your immaturity. You use it to make your pessimism self-proving. You went to that shrine of hers to convince yourself that she too must fail you. But that was unnecessary – you have decided that already. You now know that her love is too strong to let you forget who you are, for it is precisely *what* you are that draws her to you. You fear that she will force you to live with your true self whatever the price, as she will remain who *she* is, and that has a price too. You will see the proof of this very soon."

He feared the familiar's words, for they drove deep. The doppelganger was telling him that he could make Chiara follow him if he chose, however divergent her course might now be. If that meant self-examination he recoiled from it. It was preferable to drift on the meandering stream of desire, postpone responsibility. A demon mocked him – these were the intimations of fading youth! No, that thought was absurd. He paced the shadowed room waiting for her soft knock on the door. The doppelganger was right. He *was* running away from himself as Hoffman had done, pretending he knew what his spirit wanted, when in truth he had only the haziest of notions, dreams chasing dreams. Did one really have a choice – or was that another of life's tricks?

When she entered the room, instead of her usual gleaming smile and instant surge towards him there was a fraction of a second's pause, a new curiosity in her look, a new assessment. Then tender confidence returned and banished all thought from both. Desire

151

burned high. The ribbons of sunlight moved across the walls.

Later the doppelganger's words about bending her course to his own returned. Again he rejected them. The fire of life was in the present, not in the future. He clung to the ghost of his youth.

She knew there was a question she must ask, but it drifted out of reach.

Chapter 11

The next evening, slanting orange stripes of late sunlight marking their bodies as they lay together half-wakeful, something disturbed the velvet tranquillity. It hung in the air demanding to be recognised. He knew this moment from past affairs, when the future insisted on intruding. That moment was always unwelcome, but not so for the woman. She always *did* want to think of the future. But this early? Well, it was to be expected. He was leaving Rome in two days and what was to happen after? Yes, she was about to talk about it, and he was sure, as so often before, that he did not want to – he needed more time.

Lines of golden light slowly changed position on naked flesh. The days had passed too quickly. What did *she* want to happen? What did *he* want?

The doppelganger said, "A few days ago you were certain! Now you are not. I told you so."

You are wrong. There *is* something perfect here. I can't put words to it, but I know it is so. But it is all happening too soon. I don't want to think of any future – I fear it.

The other chuckled but not with pleasure. "Did you ever want to? You use different words but the truth is

153

the same. Wait. She is going to put the question to you in a form you never expected, and you cannot evade it."

Once more she drew her finger tips over his quiescent flesh. A breathless thought checked her. She raised herself on an elbow and looked down on it and with a little gasp whispered, "You are Jewish!" The unguarded observation was addressed to herself. She knew she must adjust her whole being to a truth she had only that moment allowed herself to discover. The Furies shrieked as they had in the plane, and nothing was safe, nothing predictable. She did not know how to begin.

What had brought Jewish to mind? She knew she had heard the word from him, but when, in what context, she did not know. Had he murmured it in one of the half-waking moments when dreams were spoken unawares? He must have done, and though she had heard, it had made no impact. Where had she heard about circumcision? She could not remember, but she knew. This fleshly recognition must have germinated slowly, questioning her beneath the surface, and now could be denied no longer.

He heard the quiver of panic in her voice, and lay looking up at the shadowed ceiling, his hand limp on her satin hip, and wondered in foolish anger why she had not noticed it before. What sensible response could he possibly make? None of the others had referred to it. Had they been more discreet, more sensitive, or less innocent? Or had they simply not cared?

She had felt her words shatter the mote-laden tranquillity of the room. Here was a further permutation in the riddle of this new phase of her life, inexplicably more daunting than the rest. Here was the sign of an unknown world to which, whatever she did or said, she was irrevocably joined. Tenderly she said, "I did not mean to say it like that. I am so innocent. Forgive me."

Automatically he caressed the narrow waist and jutting hip. He pulled her down to him and held her close, partly to comfort her in her confusion, partly to postpone saying anything. On a rough impulse he put his hand upon hers where it rested on him and pressed it down. She lay still. Perversely his embrace emphasised her inadequacy. The roughness with which he pressed her hand upon him was eloquent, as if to say, "It really is you holding me. Yes I *am* a Jew and you *did* know it. Oh yes you did! I said it. I know I did. Now you must make up your mind what it means to you, what it *must* mean to you in the future – that is if there is to be a future."

Now she was thankful that he imprisoned her hand, but angry with herself that it should be necessary. He was right; it *was* necessary.

She thought about it. Where had she heard that Jewish men were like this? Had it been from coarse talk among the girls in her circle? Perhaps. But how did *they* know? It could not have been from the nuns, who had talked of Jews – and only in passing – merely as misguided people unfortunately removed from the true faith, to be kept at a distance. Young and impatient girls, they had been too shy, or not interested enough in the nuns' convictions, to ask in what way Jews were different as people. Even if they had, the nuns would never have referred to *this*! She could not remember the nuns' words; they must simply have repeated what they had blindly learned. Leo's personality was unlike that of anyone she had ever met, but was that because he was a Jew? She did not want to think about it. He made her feel complete, and that was blessing enough. Yet she *must* think about it. Certainly he saw life with a new, dazzling simplicity. Being with him was a fusion more profound than anything ever imagined, every vision, every dream permissible, exciting. One thing she was sure of. That he was a Jew must not change anything.

Again she asked herself which of her "new woman" friends had said that Jewish men were different *this* way. As for the "difference", with other adolescent girls in the extended family she had often spied on the youths of the milieu undressing in the bushes at the makeshift swimming pool on the family property – and now it was plain. One of her friends must have "strayed" with a Jewish man! The thought filled her with a hot inner blush, partly shame at her unworldliness, partly envy – yes, envy! She thought of the wildest girls in the milieu and could not make up her mind who it must have been. How shocked the nuns would be if they knew that one of their girls had done that? To stray at all was a sin, but with a Jew! Perhaps she was wrong – the source might have been coarse talk overheard between Mario and medical student friends? What did it matter now? Why was she so disturbed? She knew why. She had seen, and yet refused to see! She must have been aware of it during the first hours here with him, in the intervals of his quiescence. Well, perhaps not – she had at first lacked the assurance to look at him in open curiosity. All had happened blindly. In the first delirium of fulfilment, awareness of his Jewishness must have questioned her too deeply, and she had suppressed it. Now, possessing all of him, giving and taking in wifely assurance, fleshly contemplation ranged freely. She raised herself again and lifted his hand from hers and considered his flesh with a new sense of possession.

She looked at her predicament with new realism. In the milieu, if a girl broke the rules there were "ways and means" of wiping the slate clean provided she could be respectably married off soon after. But to bend the rules to admit a Jew! She was considering it, not calmly, but with something like terror – and that thought made her ashamed – but nevertheless with determination. Yes, it was early days to be making this calculation – well, it would be early if things were normal! But these days nothing was normal despite the older generation's talk of how things were before the war, trying to run everything in the old way. She had gone too far to turn back, that was sure. She had not known this compulsion before. That he was a Jew did not change anything, not for *her*. And so her thoughts were drawn in one direction only – what she had done must be made "respectable". There must be a way. She would find it.

She wondered why he said nothing, but her thoughts ran on. Instinct, innocence, gave her confidence. There was no room in her mind for anything else. Above all they needed time – especially time to talk. Yet this was the wrong time for talk, out of key in this warm cocoon of crumpled sheets and shared sweat and possession. She wished she had not let him see how discomfited she was. If only she could retract those words? She said to herself, "What is this wildness I feel in me? Something is warning me – what is the warning? I cannot draw back. But how can I tell them at home that he is a Jew! How ignorant I am of so many things? I do not really know what being a Jew *is*! Or what it means to marry a Jew. What would he expect of me? I do not even know how to ask him such things. God, how can I be thinking so far ahead, after only a few days? But I must, for if I knew it was going to be impossible how could I go on? Not like this, in secrecy, in fear all the time, with no future? I would be ruined! Everything was so easy till this moment, so beautiful! Why need it spoil things? If only he lived in Rome and we could meet easily, take our time, make sure of ourselves step by step – I could in time arrange things at home, I would find a way somehow – later on when they had got to know him. Even about his being a Jew? There must be a way! Oh time, time! Even so I will not let time defeat us."

Timidly, hoping to share the thought with him, she whispered, "I wish time was not important for us now – but it is."

It was the word "now" that made him mistake her disquiet for retreat. A tremor ran through her, intertwined as they lay. Why had this recoil from him come so late? She *must* have noticed it before. In spite of the "new woman" in her, the currents of Catholic faith and tradition ran deep. Perversely they might even have fanned the fires of lust and rebellion! Now, thinking of her future – why did women project the promptings of desire so far ahead! – she drew back from the enigma of his Jewishness. The nuns she had spoken of had done their work well! Here beneath her

158

hand, acknowledged at last, was the physical sign of his Jewishness, already accepted in one fashion but not in any other – and he felt the power and tumult of the atavistic fear in her. And so he heard defeat in her mention of time, and was angry, for time was surely a mask for many other things, as if she said, "Your being a Jew makes a future impossible for us. So all we can do is enjoy what little time remains to us. There is nothing else."

How little he had tried to understand her? He was judging her by some of the less innocent women he had known, hard, hedonistic, who had used him as he had used them – or so he had thought. For them the sign of his Jewishness had been only a passing curiosity. For her it suddenly questioned all dreams, all the bright horizons.

That he did not speak these thoughts was fortunate, for the cold assessment would have wounded her. She sensed that he had misunderstood, and she wanted to say, in full contrition, "I am ashamed of my fears. I am trying to understand what your being a Jew means to me. I am frightened of what it will mean to my family – and I do not want you to be hurt by that. I am afraid that that will destroy what we have found together. We need time if we are to avoid that. But we have so little time – and I need you to tell me that *you* want more time as much as I do." She shrank from saying it. She knew that in some part of him he did understand, and she was dismayed by his silence.

One day he would realise that her fear had touched deeper feelings in him than he had ever allowed himself to know. It would strike him as strange that he had never lain with a Jewish girl, and stranger still that he had never asked himself why? Only then, too late, would he begin to understand what had driven him to defy the tradition that had bred him – as she, in lying with him, was driven to defy hers.

The doppelganger's calm voice returned, "You are making too much of her shock because it suits your purpose. It is not a judgment on you! With her upbringing she cannot help a moment of recoil – and doubtless she had preferred *not* to see it at first, for she needed time to admit it to herself. And what of it? You will go on your way as you have done before, and her sorrow will inspire in you a little dutiful guilt – all par for the course! But I did warn you."

She buried her face in the hollow of his neck and her silky bronze hair lay caressingly on his cheek. She murmured, "I wish I could bring you to my house. I want to very much – and soon. I am sad that I can only be with you hidden away like this, and that I can only be here at all because my cousins and friends tell lies to protect me."

She was ashamed to have referred to the deception in that manner, for the conspirators in the network practised it happily enough; it was a piteous attempt to make him see how great was her sacrifice, how solemnly in her heart she was already bound to him – which she could not confess openly, not yet. It was too mysterious, even a little frightening. As for the concealment, he must already guess that it troubled her. In any case it could only be a temporary "solution", in truth not a solution at all. The problems it compounded, let alone the sins, would grow the longer it continued. Why did he remain silent, he who gave her such sweetness, such understanding, such tenderness? True, being an outsider – how she hated that thought – he shared nothing with her rigid old world, with its fears and doubts, the centuries-old barriers that were part of her too. Yet it need not be so; the barriers were wicked, and she would fight to defeat them, but only with him at her side! Again she heard the voices of the nuns, and she raged against them for what they had implanted in her, and against herself for believing she was free. Their voices battered her spirit, telling her that her "honour" was gone. With that thought drumming inside her head she clung to him even more tightly, as if the rest of the world had suddenly become insubstantial. Afterwards she would remember that his touch, the way he held her, had in these few seconds inexplicably changed.

At last he said, "We will find time – we must."

Here was the assurance she needed; from now on everything was surely possible? Inside her, however, hidden far away, a shadow remained.

They did not speak again about time and the future that evening. They lost themselves again in perfection, in forgetfulness, till the chaperones summoned her away.

Chapter 12

When she had gone he paced the room in a fever of deprivation, sadness, guilt. Of course they would not find time. He had lied to her as he had lied to the others, to prolong pleasure without commitment – but the lie had never before brought the burning sense of self-betrayal that now possessed him. The room was suddenly stifling. He threw open the shutters but felt no relief. He left the room and ran down the three flights of stairs and out into the velvet night, consumed by panic. The sweetness of her imagined presence, that had sustained him on previous nights, was gone.

He walked across the Piazza past the *Il Tempo* building that divided Piazza Montecitorio from Piazza Colonna and on into the Corso, and hurried through the slow-moving evening parade as if the vigour of his step could free his mind. The doppelganger had warned him that a new test was about to come from her, and now it *had*, and his unfeeling response lay heavily upon him like a Sibylline curse, its meaning understood yet rejected. After all he had gone into this affair with complete sincerity, letting his innocence run free, believing it blessed as none of the others had been. Yet, inexplicably, it was going the way of them all. Chiara was taking flight, using his Jewishness as the excuse.

No, that was not it – that was not it at all. She was good and innocent – yes, too good! It was *he* who was in flight from his Jewishness, the burden he had been trying to shed all these years. He was using it to make *any* commitment impossible, a shield against redemption! Therefore this attachment, like all the others, must not be allowed to prosper, for if it did he would be denying his Jewishness totally and he could not do that either. At last he saw why he had never been with a Jewish girl. That commitment would have been intolerable too, for how could he pretend to accept their common heritage while secretly in flight from it? He was in a trap of his own making. He had turned the ancient taboo in upon itself and used it to deny *himself* – and in doing so, deny hope. So, punishing himself, he could always blame the woman, as he now blamed Chiara, for his betrayal of himself. How could he have been so blind for so long ". . . *imprison'd in the viewless winds . . .*"?

Over the years he had made himself believe, despite so much evidence to the contrary, that he was not prone to soul-searching. It was an unmanly preoccupation with the self. It drew you inwards too much. Usually clear-headed, incisive in bearing down on practical problems, when he found his thoughts in disarray he mentally shook himself like a dog to throw off the demonic clamour. He did so now, and was angry at not succeeding. He was amazed to realise that Chiara's atavistic fears were in a sense his own but reversed as in a looking glass. Long ago in childhood he had made up

163

his mind that being a Jew, one of the persecuted People of the Book, was unfair, and as he grew into manhood he had decided, instinctively, not consciously, that the only way of escape was in commitment with a woman "outside". There was nothing novel about this; some of his contemporaries had taken the same route, not from theological conviction but pretended indifference, sheltering behind desire, affinity, perhaps even love – the label was immaterial. It was unnerving to have to admit that he had deceived himself all along. He had merely pretended to escape. Though most of his women had not even mentioned his Jewishness he had told himself that they were silent from delicacy alone, which he had chosen to see as retreat – a perfect excuse for making the affair fail, accidentally on purpose! The circular reasoning was convenient. With Chiara he had begun once again in certainty, with exaltation, and the pre-ordained misery had come, earlier than usual it was true, but as necessary as it had always been, and as inevitable – the poison of the centuries for which there was no antidote.

Hurrying in fury through the crowd in the Corso. he had now torn away all the old excuses. Chiara the innocent was completely his – which made matters worse, for he could not, should not, let the affair continue to the ordained breaking point. The doppelganger was right of course. He must end it before she accumulated too much hope – and what torture disappointed hope could be? Oh yes, he knew that only too well. Some sense of decency reasserted itself, and that too brought shame. The burden of his Jewishness was his alone. It was too heavy for her. He must not let her even try to carry it.

Yet it was not enough simply to turn away. He must know, once and for all, what his Jewishness meant to him, and now to her? What awe, what challenge, long buried within him, had he communicated to her unawares and made her recoil? And made *him* recoil too, in a sense from life itself? He wished he knew. The demon that had made him retreat, inspire love and then reject it, inflict pain unknowingly, he now confronted at last. His scruples were rusty from disuse, but the things of the spirit must surely retain *some* claim on him after all.

'*All things betray thee, who betrayest Me.*'

He should have understood that long ago. The spirit did have its supreme rights. In these few days, Chiara in her simplicity had taught him that. Why could he not accept it with equal simplicity? The question halted him in his tracks on the narrow pavement, and astonished strollers collided with him and made their way uneasily ahead with fearful glances behind them.

The doppelganger said, "You ought to know why. You have always known it. You envy her that innocence. You have used your women not only from desire, but to drink at the fountain of their certainty, but resented their possession of it – as you resented your need to seek it in them. Yet it is there within you, shut away somewhere, and you know that too. Somewhere along the road – I cannot tell you where – it is waiting for you."

He walked on again, squaring his shoulders, tightening his lips, as if somewhere on these crowded pavements on this hot summer night, that discovery awaited him. But he knew there was none. The doppelganger was giving him false hope, though that was unlike him. His position was impossible if he punished women for giving him the certainty he sought in them! If that was true, there was no hope at all.

The slow pace of the couples on the pavement touched raw nerves. He turned away from them and entered the gallery flanking the Piazza Colonna, in effect a covered piazza where wide promenades of shops, now shuttered, stretched away into shadowy half-light. In a corner beside the entrance, golden light from the Cafe Berardo's interior blazed out through broad windows upon round white tables spread in an arc on the gleaming stone floor, most of them occupied by middle-aged couples. Facing them stood a stocky man in shabby dress suit, in his forties, with greasy grey hair, sallow features drawn, giving a creaking rendering of *"Funiculi, Funicula"*, his weakened voice barely holding its own against the chatter at the tables – another sad reminder of the mutability of hope. Leo found a table on the edge of the semi-circle and ordered Grappa and *espresso lungo*. Much as he disliked feeling sorry for himself he let the mood capture him. He did not see the waiter place the glass and thick cup and saucer before him, nor hear the rest of the singer's tired offering.

He saw now that he should have run for his life the moment the plane landed in Rome and Death had retreated. Chiara had warned him to draw back in those final moments; and now, unawares, she had warned him again. And so he must go. Would his heartache remain? Yes it would, as it always had in the past, heartache not for lost love but lost certainty! The doppelganger's prediction was vindicated. It was not her fault. He had tried to lose himself in her, as she must have tried to lose herself in him, each seeing in the other a magic land that appeared only once in a life-time, where every step and vista was dedicated to their happiness alone, where they would find their true selves at last. But the mirage had danced away as it always did, and always would.

He noticed the coffee and Grappa on the table before him. The coffee was cold and he put the cup down. He sipped the Grappa in its little balloon glass expecting the accustomed lift from the fiery spirit, but none came. All was quiet except for low murmurs at the few tables still occupied. The sad singer in the shiny old dress clothes had gone. The waiter, also in shiny black, also tired, hovered near. He paid him and made his way out into the nearly deserted street and across the two Piazze to the hotel.

In his room he stood at the open window looking out at the silent courtyard, and beyond to the gleam of the city reflected in the night sky. Two evenings were left before he took the plane to London. Tomorrow he would begin the charade with which he had ended affairs in the past; his sardonic name for it was "playing himself out". Cowardly, yes, but he hated unpleasant scenes. He would talk about their future, how soon he could return to Rome so that they could be together again, the plans they would make. Yes, they would find a way for him to be presented to her parents so that subsequent meetings could be on a "proper" footing. With these thoughts to sustain her she would be at peace for a time after he had gone; and then his silence would tell her the truth, and that would be the end of it.

The doppelganger was upset. "You cannot do that again. It is childish! Very well, you made a mistake going into this affair! There is no shame in that. But this is a *life* you are playing with! Do not make her suffer the slow corruption of fading hope. Tell her the truth and be done with it. Do you want her to think of you in the future only as a liar and a coward?"

Grudgingly he answered. All right. But I want to do it without hurting her feelings – after all I do love her really. But she has taught me this – and it has been a shock, though it shouldn't have been – I must learn to live with my Jewishness, for if I don't, nothing will ever work, not with her, not with anybody. I will tell her that I am troubled because I can see that my Jewishness will make life hard for us, that I want to think it all through before seeing her again. That sounds sensible enough, don't you think?

"Your words depress me. You are still going to tell her a pack of lies! The truth is you will not finish with her completely. You will leave yourself an excuse – an escape route – to come back if you change your mind and lust for her again. And so you *will* be giving her false hope after all. That, you must not do."

I can't do it any other way. And it is not a pack of lies. Anyway, I owe something to myself!

"Do not speak of being owed *anything*! You have been accumulating moral debts for so long that you have run out of credit. You have reached the end of that road – the road of youth, of no responsibility, which you imagine you can prolong for ever to suit your capricious dreams about yourself! You will suffer for this. I will see to it that you have some very bad dreams. The day will come when they will be unbearable, and you will wish you had acted with courage, with honesty – honesty to *yourself*. But it will then be too late to retrace your steps and change anything. Think about it."

Go away, you and your threat of bad dreams! I have had plenty already. Can't you ever see anything good in what I do?

There was no reply.

The next day he did talk to her as he had promised, when they rested in bed trying to hold the passing moments still.

She listened at first with quick breath, then spoke calmly, confidently. "I am pleased you have opened your heart to me. I am not worried about your being Jewish. Please – please believe me – I need to learn so much about it. And I *will* learn. I will learn everything that is needed. Trust me please. I love you. Love will make the road smooth. I know it in my heart."

"I love you very much. But I am looking to the future – and I must spend some time by myself thinking this through – so that we can move on together without fear of the future."

She seemed surprised at the enthusiasm with which he spoke of schemes for their future. Did she guess the truth? Was he perhaps over-acting? He spoke of returning in a few weeks' time, and there would be many subsequent visits when he would stop off in Rome on other business trips. So they would have plenty of time to make plans.

She was thoughtful. She raised herself on her elbow and searched his face. "I could visit you in London? I can do that easily on my staff pass."

"Yes of course," he said quickly, too quickly, "but wait till I get back to the office and see what I need to do. I know I have several business journeys to make very soon – though of course I can stop off in Rome on some of them."

Her great brown eyes were moist, the skin tight over the high cheekbones. She spoke gravely. "You are right. We must be free of fear for what we are doing. If I have seemed to lack courage I did not mean it – forgive me. Are *you* sure? Tell me you are sure?"

He held her tight and caressed her. "I am sure. I am really sure."

Soon after she arrived on the last day, the late afternoon sun casting warm shadows on russet walls, on an impulse he proposed a quick visit to the Pantheon. It suited his mood to create a symbolic moment laden with sweetness and hope that she would hold in her memory. Perhaps intuiting his thought but not its finality, she eagerly agreed. She too wanted to feed sentimental longings. They went and stood close together under the great dome and looked up through the *oculus* to the sky and the wheeling swifts, petitioning the future – he for himself, she for them both.

"My God this is sickening," said the doppelganger as they left the rotunda. "The bad dreams will not let you rest – ever."

That night as the conspirators waited below, they said farewell with passion. At the same time he strove to instil a tincture of light-hearted calm – the separation was a small but necessary detail, the beginning of a confident future together.

He did not see her again. She wrote often, letters of

anxiety, concern for him, and then of piteous appeal. He wrote only once, a laconic postcard addressed to her at the airline office, unsigned to protect her. It said, "I have not yet solved the problem. Forgive me."

After some months her letters stopped; but she wrote many more that he never received, for with each one she was overcome by the sense of her own failure. She kept the unposted letters in an antique wooden chest to which she alone had the key. Sometimes at dead of night she opened the chest and read the unposted letters, and then stood by the window and wept. How unfair life was. How different it could all have been if only she had had more courage that night of the discovery of his Jewishness – if she had spoken differently, showed no sign of surprise or drawing back, or said nothing at all? If only . . .

Chapter 13

"Papa – it's as if I'll never get any of it right – I mean the strange things I feel . . ."

Gideon's voice jumped again from the piping tone to a cracked gruffness. He shifted his feet, coughed to clear his throat as if that would decide the battle between the two registers, wiped sweat from his brow with the back of his hand.

Leo said, "You *will* get it right, but not as quickly as you want to. We understand ourselves a lot of the time through other people – how you treat them and how they treat you in return. That's what I'm trying to explain in this story. So be patient."

Leo had begun a parable about the affair with Chiara – not naming her – to show that you could "lose" a woman you loved for reasons you could not control; and what love and attachment meant. He wondered why he had chosen Chiara to talk about.

"*You* have not chosen her." The doppelganger drily remarked. "*She* has reached out to you from the past, as she has tried to do many times before but you have turned away. Now her ghost has trapped you, and demands that you pay your emotional debts. To yourself of course! For *her* it is too late. So for your own peace of mind you must learn from that episode at last – what kind of man you were then, and still are, and what changes you need to make! And pass on the lesson to Gideon. But be careful. He is not as innocent as you think. He will pounce on gaps in your story, or admissions that point to guilt, and challenge you to explain them. He will not forgive evasion or concealment, as you have not forgiven *your* father. In a sense it was not your father's fault either and yet it *was*, for he too was afraid to understand himself."

Did Gideon guess, Leo asked himself, that he was only now beginning to understand the Chiara episode? That cowardly postcard, for instance, had told the truth. He had not solved "the problem" of living with his Jewishness, for he had not even understood what the problem was! That truth had nothing to do with Chiara but only with himself; and it was not "a problem" in the finite sense of that word, but a metaphysical state demanding a painful reinterpretation of his whole being. Lacking the courage for that he had placed "the problem" in the pending tray of his mind, and after fifteen years, there it remained. That too was something to be guilty about. With Miriam, Jewish in a mild, automatic conformity, with no questioning and no deep acceptance either, he had felt no need to think of his Jewishness except in the details of sending the children to religion classes on a Sunday morning, belonging to the Parents' Association at the synagogue and making duty appearances at services, hoping that the children would not suspect how lost he was. With that milk-and-water handing on of tradition, he had avoided a reckoning with himself.

If he had stayed with Chiara that avoidance would have been impossible. With Miriam the subject of Jewishness, details of observance, of purpose and significance, were never touched upon, but with Chiara they would have been live issues every day of their life together, for her a constant concern as she dedicated herself – as she doubtless would have done – to smoothing the way for them both. Would that have brought him to this reckoning sooner? Probably not. In cowardice he would have curled up in himself deeper still, pushed time away, tried to live in the cloud of unknowing – that delusion he knew so well. In the background he would have been aware of a pursuing shadow, prefiguring the time when cooling desire would expose a divergence of the spirit never closed. That failure would have been *his*, not hers. She would have committed herself with all her simple determination, he was sure of that. But the guilt would have been his from the beginning, for letting her be tempted by the impossible. The doppelganger had been right about the bad dreams. They were with him now, even here under the blazing sun above the Forum.

In speaking to Gideon he was addressing *her*! No, not her alone but the shades of all his former loves. She personified all of them. Perhaps in her innocence she had had more at stake? Her shade spoke to him now so powerfully that there must be another reason just beyond his reach. Had the demons summoned him to Rome to make some kind of propitiation – to her, to himself? In this fever of the mind all reality was fluid, and anything was possible. *Something* had called him! He thought of those piteous letters of hers, pieces of her broken heart – God, how could he have remained silent? Would she remember them now? He supposed she must. Such tears could never be forgotten. What atonement, what remorse, could now make any difference? There was no answer, only an echo from the emptiness within. He was mourning *himself*, not her. The doppelganger was right in that too. He must learn what he could from his inner voices, behind the words he addressed to the boy.

He would have to continue with the story on two levels as the doppelganger insisted, the surface one for Gideon's instruction, and a secret voice piercing the dark corners without mercy, in humility, as if Chiara stood in judgment. Would new vision come? He wanted it to, but feared it.

How could he show Gideon that desire could have been so compelling as his lust for Chiara, and *not* confess that it was suddenly as strong now as it had been then? And how could he avoid letting the boy see that Miriam had never taken Chiara's place?

Gideon interrupted, and again the struggle with his voice silenced him. Leo saw that the boy was finding the story too taxing. Gideon craved simple answers, the child's answers. At first he had responded eagerly to the parable – the excitement of his father opening a window on himself – but now these feelings seemed dulled. Did he guess, Leo wondered, that there was an "inner" tale he was not being told?

"Wait," he said. "The things I'm talking about have deeper meanings than you think. Soon you will feel your understanding opening out like the sky at dawn, and you will feel more confident. But you must take that on trust."

With a frown of impatience Gideon shook his head and rushed on, his voice now free of the rusty gruffness. "It's hard to explain what I want to know. When Aunt Frances tells me things about – I mean – well, it makes me . . ." He had tugged a crumpled handkerchief from his trousers pocket and now mopped his face, giving himself time, then said with sudden violence, "It makes me boil over!" He gestured hopelessly to his groin and looked away at the glistening metallic greenery of the sun-scorched hedges. "I don't know how to tell you, but I can't *not* tell you! And dreams at night make me boil over too. It's sort of nice but frightening as well and I don't know why – and I don't even know how to ask you or *what* to ask you. And it's terrible not to *know* what it is I need to know! I want to know *everything* – everything."

The appeal behind the words shouted out to Leo, "Tell me what my feelings mean. Tell me what to think!"

With a shock it struck Leo that he was envying this slim Hermes poised in the shimmering sunlight eager to fly beyond the horizon, held here by an unbreakable thread of wonder. Envy his own son! Grudge him his youth and innocence? What damning thoughts these were – pessimism of age and its futility and fear? In heaven's name he was not an old man! How long had that envy possessed him? What damage had it done, to the boy, to himself? He must not let Gideon see it. How cruel of the demon to drive him to strengthen this ardent spirit, help him master the awesome forces awakening

176

within him so that he would envy him all the more? For he himself had failed to master them, not then or since – and could only keep them imprisoned, fearing to confront them.

He ought to tell Gideon that there could never be an "answer" – a single, complete answer – to *anything* in life, but was it fair to burden him so heavily so soon? Was his envy tempting him to destroy that young spirit! No. It was the truth and it would be unfair *not* to warn him. Gideon clung to the child's egocentric faith that "purity" must always triumph, whatever mistakes you made – you and all the rest – and of course that was nonsense. He must tell him.

"How selective your conscience is!" the doppelganger said sadly. "You have played that trick on yourself all your life, the pretence of "purity" getting you through to what you want – except in business where you are ruthless and calculating and successful and good luck to you. But with women you pretend to be "pure" as you call it, because you want unlimited tenderness from them, as a child does. You succeeded in that confidence trick only with women whose illusions blinded them to your total selfishness – like Chiara."

You mean I exploit women, that I go for the ones I think will forgive the soft centre in me – even be charmed by it – which I dare not show in business? That is unfair. It's not all one way. Women can be ruthless too. I must find a way of telling him that.

"You do not like the word pretence, but it is time you called things by their proper names. You have always been ruthless with women as a child is ruthless; but a child has no other way of getting what it wants, so

177

one cannot call it exploitation. But for an adult it *is* exploitation, and it is destructive and self-wounding. You may have infected the boy with it already – so take care not to pass on any more of it."

You are too hard on me. There really is purity in me, locked away somewhere, if only I dared set it free. Besides, women exploit men to get what they want and don't think twice about it. In any case, life *is* hard and I must show him how hard it can be.

"But do not go too far and frighten the spirit out of him – as your father probably did to you. It is time you dropped the fantasy that you are innocent and the rest of the world is predatory. Apart from deceiving yourself, Gideon will soon see it for the self-delusion that it is, and it is not good for a child to suspect his father's integrity."

Perhaps the doppelganger was right about Father, who in his anxiety to arm his little son against the cruelty of life might have spoken too harshly and too soon. He must tell Gideon about it with care, slowly, gently, lest he snatch the wings from the young Hermes before he had even tried to fly.

He said to Gideon, "I felt the same way at your age, bewildered, fearful, getting no answers. I will tell you all you want to know." He saw that Gideon's attention wandered, and wished he knew how much Frances had taught him; but the boy would be embarrassed if he asked directly. He must wait for further hints to emerge. He broke off, "We'll come back to that. I'll go on with the parable. You will see why Aunt Frances calls it 'boiling over!' But the story itself is even more important than that, and this is

178

probably the best chance we will ever have to learn from it."

Trying to explain what "loss" meant – and love and attachment – he saw that Gideon's features, glistening damply in the sun, had closed as if shutters were drawn. Leo thought of their visit the day before to the sacred lake of Nemi in its crater in the Alban Hills, its lucent surface still, an eerie vibrancy in the air, ancient magic awaiting its time. Gideon had felt the spell and whispered, though there was no one to overhear among stunted trees leaning in the mist towards the steep hillside, "I feel it's saying something but holding back a lot more! I wish I could hear it speak out loud." The boy's blue-grey eyes spoke of a like magic within himself, just beneath the surface, too potent to be revealed.

Again Leo recalled his own state at that age, thrown about by viewless desires, wild thoughts impossible to reveal, perplexing happenings at night and sometimes in the day. Grown-ups had talked with excitement and longing of love and attachment but with no explanation, and he had imagined them driven by simple hunger as for food; but how could hunger explain the play of the flesh and the turbulence of the heart and the mind? He must already have glimpsed, in a prefigured future, the peremptory enchainments awaiting him along the way, and been burdened with inadequacy as Gideon now was. Grown-ups had said he would understand "certain things" at some unspecified future time, but the vagueness had increased his anxiety. He had taken refuge in formless, tantalising fantasies, henceforth locked forever within him. What the older boys said they "knew" was not convincing either; which was even more disturbing, for if *they* could not explain in language he understood – near to him in age – what hope was there? Yet he had been sure of one thing. Somewhere in that miasma of dimly perceived meanings was the terrible secret of life itself, the force that made people what they were, that made *him* what he was! He had known that the blustering talk of the older boys was *not* meaningless. In sadness he had told himself that he had yet to learn how to read what his senses were telling him.

Was that why Gideon asked these arcane questions with such urgency, and so prematurely? No, there must be something more, some knowledge that had come to the boy too soon, not yet comprehended in his own spiritual language. Did it come, mysteriously, from Frances? That was worrying, but he would think about it later.

He said, "I feel I'm not explaining things as you expect me to. Gradually you will look at things in a new way, and feel a new confidence as a result. You must trust me."

Gideon nodded, eyes lowered, and mopped his face again, and Leo saw he was not convinced. He persevered, and was disconcerted when some words caused him to stumble, as when he tried to say that love was not a simple craving like hunger – remembering his hunger for Chiara, and feeling it return even as he spoke. He hoped Gideon did not notice. Yes, he said, love *was* hunger of a kind but with explosive emotions inseparable from it. How did one explain the word emotion! He was halted by a look of fear

180

in Gideon, of drawing back; and by something else, amazed recognition as if he listened to another voice speaking to him from afar. Yes, Gideon did know, or partly knew, but could not, or would not, accept any of it. Who could have burdened the boy with so much unbearable knowledge? Someone else stood between them. Could it be Frances? He thrust the thought aside. Gideon prayed for help and he must not hold back.

The word attachment obviously puzzled the boy especially. Had Gideon sensed the guilt behind the "improving" message? After all, the nature of attachment, the mystic frontier between lust and love, was at the heart of the parable! How could he preach the glory of attachment when he had turned his back on it over and over again – and last of all with Miriam? He wished he could cleanse his soul of self-chastisement for coldness, immaturity, cowardice? A mood of confession seized him. Certainly not to the boy! It would be madness. He had not done so even to Moorlock, who probably suspected most of it anyway. They had long ago agreed that guilt and remorse and waywardness – when you *knew* what you should do but indulged in selfishness instead and punished yourself for it afterwards – were par for the course. Gideon must not know any of that.

He ought to warn the boy about the "problems" attachment brought – though "brought" was not the right word; you ran to meet them heedless of the wreckage that would result! How could he extol the precious quality of "care", at the heart of attachment, when he had always regarded caring for a woman as simple self-interest, to ensure that she would be well disposed, tender, pliable? That was not as bad as it sounded, simply a healthy necessity, like watering a plant so that you could continue to enjoy it – but to put it into words would be damning.

The doppelganger was infernally right again. Making his way through the real story beneath the parable was bitter. Why had he persistently gone against what he knew was right? Chiara had told him of the nuns telling the girls at the Magistrale that invincible ignorance was a possible "excuse" for sin. Was that the explanation for him? Of course not. He had always known what he was doing, yet had behaved as though he did not. What difference did it make now, at his age? The doppelganger thought it did make a difference. So be it.

Still, Gideon must learn the rules of the game. He must be made to see that the temptation to deviate from what you knew to be right was insidious, that the briefest moment of inattention could bring disaster; and afterwards you would be appalled to realise what damage you had done to your own interests. No, he must not state the lesson in terms of self-interest. That was giving himself away again. He must tell the boy that you must always do the right thing because it *was* right. God, did he really believe that!

Had he already told Gideon too much? To say that he had truly loved the woman in the parable but that the temptation towards wrong action had made him leave her, would excite suspicion, for to the boy's uncompromising logic *one* of these statements could not be true; if he had loved her he could not have left her, and if he had left her he could not have loved her!

He saw that Gideon was considering the contradiction. Very well, he must make the truth respectable. He laid the blame on her recoil from his Jewishness – the continuing magic of tradition and religion, such as they had felt vibrating in the air on the hillside above the Lake of Nemi, always present, never weakening, always ready to influence you. Gideon seemed to chew over this too but said nothing.

The doppelganger interposed sourly, "You know perfectly well she did not turn away from you."

I know, but something makes me want to cling to that excuse – I suppose because my Jewishness is still an unresolved problem for me. I should not have tried to ignore it yet again. I should not have gone with her. And so I am warning him to be aware that he too will carry this burden with him. In telling him, I am trying to confront myself at last, find out where I stand.

The doppelganger was thoughtful. "I have been waiting a long time to hear you say that. I hope you mean it. But do not let him guess how unsure you are."

Here was something else to settle with his conscience; did he really want Gideon to believe in the prior claims of his Jewishness however much they limited his freedom? The answer must be yes – even though he himself was no paragon! To stress the power of the ancient taboos was not an excuse but the simple truth. He felt a sense of release. In spite of himself he must be a believer after all!

There were too many voices, hard to live with in peace, impossible to explain to the boy – not now, perhaps never.

183

He must give Gideon solid ground under his feet, even if it must prove temporary – though the boy must not know that! Therefore he could follow the taboo route with an easy conscience.

Gideon's face creased with impatience. "But Papa, if love has all that power, why couldn't it just blot out the difference of religion and so on, and make everything all right?"

Trust the young mind to catch him in that trap! Chiara had sworn that her love would triumph over every obstacle. Once again he heard the conviction in her softly resonant voice as she said it, and saw the confidence in her great dark eyes. Oh yes, she had meant what she said, but he had not believed it *could* be done – or had not wanted to! Did he still think it would have been impossible – for that was what the boy was asking him? He was not sure. That certainty of hers haunted him again. As the doppelganger had said, he was still in flight from it. He could not tell the boy that. He must not even hint at it.

Perhaps he had been foolish to choose this parable, or a parable at all? It might have been wiser, and easier, to continue the line he first thought of – talk of desire, seduction, detumescence, illustrated from Ovid. But even from there, guilt would have led him to the tantalising question, did you love her or simply lust for her – or any of the others? And should you care? To Gideon such a question must be incomprehensible – as it must have been to him at that age. What youngster had time to wonder whether love and lust were not one and the same – and not only youngsters? Had he loved Myrtle or lusted for her – the agony of her rejection would have been the same! Was it really too early to explain to the boy that lust suited many a man well enough; but although a man's desire alone might please a woman for a time, she would soon need something more if he wanted her love – and thus his freedom to enjoy her – to last. What was that "something more"? That question would bring him back full circle to the crux of the parable – the enigma of woman.

He was tempted to say that no man ever solved it. There was no relief from it, no settlement, no truce. Nor could you refuse to try, for you could never turn your back on it. Certainly it was tiresome to pretend to love a woman, but it was the price you had to pay for the pleasure she alone could give you. However you must not let desire trick you into pandering to *all* her fancies, for then she would rule you mercilessly, which would in time kill all sweetness.

Some of this he did try to tell him, but hesitantly, and he was not pleased with himself, aware that bitterness was ready to spill over. Sooner or later he would be forced to tell Gideon that all relationships had a selfish element, that it was for your own protection that you forever sought the elusive heart of a woman but doomed to failure; and there were times with a woman when you felt an intractable loneliness, and that was par for the course too.

That sombre thought must have prompted him to switch to a superficial course he had rejected before, roguish banalities from student days – and he stopped, ashamed. The little clearing was filled with voices clamouring for release, and he was talking to drown them lest Gideon heard them too – moral creditors from the past, dunning for quittance. How bizarre at his age to imagine that those careless days of wine and roses, were still potent within him! Something told him it was time to move from the little clearing. The halt in this reminder of Arcadia, among old green dreams, old regrets, old pain, dusty joys, from a time when he still believed in his indefinable quest, had served its unknown purpose. The voices of the girls had faded into the glistening foliage.

He was about to rise but Gideon was bracing himself to speak, swaying in the heat. "Papa, I don't understand a lot of what you were saying, I mean in the story – well, no – I do understand in a way, but it's all so strange, like a different world. But you're not answering me really – about, well *things*!" He gestured again downwards, and looked at Leo sideways, his damp features reddening further.

How neatly, how implacably, the boy brought him down to earth – as *he* wished he had had the courage to do when Father had talked to him at that age – yet not really talked? "I'm sorry," he said. "I *will* try harder. I will try to remember how I felt at your age. I promise. Anyway let's move. It's got too hot up here and I'm parched. We'll go down and get a cool drink."

Gideon pretended to look at his sketch pad, hoping for delay, wondering if he dared say more. He pulled at his sweat-soaked shirt where it stuck to his chest and said, "I suppose you're wondering . . ." He checked himself. He was thinking of recent sessions with Frances, when her words had set him on fire, and his body had been uncontrollable, almost terrifying – and she had laughed, gently it was true but laughed all the same, and said everything was natural. He had asked so many questions she could not answer them, or would not. He wanted to shout those questions out loud now, and tell his father that Frances had drawn them from him, but he sensed that it would be unwise, and that was worrying.

Leo thought he knew what the unfinished sentence was. "I suppose you're wondering how I know so much?" He did not want to confront that question yet. There was fear in the boy and he must approach it gently. The thought of Frances crossed his mind again. He pretended not to have heard and stood up, trousers sticking to his knees with sweat. A black cat darted between his feet from under the bench, sinewy form shimmering in the fragmented sunlight under the tree, and fled across the sand-coloured earth and glided into the hard-edged shadow of another bench of sun-baked stone and stood still, swung its tight smooth head in slow scrutiny, ears stiffened, greenish-yellow eyes narrowed, then subsided with forepaws extended, to out-stare the world.

Emerging from the tree's shade the sun seared his neck like a fiery breath and his steps were sluggish from sitting so long in the damp heat. As they made their way in silence between the high hedges towards the stairway, Gideon unclipped the curved metal water bottle from his webbing belt – part of army equipment issued to his school cadet unit – and with a flick of the thumb unscrewed the stopper so that it clinked down the side of the bottle on its short chain, and held it out. "Have a swig of this – it's probably a bit warm by now in this heat!"

Leo took a sip of the tepid contents and grimaced and handed the bottle back. "Hm! More than a bit! I'll wait. I saw someone near the gate down there selling refrigerated water – Coke or Fanta or some such stuff – anything will do so long as it's wet and cold."

Gideon said thoughtfully, "It'll be expensive down there Papa – with no bar nearby. Those street-sellers sting you in this heat – I heard them asking four thousand lire a can when we came in."

"Oh well – needs must when the Devil drives – that's something else you're learning!" And in more ways than one, he added under his breath.

Down in the Forum they threaded through the crowd moving respectfully among clumps of grey debris separated by patches of spiky grass. Corpulent tourists in bulging checked shirts and peaked caps paused and leaned on the nearest piece of ancient masonry to catch their breath in the heavy air of the late afternoon, weary gleaners in the derelict field. Leo wondered what they sought among these imperial echoes, tramp of soldiery, pomp of power? What voices spoke to them from fissured column and broken arch? Did they come to hear certainty reaffirmed, reminders of questions that had once been settled here it seemed for ever? Suppress what you cannot solve? A poor answer to life!

The doppelganger said, "Do not be superior. Look to your own case. Certainty of a kind has been waiting for you to grasp it all your life – but you have fled from it. *You* must decide what it is and reach out for it. And you must find it for Gideon too, and hand it on to him."

If certainty does come to me now, he answered, it will be too late to enjoy it. As for Gideon there's no communication, just as there wasn't between father and me. I cannot give him the experience with which to understand what I am saying! And yet something compels me to continue saying it. Anyway, you have changed your tune. You say I am doing this not for his sake but mine?

"I have not changed my tune. In speaking to him you are redefining who you are *to yourself* – and you need that image badly, as Hoffman did, to navigate at all. So it is not too late. As for helping Gideon, it is the Life Force compelling you – or God if you prefer, the name is immaterial."

He had no energy to reply. He had been on a long route march through unknown territory, and he needed time to discover where he was.

When they had trudged to the gate he was ready to pay any price for a cool drink. Some fifty paces beyond, two boys stood in the glare against a low wall topped by grass, the cold-drink sellers they had seen on their way in. They were about thirteen and fifteen, naked to the waist, wearing skin-tight jeans and open leather sandals on bare feet, emaciated flesh burned nearly black by the sun. They guarded two plastic picnic boxes of the type cooled by bottles of frozen liquid, that stood in the only shade available, the low shadow cast by a piece of broken column lying on the parched grass behind them. The older boy hailed him with a great grin of thick lips and large yellow teeth. "American – yes? You want Coke – ees cold OK?"

An absurd sense of offended dignity took hold of Leo, pique at being taken for American, and he replied stiffly, '*Vogliamo due per favore. Quanto costa?*"

The boy looked blank. Gideon said quietly, "They're not Italian – they're from North Africa somewhere – I've seen a lot of them about."

Leo tried French, "*Deux Cokes s'il vous plait. Combien?*"

The toothy grin opened out once more. The boy obviously understood, but insisted on testing his English: "Ees feef towsand plis – you no American?" He sounded disappointed.

Leo was a little light-headed now from the heat, and as he fished out a ten thousand lire note he succumbed to the silly temptation to reply in pidgin, "Me no American – me English."

The youth looked thoughtful, perhaps considering that his English was after all quite good if the Englishman spoke similarly. But business obviously came foremost, for he shrewdly twitched the note between claw-nailed finger and thumb while his ageless eyes studied Leo in triumph and contempt – this stupid foreigner had accepted the price without even trying to haggle!

The look hit Leo hard. As a business man he should have tried to beat him down even though his bargaining position was weak and the young merchant knew it. The nearest alternative source of supply was a bar about a quarter of a mile away, which in this heat might as well have been ten miles. These boys enjoyed a virtual monopoly here. But you never accepted the first figure immediately, and certainly not in this buccaneering culture of the streets! You owed it to yourself even if you knew that you were going to accept the deal. He wished he could wipe the triumph from the sun-dried face before him, old before its time.

The temptation to drink from the cans then and there was great, but pride demanded that he distance himself from the two young merchants and their victory. Some distance down the steeply cambered entry road between old cracked grey walls of bulbous stone and banks of dry grass, they found shade in a doorway. Gideon took the can from his lips and covered the opening with his hand to keep the hot air out and said thoughtfully, "You know they're clever those two. They were asking *four* thousand a can when we came in, because most people coming in had just had lunch and weren't buying because they weren't thirsty yet. But now there's no one going *in*, only coming out and dying for a drink and don't care about the price – like us! So they put up the price to five thousand knowing they'll get it!"

Leo nodded approval. "Well done! You've grasped a basic principle of business. Pitch your price at what the market will bear! If you catch on as quickly in everything else in life, you'll do all right."

Gideon blushed with pleasure, but Leo saw a shadow of uncertainty in his face too. He wondered again whether the boy detected envy in his voice.

They were only partially revived by the sweet drink. They were dehydrated. Next day the *Corriere* was to report that it had been Rome's hottest June day in living memory. In a cafe some five minutes away, Leo ordered mineral water and shook a generous amount of salt into his glass and persuaded the boy to do the same. Soon the weariness faded. Leo had had enough of the heat. He must make for a cool place indoors that would interest Gideon. The Pantheon would do; it was always cool in summer. He had not yet shown Gideon the mysterious structure that had captured his imagination on his first visit as an undergraduate. When in Rome on business, if he had time to spare he sometimes found it soothed the spirit to sit on a low shelf along the concave wall to the left of the great doors and marvel at the genius of the pagan builders in creating the sensation of being under divine scrutiny. Going there now would be a rest from the "lesson". The waiter telephoned for a taxi.

Gideon was disappointed at the interruption. Whenever Papa seemed about to answer an important question he veered away to talk about obscure things in books, stories about love and something called attachment, meandering asides about your body, what you were expected to think and do and say in such and such an unlikely situation. Papa was usually so perceptive, aimed straight to the mark! There was something different about him today. Still, the Pantheon might be interesting, if only to see why Aunt Frances got so excited about it.

Leo led the way to the stone shelf. Gideon's thoughts flew up and round the dome. Yes the building *was* virtually one huge dome as she had said. His imagination turned to the meaning of the name. He thought he would try to impress his father with his general knowledge. "Papa – Pantheon means 'all the gods' doesn't it? But this is a church, though it's a funny-looking church! So how can a church be called a place for *all* the gods?"

Gideon did not understand the exhilaration he felt whenever he prompted his father to talk about the poetry of things, the romance of ideas and legend.

He only knew that he soared with him up into the sky, far from ordinary things. Leo talked of the Pantheon's conception in paganism, the power of mathematics and the human imagination to conjure divinity with this mighty structure, according to legend originally dedicated to the Asian goddess Cybele, mother of the gods, and of its ultimate consecration to St Mary and All Saints. "All Saints you see! Not far from Pan-*theon* as you said! So its original purpose in a sense continues unchanged, celebrating the truths of life as men and women have seen them through the ages, the earth's nature the source of them, and our commitment to be in step with all of it."

Gideon's excitement bubbled over. "What about *us* in all that – us Jews? Did *we* borrow from other religions or was it the other way round? It *had* to be the other way round I suppose, because we were Jews before all that weren't we?"

"This is the year 5727 in the Jewish calendar – think of that! Yes, we do go a long way back. Still, at the heart of the great religions the understanding of life and how it must be confronted – the rules of living – are not very different. How could they be? For they bring down to us the experience of countless generations of people who distilled life's lessons for those who followed after. And they did it in the most potent way they knew, through magic, legend, poetry, in celebrations marking the ebb and flow of the seasons, the fecundity of the earth and the will and wildness of people fertilising and sanctifying it. And all of it paying homage to the will of God – which must be true for everybody, whatever poetry of the mind and the heart

193

we use to describe it, whatever the songs we sing – in every sense!"

Leo was astonished by an exaltation that sparked like static in his mind. If only he could live by it forever. If only scepticism would not return and spoil it all. But he knew it would.

Gideon's face shone. "Fecundity! I remember that word from when Aunt Frances was talking about this place and what it means to her – " He checked himself and blushed. "I mean when she says – no I can't remember the rest!" He managed to change course. "But I can't get over the way everything you say fits this place! Can you explain a bit more though – how the things it stands for could stay the same for all the centuries? One minute I *think* I understand and then it slips away. And *us* – the Jews – Abraham and the rest – did they really put it down in words long before? When I think of them sitting in their tents all those centuries ago writing it all down, and us here in this place talking about it – it sends cold shivers down my spine."

Leo talked on, and Gideon heard Frances talking too, and his excitement was mixed with the physical. To quell the arousal he glanced away at the crowd whispering and shuffling amid the gigantic susurration echoing round the concave walls and up into the mighty dome and down again. Tour groups chattered in diverse languages, scurrying after their lecturers like flocks of sheep; and from moment to moment vistas opened up straight across the floor to the far wall and closed again. In one of those clear views his attention was caught by a woman standing alone at the central point directly under the hole in the dome. She was about Mama's age,

194

dressed in cream linen jacket and skirt. Unaccountably he could not take his eyes off her. She turned her head and he saw her full face, and it seemed that her features contracted as her eyes rested upon him. A surge of the crowd hid her from sight, then he saw her again, and she was walking quickly across the arena, and he had the dreamlike feeling that she was making her way towards them. She had a neat, slim figure, round face and high smooth brow, eyes set wide, full lips slightly parted, an expression partly smiling, but also – and this disturbed him – tinctured with anxiety. Yes there could be no doubt now; she was aiming for *them*.

Leo, in full flow, was seated on the bench half-turned away from the arena. Gideon tugged at his sleeve. "Papa there's a woman coming straight for us – and there's something strange about her. Look!"

Leo did not immediately glance round. He thought of all the times he had come here in the last fourteen years and nothing had happened. What was he to say now? What did he want to happen?

The doppelganger's voice was hard. "At any time during these years, with a little trouble you could have found her, but you did nothing. Soon after your marriage, the compromise solution as you called it, you *knew* you had made a mistake and you thought of finding her again but you lacked the courage. Like a child you left it to Destiny, or chance, anything that did not demand a decision! So you threw away the years. And now against all the odds it *has* happened – I must say you have the Devil's own luck! You must dismiss this ghost as best you can. And then you will be free."

195

He turned and Chiara was now a few paces away. He looked upon her in wonder. The doppelganger was right yet again. He had chosen to wait for the million to one chance – to seek her out would have meant taking a decision, and that had been beyond him. Now it had happened and he was no further forward! He felt his features freeze, unable to shape any expression. She was the same yet changed. No, not changed – the features tighter, that was all. There was a wariness in her, less of the softness imprinted in memory. He forgot that Gideon was beside him. Lamentations clamoured for release but the words were unreachable.

She halted and stood almost at attention like a soldier reporting after a mission accomplished. Her lips tightened, and then a timid look of compassion crossed her face. With a glance at Gideon, she said in Italian, "My dear, where are we?" She shook her head slowly, and her lips trembled. "Oh my dear, my dear – yes, I have said this so many times – where am I? Where are you?" She uttered the words as if they were forced out of her in a dream, and he was in the dream with her.

When he did not answer at once she said softly, still in Italian, a tremor in her voice, "You wonder that I still say, 'My dear!' How could it be otherwise? How could it?"

Seeing that he still strove to find words she added, "But you *are* here! I wanted this to happen! I swear I did – and one day I knew it would. I prayed and I prayed! For I must *know*! I must understand. And so it had to happen."

At last he said, in Italian, his face turned away from Gideon so that the boy should not see him blinking, "Yes I am here, and what you say must be true. But it should have happened differently. I should have had faith. *Mea culpa – mea culpa*."

Chapter 14

For Chiara, in the years since Leo had gone, the celebration at the Pantheon had become an even greater compulsion than before. It followed no pattern of the moon or the sun or the seasons, but each time the summons was inescapable. Sometimes a month or more passed without one, sometimes there were several in a single week. The ritual kept her vision of herself intact. That it kept the flame of him alive was also true, never to be disowned. She offered up a pledge drawing past and future together.

When she walked between her boutique in the Via Condotti and the apartment behind the Piazza Navona, as she did most days, the Pantheon, even when it did not summon her, was an important presence. Whether its proximity had influenced her choice of the apartment when she married she had never asked herself, but it must have done. She knew only that on some days, as she passed between the fountain in the middle of the Piazza della Rotonda and the blackened portico of the Pantheon, she felt its magnetism, and was drawn in to that personal communication with the brooding influence she found there. Sometimes, standing under the *oculus*, the moment had Delphic significance and she trembled at the touch of a sacred wind though the air was still, or heard a poignant cry from afar, a tantalising whisper, a sigh, or was aware of a silence as of a deity stilled in meditation; and she imagined a mirror turned towards her to reveal an unfamiliar image, herself yet different, the old and the new joined – a rite of passage from one trial of the spirit to another.

That day she had sensed a new note often foretold in imagination. A chill went through her. She bit her lip and scanned the faces nearby in the shambling crowd. The signal was insistent. She could not see him. A fearsome thought struck her; he *was* there but some terrible injury rendered him unrecognisable. She wanted to shout his name, as she had done many times in dreams when she had sought him in vain though he had been standing before her. The restless groups opened on either side of her like retreating waves and suddenly she had a clear view across the concourse and trembled with fear. There on the far side, seated on a stone bench on the concave wall sat the erect figure with its unruly hair, head held back. Time had touched him lightly. Then she realised that he was talking to a slim boy beside him, and an iron door slammed shut within her. Before she knew it she was almost running towards them. There was no pause to reflect, and no time either – the movement obeyed a higher power. She must reach him before he moved away, for this time it would be for ever.

She fixed her gaze upon him as if that alone would transmit her emotion and hold him fast there. Only as she drew near did she ask herself, what *am* I going to say? What *is* there to say to a vision I have talked to constantly through the years in imagination and in dreams? Thoughts flung themselves about in confusion, with no clarity to fix upon, no vision, only a formless hope. She must find words of power, a magic that would bend Fate. If he had heard a fraction of all she had said to him over the years there was nothing fresh to say now. Did he even know she was alive? Or that she still lived in Rome? Heaven had at last shown mercy and allowed their paths to converge! Yes, if it was ordained to happen at all, it had to be in this place; and he, being the spirit he was, would understand that too. Oh where are we *caro*? Do we still exist! No, not *caro* – have I the right to call you that when it was *my* fear that drove you away? Tell me we still exist!

When he said, "*Mea culpa – mea culpa,*" she shook her head, breathless. "No, no – it is not true! It was I who sent you away – with my fear of . . ." She glanced at Gideon, wondering if, after all, he did understand Italian. "I did not hope for this – and I had no right to hope – I know that. But tell me, are we still alive? Sometimes I do not know." She knew her words were bizarre, but they expressed incalculable longings and they must stand. When she said, "I did not hope for this," she meant that hope itself had been ill-defined, hope for quittance for her pain, for the wounded past to be healed by some unknowable magic.

On impulse he held out his hands and she took them, and so they stood for some seconds in silence, looking deeply into each other. Gideon had never seen grown-ups so upset and yet pleased – no, not pleased exactly, but relieved, and stirred.

Leo half-expected the doppelganger to say something

but there was silence. What he wanted to say felt ineffectual, naive, silly, but he could not resist answering her in her own dreamlike fashion. "Oh yes, we exist! But where *are* we? I wish I knew – I wish so many things. I wish I had possessed more courage."

He sensed that she understood, and that she waited for some other sign. Here in this noisy market place, with Gideon at his side, how could the demons be set free, debts of remorse, guilt, desire, be redeemed? He said, "How misleading life is; how one fears the wrong things! I want to say so much but it is hard to say *anything*." He made a sign with his eyes to warn her that Gideon might hear or see too much.

She turned a little to the side so that Gideon would not see, and took a handkerchief from a pocket in the waistband of her linen skirt and wiped her eyes. As she turned back to face him, they both spoke at once in an outpouring of excitement and urgency, the words leaping between them as if speech were too slow for all that must be said, a fury of emotion, confession, remembrance, regret, mingled with a headlong account of time and chance in the years between, the progress of the soul laid bare. The momentum threw them together with no pause for questioning or doubt. At last they stopped, breathless, and looked at one another in perplexity – the past had been joined to the present, but something was still owed to it; an unknown quittance must still be found. She leaned towards him a little as if she wanted to cling to him but dared not, saying, "There is more to be said. I know it. And you know it too." She held her breath, waiting for his answer.

In speaking Italian, their hope that Gideon would not follow what passed between them, least of all guess its poignant undercurrents, was only partly fulfilled. They reckoned without his acute mind, his sensitivity during these days in Rome, his determination, and his skilful adaptation of school Latin. On the flight from London he had memorised stretches of an Italian phrase book he had found at home. He had Leo's good ear and mind for language; and here in Rome he listened carefully when his father spoke Italian, in hotel or restaurant or shop, and noted the replies, afterwards questioning him about them. And so he did understand random phrases that passed between them, especially in their halting exchanges at the outset. More to the point, however, he caught the emotional harmonics that flashed between them; and though he could not read them fully they disturbed him. Why was Papa shaken as if a ghost had materialised? Why was he saying *mea culpa*? To what awesome time in Papa's life did this woman belong?

More extraordinary still, despite his father's obvious amazement it struck Gideon that Leo had been in some fashion prepared for this encounter. How could that be? And while it was plain that they did not want him to understand what they were saying – continuing in Italian – he sensed that he was not even supposed to know that this meeting was taking place! Was something bad happening? Was it an example of the quicksands Papa had been talking about? When would he have a chance to ask him about it – for he guessed that it would not be right for him to ask Mama when he got home, or Frances. But why? He was being hurled forward into grown-up life, and though that was exciting he knew he was not ready for it, and that thought made him unhappy. He needed help to leap that far ahead, and Papa *had* been trying hard to give it, and so he wished under his breath that this woman would go away and let the lesson continue.

Leo saw, but did not see, the tiny lines at the corners of her eyes, footprints of time. She was as she had been. He had not realised till this moment how often he had re-lived those days. He did not know that he was blinking hard to hide tears and that she nodded in sympathy. He said to himself, or thought he did, but the words came out unchecked: "What a foolish thing life is!"

She spoke now in more measured fashion. "I did not know I would come here today but something made me, for I am powerless *not* to be here when the call comes. True I have often dreamed of this happening. But often I have told myself it would be better if it did not happen, that the past is best left undisturbed. Look at me – I am thirty-seven!" She shot a glance at Gideon and shrugged. "Yet the heart will not be made quiet. And what has happened now must be answered with courage."

The round, taut face, high cheekbones stretching the lightly bronzed skin, quivered as pride fought with emotion, as if she said, "I ask for nothing. I say what must be said." Then a timid smile broke through and she put the handkerchief to her eyes again and said, "The truth is this – you *are* here!" She shook her head. "I do not want to talk of the past. I want to understand what I feel *now* – and what you feel. That is the important thing. Nothing else."

Leo wanted to take her in his arms, let all the unidentifiable disenchantments fall away, the years of living with the "might have beens" appeased. Part of him was glad it was impossible, not in this place, and certainly not in Gideon's presence. For this was happening outside time, and he feared the return of that Siren song so intoxicating in the days of youth, which drew you into the imagined emptiness between two moments of time where no responsibility could seize you. Now, when time did not exist, logic was irrelevant, all impossible dreams were suddenly valid – and therefore awesome! Yet he saw in her a grain of certainty that insisted on having its way. What was it? The answer hardly mattered. Her eyes told him she willed it, or half-willed it. No, it was not desire, nothing so trivial, but a link of far greater power. It was all beyond him. He tried to think of an immediate step and could find nothing. What could be done in this freak moment? How were they to make a bridge between this highly charged, fantastical encounter and its sequel – for *something* must follow? It was banal to think of going to a cafe for a staid social threesome!

He realised that he was about to say something important that was unconnected with that thought – though it was! In his confusion he was not sure if he had already said it. "It is too late to beg forgiveness but I do, with all my heart. I did not know that I was hoping for this, but I am glad it has happened. So many things in life come too late. You speak of lacking courage? It was I who lacked courage. No, it is true . . ."

She shook her head again: "It was I who lacked courage – it was I who drew back from . . ." She bit her lip.

He went on, "And now I wish . . ." He checked himself. "I don't know how say it."

The doppelganger's voice was troubled. "For God's sake take a grip on yourself! Your guilt will destroy you if you go on like this – guilt and the absurd sentimentality of this simple woman. There is nothing you can do for her. You can change nothing. Whatever you are looking for is not here. The trouble is you cannot resist humouring a woman! Especially if she plays on your guilt. Now listen to me. Think of what this idiotic behaviour will do to Gideon – what a twisted sentimental education? Apart from messing up your life even more than you think it is already! So leave well alone. Say goodbye, wish her well, and get out of this quickly. It is all too late."

As Gideon studied them, a new thought struck him. They shared some mysterious knowledge, and Papa was worried about it. If only he could ask Frances what it might be. She knew so much? The word "affair" came to mind, that she often used when she spoke of a man and a woman being "too friendly by half!" – meaning they did the things Papa had been talking about from a book by an old Roman writer called Ovid, things you shouldn't do until you were married. That couldn't be true! All the same Papa does look as I suppose I do when I'm caught doing something I shouldn't! No, I think she's talking about things that happened a long time ago. I suppose that was before he married Mama?

205

Then why should it matter now? All the same they do seem worried about it – looking at me every now and then to see if I understand.

Why didn't he tell me we were going to meet her? Or didn't he know? I can see Papa's important to *her* – from the way she looks at him. Perhaps they haven't met for a long time and that's why they're behaving in this funny way, as if they don't know what they're doing?

As he strained to understand the quick, lilting Italian, the words sliding into each other, he felt breathless as he had never felt before. Tumultuous thoughts whirled in his head. As in a dream a great secret was being revealed from the very core of things, exciting, frightening. Loneliness wrapped itself round him. Papa and this woman were shutting him out. The next moment he understood something new about these days in Rome; Papa had brought him here to teach him about life in a fashion not possible at home, and to do this Papa must show him things hidden in his own heart, things he was unhappy about. He wished he could help Papa to be happy. Yet even as he knew this he was not sure *what* he knew, only that this encounter held truths reaching back to the roots of his father's existence, to an original vision of himself that had guided him long ago, only now understood – and that such a rough onset of reality would one day come to him too. In giving him this foretaste of it Papa wanted him to know how life worked its will on you, incised its truths, changed your vision of things, and of yourself. It struck him that his father and this woman "read" each other with no word spoken, and a cold shiver went through him. What magic made that possible! Would *he* ever possess it?

How unfair it was always to be too young! Grown ups told you so often, "You will understand this when you are older." But "when you are older" was a distant land far beyond the horizon and it never drew any nearer. If only he could be older *now* and not have to wait any longer!

Papa and this woman knew one another in a way he wished he could fathom but why was this knowledge important to him? The link between them was a dark magic and he feared it. Breathless again he had an intuition of how they must feel, and it seemed that he touched their very souls and felt a new power awakening in him. He hoped he would know, one day, why some part of a person remained hidden however hard you tried to "read" them. Frances said that if you loved someone you always read them correctly – and if you couldn't it meant that you didn't really love them, or love had dried up, though she had never explained what dried up meant. He had asked Mama what love was but had not learned much, and had given up. Mama was always so impatient, in a hurry, running here and there. "Oh it's something you'll understand when you're a lot older. You care about a person, you care what happens to them, you care about what they feel, you see? No, you don't see. At your age nobody understands these things. Loving someone is caring, and caring all the time."

"But Mama, I care what happens to *you* but I can't

207

marry you? I thought there was only one person you loved and that was why you married them?"

"Oh Gideon, you do run round corners to ask questions! I can't explain it any more – you'll just have to wait till you're older."

Whatever the hidden knowledge was that these two shared seemed to have transformed Papa – a moment before he had been tense, fearful; now he looked contemplative, as if great questions were being answered. What was that dark magic between them? Why did he fear it? Something they shared, experience, knowledge of each other and the world, a precious sensibility, was being denied him. He knew it was important for him, but there was no hint of what it might be, not yet. He was beginning to see that life had a habit of allowing you to understand the really important things only when it was too late to profit from the knowledge. He would be forever pursuing and never catching up. Life worked upon you inexorably, moulding your thoughts and feelings every moment of the day asleep or awake. Most disturbing of all, no experience was trivial. You could not escape the pain it brought, from however far back in time; and there was no antidote for it, and no forgetfulness either.

Papa looked perplexed once more; but the woman's face shone with a kind of uncertain eagerness. Their headlong Italian had left him so far behind that all contact was slipping away. Loneliness returned.

It was Chiara who first realised that they were excluding him, and sensed his perplexity and hurt. She said to Leo in Italian: "The poor boy is wondering what is happening!" – then eagerly in English: "I have an idea! Let us go to Ostia. The sea will still be warm, and there are swimming things in our beach cabin there. We will go and get my car – it is not far away. Please say you agree!"

Chapter 15

Leo had no idea how long they had been standing here. Even in this public place they had enclosed themselves in a cocoon of memory and emotion and speculation. He would afterwards marvel at the wildness of their talk in this space between two segments of time, when all fancies flew without restraint – elegiac visions of the "might have beens" if he had not stopped the clock of his life all those years before! That she joined in the fancies so readily amazed him; and he supposed she had stopped the clock too. The wonder was that they found enough sympathy between them to play a game of make-believe, a brave regression to a youthful insouciance in which the bitter tincture was somehow essential.

No, despite the doppelganger's admonition he could not simply walk away. Decency, to put it no higher, demanded something more. Her idea of going to Ostia was inspired! Gideon loved swimming and could spend hours in the water. He would be in the sea, in sight but out of earshot, and he and Chiara – in seeming ordinariness – could sit and talk. Even so, after all these years, after what had happened, to go for a swim like friends continuing a familiar pattern was comic, even bizarre! Well, what of it? "Good idea," he said.

"Let us go then," she said excitedly, then reverted to Italian. "Franco is away – in Buenos Aires – so I am free. We will go to find my car. It is near."

Franco was presumably her husband. To Leo's surprise she had shown no interest in his own history. Perhaps, seeing Gideon, she had gathered all she wanted to know.

She turned to Gideon and was about to put an arm round his shoulders but checked herself. "Tell me young man," she said warmly, leaning towards him. "do you like swimming?"

Something in her smile banished Gideon's isolation; he felt the presence of a beguiling female chemistry, decent, essentially spiritual, worlds away from the kindly sentimentality of Frances, or his mother's punctilious attention to duty. With her simple words, her serious smile, she reached into his heart and gave him a part of herself. He warmed to her.

"Yes I do, very much," he answered and looked at Leo enquiringly: had he said the right thing? Leo reassured him with a nod and he was happy. This woman had welcomed him into their adult world – she had "read" him!

The pause gave Leo a second wind. In these few days in Rome he had returned to the point where he had stopped the clock. Moorlock knew of the Chiara episode but it had been years since it had been mentioned between them. Long ago they had agreed that they had both stopped the clock, though Moorlock seemed the less troubled by the fact. It was

211

a condition, he said with stoic irony, that was seldom fatal, and one that you could palliate in many ways, and among the drugs you could use, women could be the least harmful if you took care not to become too addicted. Leo saw more clearly now that Moorlock had intended this trip to have one purpose only, to see his reflection again through a woman's eyes and start the clock ticking once more. Despite his blind attempt to defeat that purpose by bringing Gideon, the Fates had had their way! He would go to Ostia and see what else they had in store. Gideon's presence might even be a help.

The doppelganger laughed, not unkindly. "You should thank your stars for bringing the boy! With any luck he will stop you doing anything stupid."

He might be right. People spoke of this as the dangerous age for a man, mid-life crisis, fears of declining libido. Such talk was too facile. Even if true, what of it? Could he not win one more sojourn in the enchanted garden? What was he doing, thinking the unthinkable! *Was* it so unthinkable? Looking at her, the esoteric magnetism returned; and with it the full-blooded urge of youth with its rejection of all calculation. What would he gain from seeing his reflection anew in her? When they parted again as they surely must, would he be any further forward? No, there was nothing to be gained here, nothing at all.

The doppelganger spoke sadly. "I wish you would give me some ground for hope. Your image of stopping the clock is apt. You lacked the courage to behave with maturity and so you gave up *living*! Or tried to, thinking it easier to follow someone else's rules, which is why you married a determined woman who knew the direction her life should take, and followed her. It was spiritual self-destruction and you knew it. No one can stand aside from life, but you certainly tried. In your heart you are still trying to think as an adolescent, that you can treat people painfully – and yourself too – and not inflict pain! Even now you only *pretend* to consider this woman's feelings, or Gideon's. All you really care about is avoiding guilt and what you call untidiness, meaning responsibility. It has taken you all these years to wake up. If what is left of your life is to have any meaning you must move ahead fast. You must get rid of her."

He had no stomach to reply. Most of it was true. As for courage he had never thought he lacked *that*, but the doppelganger meant another kind of courage, the will to follow the soul's secret purpose, always there in the shadows, speaking in whispers, in signs and symbols, but insistently none the less – giving you pain when you failed. Instead, like a child he had waited for time or destiny to tell him where to go. Well, he still did not know. Was it too late? The doppelganger thought he had a little time left, but not much. No wonder he was tense! Inexplicably an orgiastic fear returned from the war, waiting before dawn for the rear guns to open up and hoping to God they had the range right and everybody and everything was in the right place and nobody would put a foot wrong. So this episode was going to be equally apocalyptic. How could that be? He would play it out decently. What did he mean by playing it out, or decently? He was not sure.

He supposed he had known all along that the soul

followed its own way in spite of you, wounded, defeated time and again but opposing compromise all the way, taking its revenge on you for impeding its purpose. How much of the truth had Gideon guessed? Probably quite a lot. She must have sensed that too, and was trying to calm the boy's fears.

As they made their way out of the cool grey shell of the rotunda and across the golden yellow glare of the Piazza into a a shadowed side street, she gave him a blunt summary of *her* journey, necessary background material only, as if the events were long finished with and put to one side.

The family had married her off quickly. She had understood his silence, and blamed herself for it. Her pride – she no more than hinted at it – would not let her pursue him, but insisted that she turn away and find a practical "escape" with honour. When she announced this intention at home she pretended to have reverted to the traditional view that a girl's value in the marriage market fell rapidly with each year that passed, and she must therefore make an approved marriage as soon as possible. Her parents must have suspected something, but with shrewd delicacy did not probe beneath the surface; instead they set the wheels in motion. They might already have had Franco in mind as a good match, a young banker ten years her senior, the son of old family friends whose country property marched with theirs. She had known him distantly in childhood days when he had seemed very old, too old for a true playmate, fastidious, careful, studious.

"For his business he travels much, all over the world. I do not go with him, for I must look after my boutique.

It is my own business, bought with part of the marriage settlement I insisted on preserving in my own name. I deal in fashion jewellery, accessories, things like that. The merchandise is expensive, very chic you understand? The business is successful, but I must take good care of it. It is for my own independence! We have no children – I do not know why."

He wondered at the words "I do not know why". spoken with slight but distinct emphasis. They seemed to say, "It is not through any defect of mine!" Doubtless her reasons would emerge.

They went through narrow cobbled alleyways where oncoming vehicles could only pass with deft manoeuvre, forcing pedestrians to take refuge in the doorways of shops or cafes. This was the secluded quarter where they had made their furtive sorties long ago, its blend of domestic smells the unique Roman persona, sharpening memory – from grocers, butchers, bakers, oil and wine shops, bars, *trattorie*; and little workshops, deep caverns dark even in day-time, where artisans bent their backs under dusty light bulbs. Here and there in the grey walls the gateway of an old palazzo gave on to an oasis of ragged lawn and shrubbery. At one of these Chiara led the way into a flagstoned courtyard where the westering sun threw slanting grey shadows like spectral buttresses. In the central grassy patch a twisted fig tree sheltered a faun pouring water from a jug on his shoulder. In the far wall an archway, wide enough for a car, led into a tunnel with a stairway at one side swinging up to apartments above. At the end of the tunnel she unlocked iron doors and they entered a vast chamber of red brick walls with a ceiling of beams and plaster, and floor of venerable stone. Round the walls stood furniture under dust sheets, and packing cases piled high. A clear space in the middle was evidently used for parking two or three cars judging by rectangular patches of black on the floor. One car stood there, a new-looking red Alfa Romeo.

"Here is my car. Franco took his Ferrari to our property in the country before he left." She turned to Gideon. "Young man, you sit in the back. But be careful not to sit on Franco's spurs! He always throws them on the back seat when he uses my car to go to the stables – it is strange that he never does so in his own car! I am always telling him not to but he forgets. *Pazienza.*" She got into the driver's seat.

The storeroom was fitfully lit. The few electric lamps hanging from cross-beams were not switched on, and the only light came from slender shafts of late sunshine entering transom windows close under the eaves, throwing a rectangular pattern of light and dark on the floor. The car stood in one of the darkest shadows. Gideon, his imagination caught by the mystery of the shrouded furniture – sofas, cabinets, tables, chairs, a piano – absently reached for the rear door handle, failing to notice a gash in the middle of the door panelling near the central pillar that exposed some of the hinge mechanism, which might have made him pause. Chiara in her excitement, had forgotten about it. With unthinking schoolboy vigour he lifted the handle and pulled. There came a groan of scraping metal as the door toppled out towards him. Red with confusion, he caught it and tried to push the rear edge back into place, but part of the broken hinge mechanism hung

216

free end was now jammed between the edge of the door and the pillar. He leaned his weight against the door to hold it fast and wondered what to do next. Chiara cried out, "*Mama mia*! My poor boy!" and sprang out of the driving seat, a box of paper tissues in her hand, and was at his side: "I am so sorry. I forgot about that door! Now I will restore it in place. It is simple – see!"

Gideon, thinking he had broken the door hinge, had begun to apologise, and perhaps his confusion summoned his gruff voice, upsetting him the more. "I am sorry. I didn't mean . . ."

"No no, *poverino*! It is not your fault! Please, I will do it."

Leo had moved round the car to help, but in those few seconds, her hands swathed in layers of tissue, she pushed the greasy levers out of the way and manoeuvred the rear edge of the door to engage the groove in the pillar and banged the door shut. Then she knelt on the front seat and reached into the rear and pressed down the lever on the inside of the door to lock the latch bolt in position. She did it all with a practised air; it could not have been the first time.

"See? It is done! Do not worry, my fine young man. You are not to blame. Franco's horse kicked it and we had not the time to take the car to be repaired. I should have told you to go to the other side. Go then – that door is all right! But remember the spurs. Do not sit on them! We go now."

Gideon took his seat warily. He fingered the spurs. Town-bred, horses and riding equipment were known in imagination only. He traced the outlines of the heel-piece, stout leather straps and business-like buckles, pushed the rowels round with his thumb, merciless spikes, poor horse! He thought of knights and squires. He was in a tented enclosure at a tournament with crested pennants fluttering. He buckled one on; it was loose on his canvas shoe but no matter, then the other, and jumped on his horse and galloped away. As he lifted in the saddle to the horse's movement he wondered what sort of a man would leave his spurs behind, far from the rest of his knightly accoutrements? The car had a strange mixture of smells, mainly perfume and femaleness, but tinctured with that of stable and mown grass and farmyard; perhaps the spurs were intended to make their special imprint, lest the owner be forgotten? That rank smell of animal and harness stirred new dreams, clash of metal, rumble of hooves, cries of battle. He was in the saddle spurring towards a bright yellow horizon, sword hilt slapping his side – but he was also in a magic car going to the sea, listening to Papa's thoughts but only partly reading them, and this strange woman driving with Amazonian verve, warm and wonderful too, who could deal with a broken door by a flick of the wrist! What were *her* thoughts? What did she think of Papa? What new pictures in the kaleidoscope awaited him? He galloped on.

In the dense homeward bound traffic she weaved through the mêlée, escaping collisions by fractions of a centimetre, accepting every challenge of nerve, the Roman way.

Leo sat sideways and studied her, each curve, each flow of flesh at the eyes, at the mouth, the set of the head, fixed by time. This seeming hardness was simply a refinement of the image he had chosen not to see long ago. Was the innocence still there beneath? He checked himself. Why should that concern him now? What was happening was still not wholly credible. With the slightest shift of the imagination all this could be a half-waking dream that he could bring to an end simply by waking up completely. He wished it *was*.

The doppelganger said, "I think you are beginning to see sense – maybe for the wrong reasons but I don't care so long as you do."

Chiara's exchange with Gideon over the car door had uplifted her, and an unfamiliar tenderness wanted to flow out to him. In a new confidence, instinct moved her to reach out to Leo through him. Though she could only glimpse Gideon's face in the rear-view mirror, she spoke to him warmly, lyrically, her voice rising to be heard above the rush-hour roar, telling him about herself, about her feelings at his age, about meeting his father on the plane in a storm long ago, how they had talked and talked afterwards about so many things; and what an interesting man he was, and that she wanted *him*, his son, to be her friend too. Recklessly she turned her head once or twice to look into his eyes and put a seal on her words.

A magical throb in her voice touched Gideon's heart. She was reaching out to him with a simple tenderness that spoke to his condition as no grown-up had ever done, except his father sometimes. She seemed to look into his soul and like what she saw. She heard his secret voices and offered glimpses of certainty. Her spirit spoke to him at his own level, far removed from the daunting earthiness of Frances, or his father's elegiac flights that sometimes troubled him. With wonderful delicacy she shared his dreams, recognised who he was, applauded his heroic visions of placing his mark on the world. She was on his side.

He could not know that the golden glow he felt was the truest happiness he would ever find, a measure he would use, unawares, for all experience in the future.

Fortunately he could not guess that in her tenderness she was unthinkingly using him as an emotional bridge to reach Leo, driven by the sense of precious time slipping by.

Nearing Lido di Ostia, the black surface of the quiet road gleamed under the brazen sun with a kind of phosphorescence, exuding an acrid vapour which, mixed with petrol fumes, gave the humid air a soporific quality whose influence may have blunted her intuition. Feeling she had achieved a strong enough sympathy with the boy, she was impelled to move closer to them both, to touch on the relationship between father and son. She glanced round at Gideon again and said: "Now that you have come to Rome, what is your Papa teaching you?"

Gideon hesitated. The question was disturbing. Should he talk about the "lesson"? Something told him he should not. His father's tensions, he had sensed, were somehow linked with the lesson, and the knowledge troubled him and excited him too. Some perversity prompted him to stir those tensions again. He said, "Papa has been telling me how grown-ups behave. It's hard to explain."

In the driving mirror she saw Gideon blush, then frown with doubt. She said to Leo in Italian, in a new tone of intimacy, her breath quickening, "Have

I walked on a too delicate path? I think you have been teaching him the old manhood things – yes?"

Abstracted, Leo nodded, then saw her cheeks tighten and wished he had paused to think; he had been misled by her seemingly light-hearted use of the phrase "the old manhood things" and failed to sense the bitter inferences beneath – the way of a man with a maid. He wished he could seize upon some antidote, but could think of none.

He had been wondering how she had created an almost familial closeness with Gideon. Miraculously she had ceased to be a ghost from the past and created a place for herself in the present, joined to them both. Did she know what she was doing? He was thrown back to the uncertain days of youth, when other people always seemed to have a clear plan of what they wanted, while he had to pause and reflect. What could *her* design be? No, he was imagining things.

Gideon had seen the sudden stiffening of her shoulders, sensed the meaning of her darting question in Italian and Leo's reluctant nod, and knew he had blundered. Why was dealing with grown-ups so full of pitfalls?

She bent her head and crouched over the wheel, making a show of concentrating on her driving.

The doppelganger said, "If she sees a distasteful irony in you teaching the boy the rules that *you* did not live by, why should that trouble you? Her moment of bitterness will pass. But you are right in one thing. There *is* a design forming in her mind, but she is not yet aware of it. It is an absurd design, but she is going to talk herself into it."

What possible design can she have? After so little time – an hour or so? – after so many years! I can't believe it.

"It is perfectly credible. Women chew over their dreams day by day, year after year, a ruminative quality that sustains them. And so the fantasy is always ready for the random stroke of Destiny. So be on your guard. You are confused. Your guilt is driving you hard. You could easily be swayed."

Chiara told herself not to be upset. She should not have asked the question when the answer was obvious. The boy could not have known that his words would touch an unhealed wound. How grown-ups behave! What exquisite irony? Had Leo told the boy how a grown-up really did behave – himself in fact? He would surely not have gone that far. Please God do not let the boy discover the truth about the affair! As for the rest he will learn as everyone else does, from life – poor boy.

If she could have heard the doppelganger's words she would not have believed they referred to her. She had no design. A new clarity was spreading within her, an admission, at last, that she was alone. Franco was not a bad man – well, she supposed not. He was attentive and kind but cold. His needs seemed satisfied by business, his horses, and a masculine life that excluded women. Suddenly she felt a wave of concern for Gideon unlike anything she had ever felt for a child in the milieu. She prayed that he would never know the desolation she had felt when a perverse demon had made her drive Leo away. Gideon, this shining boy, could have been *hers*! Oh *mio caro*, look what we did! No, not *we*. It was I who did it. You made me happy with a completeness

I had never imagined possible, and something about it frightened me. Over the years I have tried to understand what I did and that is the only answer I know – fear blinded me and I had to make you go. Gideon would have been *ours*! He would have made my heart sing. We would have gloried in him – you and I together.

Gideon must not sense these thoughts. There was so much unease in him already. Leo being the man he was, she was sure that in his talks with the boy *some* emotion had spilled over, some regret, some tremor of the heart – and this sensitive lad must have been troubled, unable to understand the cause and not daring to ask? She recalled from her own childhood that when something disturbed the grown-ups you thought first of the consequences for *your* life. Gideon must be asking himself what her appearance on the scene portended. She must put his mind at rest. Something else tugged at her heart. This miraculous meeting must not fade into nothingness. Did Leo feel this too? He was here – the turning world had brought him back. That must prove something! Some continuing link could surely be found, something to sustain her? It *must* be found.

For the moment she must send comfort to the boy, and at the same time send a signal to Leo. She caught Gideon's eye in the driving mirror. "Gideon, I will tell you something. I am old enough to be your mother so I speak to you from the heart. It is natural to be puzzled by life at your age. So listen well to your Papa. He is a fine man. He understands many things, and one of them is that people are not perfect. Sometimes grown-ups do the wrong things in

223

innocence. *Pazienza*, we say! Be patient with life! Listen to him and you will grow up to be a fine man too."

Leo, do you understand?

She was sure the words had not come out as warmly as intended; the steel of bitterness must have glinted through. She coughed to conceal her distress. Her hands shook and she feared she might lose control of the car. She pretended to cough uncontrollably and drew in to the side of the road and put on the hand brake, leaving the engine running. She made a show of blowing her nose and wiping her eyes and exclaimed, "I was going to sneeze! I once nearly drove into a tree when I sneezed!" She took long breaths. "That is better. We will continue – yes?" She drove off again. "Gideon, what was I saying? Oh yes, your Papa – he is a good man and I am sure he talks to you from a full heart as we say. And that is the most precious thing, to talk from a full heart – but it needs much time, and patience. Especially time – and there is never enough time."

Oh Leo! Please – please understand! I am lonely. I want to draw near you – somehow.

In the tremor of her voice, Gideon felt her reach out to him, and she seemed to speak to him from somewhere inside himself, gently, with tenderness, and he tasted a new, perplexing excitement. No one, not even Frances, had ever come so close, What did she mean by "talking from a full heart"? She was sharing secret truths and that was exhilarating, even though he did not understand what they were – but he would, one day, if she would only go on talking

224

to him with that wonderful warmth. Inexplicably she was adding substance to Papa's lesson. If only Mama would talk to him as this woman did – but that, he told himelf sadly, would never happen. This woman, and Mama, and Frances, were different worlds. And Papa was a separate world too. It had never occurred to him that people were separate worlds in themselves! Was he himself a world alone? The thought was a little frightening.

Leo wanted to tell her he had heard her appeal. He thought of her words to the boy, "He knows so many things." Whatever he knew was of no help. In these few days he had pulled the curtain away from his life and found emptiness, as if time itself had gone away. Yet he had filled time with hope, effort, even triumph – yet none of it had touched the inner life. How skilfully one concealed that emptiness? Good manners demanded it. Gideon would learn to conform in that respect too. What was that other essence the spirit demanded? In time one stopped asking oneself that question – or tried to; but at some unguarded moment, turning a corner in an unfamiliar part of town, or in the quiet of early morning picking up the newspaper from the doorstep, the question returned, and you were ashamed to have no answer. Judging by her coded confession, she was a similar case.

The doppelganger was right again; she did want a link, a life-line. What irony! What did he have to offer, now? All the same it would be cruel not to make an effort, even now – *pretend* that there is hope. After all, time itself has become unreal.

He said in Italian: 'I understand what you are telling me – perhaps there *is* a way, a bridge to be found. Something is better than nothing!"

She glanced at him with a quick smile and sat up straight again.

Chapter 16

At Ostia she stopped the car at the beginning of a line of private beach cabins, beside one considerably larger than the rest, painted in watery blue. A patch of sand before the door was marked out in blocks of cement, its private territory. A stone's throw away was the commercial beach with ranks of tables and chairs and beach umbrellas and bars, and stalls selling beach paraphernalia, at this hour beginning to look forlorn as family parties packed up and left. A few adults with young children splashed in the shallows, where the water reflected the evening sunlight in dappled bronze. Loudspeakers blasted a pop song into the torpid air, a version of Moorlock's hedonism, take what you can from life before your luck runs out.

Leo had often wondered if the grey sand of this ancient beach resort, lumpy, grey, soiled looking, contained the original Roman pollution mixed with recent additions. As the thought crossed his mind again he noticed, some fifty vards out in the water, six muscular young men, deeply tanned, hurling a large rubber ball to one another. One was pushed under, and as he came up for air another jumped on him with legs round his neck and rubbed his groin against his head, and the others crowded close in a libidinous cluster. Ancient Roman games too!

A little breathless, she unlocked the cabin and handed out beach chairs and a small folding table, and Gideon set them down on the little square of sand. She showed the boy where spare bathing trunks hung on a rail inside. He came out looking self-conscious in pale pink swimming trunks. Leo smiled in sympathy; the colour did look odd against the boy's hard, muscular body. Gideon returned the smile warily as if to say, "This is the least awful colour I could find!" Then he ran down the slight incline towards the water. Turning in his flight he shouted to them, "Aren't you coming in?" Leo shouted back, waving him on, "We'll come in soon."

She stood on the steps, eyes narrowed against the sun, and watched the straight, slim figure scamper into the water, then make a flat leap and swim a powerful crawl close to the beach line, away from the group of tanned young men. She nodded to herself, then indicated the group with a pointing of the chin. "We must watch these rascals. It is possible they will try their games with the boy. I will not permit it." She made a whiplash movement of the hand to the side with fingers opening wide as if discarding something. "They are friends of Pasolini, you understand."

She did not mean they were Pasolini's friends but that they shared his tastes. She added, "Let us change quickly in case we must make an intervention in the water. I know how to speak to them! Some of them I think are known to Franco." She added, tight-lipped, "I wish that was not so – but – it is true!"

228

Trembling, she slipped into the cabin and closed the door and leaned against it. In these few words she had betrayed Franco – and now that she had done it, she felt free, and bitter, and vengeful. She had confided in Leo more about her life than she had ever done to anyone else – well, to one other only, her confessor, but on that occasion she had been too ashamed to do more than hint at her sadness. Father Umberto had told her to be patient with her fate, nothing more. She had hoped to feel release, but none came. Now, though Leo had simply nodded understanding, she felt her burden shared. With this new confession she confronted truths she had refused to see through the years. She had known the truth about Franco before she married him, known and not known! Why, then, had she married *him*? There had been no shortage of "good" matches. Did she marry him in a madness of blind escape, or to protect herself from full commitment? Yes, she must have done it to keep part of herself pure. What a price to pay.

Leo marvelled at the aptness of seemingly chance events. In her haste to find privacy with him, she had chosen to forget that this was a favourite haunt of "friends of Pasolini"; what more appropriate place to let slip this fact about her husband? It had burst out of her as if it had waited years for the right moment!

Could she have married him in ignorance of his tastes? Moorlock, speaking from professional experience, had once remarked that women instinctively recognised that tendency in a man; and some preferred such men as husbands – they "bothered" them less. Moorlock, in bantering vein at dinner, his broad face lit up with good food and wine, often joked about the hidden caprice that governed the choice of partners. "It's one thing getting your end in, or for a woman to feel you fading away in her – victory or surrender according to taste! – but a lot of people secretly prefer the easier communication with their own sort, chaps together and girls together!"

"Of course," he added. "You can dress that up in Freudian jargon if you like, but that gets you no further! We are what we *are* and there's an end to it. *Carpe diem* – what else is there? Or as Matthew says, 'Sufficient unto the day is the evil thereof . . .' Good, isn't it? Leave well alone."

She emerged wearing minute yellow shorts with black diagonal stripes, and a strapless upper piece of shiny black. Her figure was if anything neater and tighter than he remembered, finely poised, the tiny waist and wide hips breathtaking. With a timid smile she acknowledged his admiration, and sat down on the chair nearest the door of the cabin, following Gideon's vigorous progress up and down the shore-line with an unfamiliar emotion, her stomach muscles tight.

He went into the cabin to change. It was spacious and surprisingly well equipped. There was a toilet compartment and shower in one corner, and in another a small kitchen with compact cooker, glass-fronted cupboard containing crockery and glasses and plates and bottles of drink, tall refrigerator with orange pilot light aglow, electric coffee machine. A large wardrobe occupied another corner. With infra-red heaters on the walls for cold days, the cabin could serve as a large bedroom; several inflated air-beds, of double-bed size,

230

leaned against the stucco wall behind the door. He recalled her acid tone when she remarked that some of the tanned young men were known to her husband. Presumably he entertained them here.

He contemplated three pairs of swimming shorts hanging on a rail – pale pink with large yellow spots, cream with purple stars, white with black vertical stripes. He chose the one with black stripes.

Emerging, he stood for a moment looking down at the water, reassured to see Gideon cleaving the sluggish shallows well away from the young men. Hearing him close the cabin door she started as if drawn away from deep meditation, and said quickly, "You look the same! Is this the only way we have not changed – you and I – on the outside?"

He said, "I am not sure I *have* changed inside – I've got to admit that."

She looked startled and seemed about to question him but checked herself. She locked the cabin door with a key on a rubber band which she put on her wrist, and gave him a similar band with a duplicate key. Then they sat down at the round white wooden table and watched Gideon in silence. To a casual observer they could have been any couple contentedly watching over their child in the water.

Each wondered how to begin their meeting anew, for this change of scene, sitting together in temporary alliance, was a challenge quite different from that of the first shock in the Pantheon. Some understanding had to be found. What is to be said? How can we move from this point? For something *must* be said – we owe it to ourselves! The silence weighed upon them.

Gideon swam back and forth parallel to the beach. At last he stopped and waded through the oily water towards the shore till he stood waist deep. He looked up towards where they sat, and seeing that they were settled, turned to watch a group of young children alming brightly coloured rubber quoits at a red pole floating on a round rubber base. When one of the children threw too hard and sent the quoit into deeper water he swam after it in his burrowing crawl stroke and when he returned with it, stood up and put the quoit on his head for them to jump up in competition to retrieve it, laughing and shrieking at this embellishment of their game. A few adults standing near, evidently part of the family party, looked on approvingly.

"He could have been mine," she said in a great sigh. She did not know she had spoken out loud.

The words cut into him like a knife, fury at life, at the inescapable reach of Fate. He had given "her" child to another woman! What answer could there be? Of course she was right. What could he say that would not sound mawkish? He remained silent.

Yet every flight of the imagination, every invocation of the "might have been" had a right to its moment now. There was no way forward. Where was reality! Where was time? Her feeling about Gideon was understandable. Why not acknowledge her dream with all its bitterness? At last he said, "I am sorry," and was ashamed. How banal that sounded, how weak, how insincere? How many "wrong" meanings could be seen in it? Did he really want her to think that he wished Gideon had been hers?

In their hectic exchanges at the Pantheon, what had

he said about his marriage? He could not remember. Had he told the truth! It was possible. If he had, so be it.

The doppelganger said firmly, "She is playing on your great weakness, sloppy sentiment! Women know how to work on it! 'Pity me! Gideon could have been mine!' What rubbish!"

For the first time in years he thought he could see his familiar, a tall, angular shadow at his side, darkening the fire of the evening sun. He had seen the shadow before, long ago, but dimly, a trick of the eyes, never as hard-edged as now. He had thrust the vision aside then, and wished he could do so now.

Why are you so certain it's rubbish? Come to think of it, you never bothered me as much as this in the past? For that matter why do you never interfere in my business life?

The other laughed. "In business you think clearly and coldly, never troubled by doubt, entirely ruthless. But you have paid a heavy price for success. In the things of the heart you are unsure. What sensitivity you once had is rusty from disuse. There are so many questions about yourself you are afraid to answer, or even acknowledge."

Bitterly he said, Why did you let me sink this far? Why didn't you tell me all this before, all those years ago?

"I *did*! You would not listen. You turned your back on life. You rejected sensibility because you could not stomach what it told you – about other people, about yourself. I hoped that when you had proved yourself in business you would turn back again and confront

233

your immaturity – and grow beyond it. But riches and power held you fast. In desperation I gave you bad dreams. Only in the last few months did you wake up, and you saw that you were only partly living. And now the demons bring you terrible questions. Dare you accept awareness at last? Can you accept love any more now than you could all those years ago? Alas the time to take great risks is when you are young and resilient, not in your middle years! That is why I am here so much these days. You worry me."

You paint a diabolical picture of me, ruthless, cold, calculating, selfish – no use to anybody! If that's how things are with me, you are wasting your time, and so am I to listen to you!

"That is just another excuse. Life does not accept excuses. I have to frighten you, for you are in danger. My duty is to steer you away from this woman. Her predicament is *hers* to deal with, not yours. Emotionally you are lamentably naive."

But Gideon *could* have been hers! Another of life's "might have beens". What is wrong with being sorry for her?

"You refuse to see what a woman is capable of. She may not be thinking it consciously – not yet – but you do see where this line of hers is leading, do you not?"

It's leading nowhere in particular. It is simply gloomy self-pity – understandable enough.

"You try my patience! I will ask you this. Are you willing to give her a child, answer me that. Do you not see now?"

You can't be serious!

"Of course I am serious. She does not realise it fully

yet but the possibility is taking shape in her mind. Meeting again was a cruel trick of Fortune for you both. It has sent her into a delirium of despair and recklessness – the absurd fancy that *any* risk is worth taking to retrieve the past. You must not let that delirium seize you too. The past can *never* be retrieved."

I still can't believe it. It's absurd – grotesque!

"Quite so. Wait. You will see."

She wondered why he had said "sorry", and only then realised that she had spoken out loud. It was true. Gideon could have been hers! This was surely a moment – never to be found again – for wild thoughts to be set free. She pictured a life in which Gideon really was hers, and felt a glow of completeness often conjured in dreams. She said to herself: "What does he mean by 'sorry'! He still does not understand." Aloud she said: "God makes a woman to create life, and we are incomplete if we do not. *Mio caro* – it is not easy to find words. When I look at the boy, and you here beside me, I can see him as mine."

"Tell me— " He stopped, for the question must not be asked. But it was too late to retreat. "Did you *decide* not to have children?"

With a wistful smile she leaned over to touch his hand lightly then drew back and sat erect in the white chair, hands on hips, flowering girlhood bravely resurrected. "You are thinking: 'Did she hope for a miracle, a chance to start again – sometimes afraid she was losing her reason?' Yes, I did punish myself for driving you away, but you remained with me always. You are right in one thing." She sighed. "I did sometimes think I was going out of my mind."

She looked down at herself and stretched out her fingertips to her knees and drew them back along the outside of sun-browned thighs to the hips as if tracing a secret sign. Without looking up she said, "I must be a little mad. I am not happy to have failed to have a child, but there *is* something else – and I I would not say it if you had not asked." She gave a start and put her fingers to her lips but it was too late. "No, you did not ask, but I will say it. It was always *your* child I wanted. Yes, that was what I felt and – and – " She blushed and went white and blushed again. "We are not reasonable creatures, are we?" She looked past him down to the sea.

He contemplated the bronze sunlight on her still flesh, a breathing statue glowing in the sun against the dull sand, exemplar of courage, defiance, hope. Guilt returned, and compassion. Was there *nothing* to be done?

She faced him. "How can I say it all? But I must try. There is so little time. Wait! Tell me." She leaned close and whispered, "How much time have we?"

In a shift of torpid air the warm smell of her enveloped him, recalling memory and desire. He said, "We go back in two days, but we could . . ." He stopped, but could not draw back. "But we could meet again? I would come back alone. I want to do that."

The doppelganger broke in angrily, "There's your weak sentimentality again – taking the line of least resistance as you call it. She is leading you by the nose. Her siren song is more dangerous than you think. If you go any further you will be in a battle of guilt and remorse where there can be no victory, and no escape either."

236

But I can't simply turn away – that would be heart-less.

"You have another motive, deeply hidden, even more dangerous, suppressed since student days; the romantic dream of resolving in your own life the historic predicament of the Jew, to reconcile the private identity with the secular world's recoil from it! With her you came very close to it, or thought you did, but at the crucial moment you found an excuse to flee. And now you are tempted again! It was madness then! It is madness now even more."

Yes I did have such dreams long ago, but no more. I only want to be kind to her, be a friend if possible – do *something* in compassion.

"You want to prove that you are not a villain after all! Now that you are in the middle way of life, with money and power, you imagine that nothing can touch you; and so you toy once again with extravagant dreams of youth. Leave well alone."

I still don't believe you. I may want too much, and too late – but I am not as daft as you think. Go away.

She said, holding him with that poignant, pleading look, "Will you really come back – and soon?"

"Yes. We can decide the dates before I leave. I want to cancel the years of silence – I want to – how can I say it – I want to know you again."

She studied him, lips pressed together. She wanted to believe. Yes, it must be so. Solemnly she said, "Then I am glad. We need much time, for everything that needs to be said. But we must begin to . . ." She gasped and jumped to her feet and the next instant was running down to the water screaming in Italian, "Stop! Help!

Murder! Assassins! No, No! Leave the boy alone you villains! . . ."

Gideon's shrill, fear-stricken shout was just audible against the boom of the loudspeakers. "Papa help – help! He-elp!"

Leo got up violently and his chair tumbled over, and ran after her. The tanned young men were clustered round Gideon, pressing upon him, laughing in private joy. Gideon's voice rose to a scream. "Don't *do* that! Don't! Get off!" One of them ducked under the water with his head against the boy's loins and Gideon kicked out and two others lifted him horizontally out of the water showing his swimming trunks pulled down; they were about to carry him away. Gideon twisted and broke their grip and hurled himself sideways kicking out as he fell back into the water, and one of the men cried out and held his hand to his eye. Before Gideon could stand up they closed in on him again, laughing in orgiastic hysteria. Chiara had run along the sand till she was level with them, and now splashed through the viscous wavelets, waving her arms and shouting terrible curses, an avenging Fury. Two of the youths turned their heads and jeered and returned to their libidinous frenzy. Now within arm's length she struck out at heads and faces with her fists and shouted, "Bruno, Marco, Ricardo! Leave the poor boy alone or you will suffer for this! Leave him now! At once I say!"

Three of them instantly drew away, calling to the others in surly tones, "Let him go. It is the wife of Franco! She will make trouble for us! Much trouble. Come on!" The other three eyed Leo warily.

Leo considered them with steely calm. In his boxing

238

days he would have sailed in and taken his chance, but that was out of the question now. He would use bluff, and his still fluent grasp of Neapolitan dialect – he had spent a year in Naples after Oxford. With a sudden lunge he seized one of the hesitant three by the upper arm and pressed hard on the nerve at the root of the biceps, and hissed in slurring Napolitanese, "I have some people who will deal with you and your friends. They know where to find you. I advise you and your friends to go – at once. Understand?"

Chiara stifled a gasp. In that dark world you must tread with care. Still, such things did happen, and they must know it.

The young man jerked his arm free, pushed out his chin in defiance and leapt away and the others followed; they ran through the shallows and up the incline of the beach and through the line of kiosks and were quickly out of sight.

Gideon pulled up his trunks, angry, ashamed, confused. What had befallen him had been disagreeable, and mysterious in the orgiastic transports of his attackers. He was close to tears and ashamed of that too. He glanced at the grown-ups who had been standing nearby with their children – why had they not come to help him? Instead they had herded the children away and now stood protectively close to them, looking at him accusingly. But he had done nothing wrong!

Chiara put an arm about his shoulders. "My son, do not be unhappy. What they did is not your fault. They will not come near you again."

She would tell Franco to stop giving them money.

She blinked her tears away. One thing was certain

now – she would change her life with Franco, and do so without mercy. She turned, still holding Gideon close, and said to Leo in Italian, "Why do we do things we know in our hearts are wrong for us?"

He nodded in sad agreement. She seemed to echo the doppelganger's words.

Chapter 17

Gideon wanted to remain in Chiara's embrace where they stood, the warm shallow water lapping round his legs, the summer beach sounds returning, a maternal closeness, natural, protective, safe. That she talked to Papa in Italian no longer worried him. Here, for the moment, was his rightful place. He thought of Mama, and why this was different – a sweeter embrace; no, not sweeter but more lasting in its intensity. As he wondered why that was so, he pressed himself closer and Chiara hugged him even more tightly, and the question drifted away.

The shock of the attack returned. He needed more explanation than she had given him; but it must come from Papa. He slid from her embrace and moved to Leo standing near and leaned his face into his shoulder.

Leo felt the boy's tears on his neck. He held him close and tried not to show disquiet. "Don't be upset. One thing you must take my word for – it was nothing to do with *you*! None of it was in any way your fault."

Gideon said, 'I suppose they're what boys at school call queers.'

As he said the words, hearing echoes of schoolboy raillery, Gideon felt once again that he was being

241

thrust away from one phase of understanding into another, through a doorway that would close behind him for ever. All perspectives would go on changing and there would never be time to catch one's breath before the next change happened. That too needed its proper moment to be understood. Everything needed its proper moment! Why did one always have to wait?

He wanted that door to close and yet *not* to – or rather he wanted it to happen without having to leave behind the person he had been, but he knew it was impossible. A divine hand had drawn a line in the sky between past and future, and life would make its special mark upon him in its own inescapable time.

He glanced round at Chiara. She was regarding him with an intensity as eloquent as speech, reaching out to him, telling him that he was important to her, and he felt an excitement never known before. Her soft brown eyes spoke of a longing he could not understand. He knew only that it uplifted his spirit and that he wanted her to reach out to him always.

He wished Frances was here and that he could tell her what had happened, and try to describe the mysterious new visions that were coming so quickly, too quickly, so hard to fathom. Then he had second thoughts. She would make a joke about it, and he would feel he must laugh with her, though sad at being unable to explain that there had been nothing to laugh at. With Frances there was always a curtain between what she said and what she really felt – only now, at a distance, did he see that clearly. He wished it was not so. With Chiara, if he could ever be close enough to her to talk from the deepest recesses of his soul, he was sure she would never laugh at him – she would speak to him from the depths too. He longed for that to happen. Frances, he sensed for the first time, never moved towards him in that complete way; she always seemed to be playing a game with dreams, *her* dreams, not his! Chiara was different, reassuringly so, even though her perception was unsettling, as if she saw all the way into him. Perhaps she did? He wanted to send her a signal of acceptance, of comradeship. He held out his hand and she came close and put her arm round his waist, and Leo did so too, and they both hugged him, and thus linked they walked up the little incline of dark sand to the cabin.

The communion uplifted Chiara too, a 'might have been' made real. For these few moments Gideon joined her to Leo in the present, and the past fell away. Holding Gideon's muscular young frame at her side revived a cry in the secret kernel of her; and the demon sent her the dizzying illusion that the boy was in truth her son, hers to glory in, his soul part of hers. She wanted to go on holding him tightly as she held him now, love him, protect him.

Wildness possessed her. What should she say to Leo now? What dared she hope for? What could be done? Steely thoughts of Franco returned. She owed it to herself, before it was too late, to answer *her* needs, as Franco had always followed *his*.

If only Leo would lead the way! He said so little. What did he want to happen? What did he want her to do? One thought brought hope. The past lived in him again, as it lived in her. He was waiting for her to reveal what *she* wanted? So be it. Suddenly all was malleable.

243

That cry from her viscera banished self-questioning. She began to consider possible ways forward as coolly as she did in business. Above all, Gideon must not know – perhaps never.

She went into the cabin and dressed quickly and made way for Leo and Gideon. She sat outside at the little table, chin on hands, watching the slowly moving water, bronze-dappled by the sinking sun, shimmering gleams diffracted in the heated air. Her mind moved with an equal inevitability towards something unthinkable – a temptation that had tantalised her in many restless nights. Why unthinkable? It must have happened in many families down the generations! In the milieu it was bad manners to comment on a likeness between members of different families, or an unlikeness *within* a family. Imperfect her life must remain, but if she could satisfy that labyrinthine hunger inside her once only, how enriched she would be! Leo was the same as he had been, and so was she – time had made little difference, except that each was now encumbered. Well, such "problems" could be managed as they had always been, by craft and compromise. She would find a way. She had nothing to lose.

She saw the faint outlines of a plan. Her cheeks burned and her breath came faster. How strange that it was suddenly so clear a possibility? Yes, there were dangers, but she would see to it that Leo was protected. For herself she must risk everything. At her age it was her last chance, her only chance, to redeem the past.

Leo blamed himself for the attack on Gideon. Knowing the evil genius of this spot he should have been ready for it. The boy's disquiet seemed to have subsided, but

244

sooner or later Gideon would want to be told more about the *louche* culture these young men inhabited. ". . . *the contagion of the world's slow stain . . .*". There were so many contagions! If only Gideon could learn about them without pain? There was little hope of that. The pain was part of the learning.

Each looking inwards, they put the chairs and table away in the cabin, hung the swimwear on the rail inside to dry. Locking the door, she glanced down at the rubber ball bobbing on the slow swell where the young men had been, and pursed her lips.

As they drove away, Leo felt the touch of the ancient spirit of the place. On the horizon the sky was furnace red. Bloodshot rays of hard evening sunlight pierced the car's dusty side windows. He saw Aeneas's ships becalmed in the offing, their dun-coloured sails dark patches against the angry sun, awaiting a propitious sign to pull for the swift landfall and the merciless assault. Predatory conquest, savagery, desire! *Carpe diem*? Why not?

They drove along the line of parked cars. The fiery rays gleamed on sun-glasses and reddish-brown limbs as family groups in multi-coloured playtime costume loaded the equipment of another beach day. He glanced at his watch. It was little more than a couple of hours since Chiara had appeared out of the past, but it seemed that she had been with them beyond all time and memory. The three of them could have been one of these commonplace families heading for home.

He knew she waited for him to speak – where they should go, what they should do. Silently she begged him to play his part. What were they to do in this

Pirandello-esque play – waiting to invent their parts? Again he thanked his stars that Gideon was with them. Gently he said in Italian, "There is much to be said. I have an idea. Let us have dinner at our hotel. We will be alone most of the time. The boy is enchanted with Italian television! He will eat quickly and go up to the room and watch for the rest of the evening. We can take our time over dinner and talk in peace. We are staying at the Nazionale – remember?"

She made an exaggerated show of surprise at the name of the hotel. "Ah yes. Of course! It had to be so. See how everything fits!" There was pain too, but he must not see it. The Fates were driving them.

She stared hard at the little cloud of dust thrown up by the car ahead. At last she forced herself to speak. "It would please me if you came to my apartment. My family bought it for me. So it is truly mine – truly me. Please come."

"Yes of course," he said quickly. "But the boy has had enough excitement for one day. Perhaps tomorrow?"

She said to herself, wait – let the thought take root.

What answer would he have made, he wondered, if Gideon had not been there? Nothing was clear now, not even temptation! Had his fires burned so low? They passed a roadside cafe where mini-skirted girls sat with legs crossed high, and the tactile fantasy wandered urgently over shadowed thighs. That proved nothing. Old men employed such fancies to avoid self-knowledge! The true comparison could only be with the days of hot youth, when the blood rose and you rushed ahead to bring down yet another quarry!

Oh yes, the good days had lasted a long time. Then imperceptibly the glory of the hunt was dimmed by thought – of compatibility, whatever that meant, of true communication, of a certainty you called love when it was ownership you wanted, which you called fidelity, meaning *her* fidelity! You knew, then, but preferred not to dwell on the knowledge, that the careless days of the chase were over. How bitter to lust after those young thighs now?

He thought again of that mirage of youth, "she", the unique soul mate. How wonderful it must be to be young and believe in the impossible! He must tell Gideon: do not fear your dreams. Follow them with all your heart in the days of your innocence. You will regret it if you don't. As I do now. Well, he would not say "as I do now", for that would tell the boy more about his father than it was good for him to know.

Of course it would be wonderful to have Chiara again, but what would follow after? The "but" said everything! That was something else he must warn Gideon about. If you are not sure that you want something, then you do not want it enough, and you had better forget about it.

Suddenly he wanted to shout, "By God I envy Gideon for being young and strong and full of hope. Why should *he* have so much pleasure ahead of him! What am I to do with myself? I am not old enough to *feel* old. It's not fair. Why can't I gather rosebuds as I used to, and to hell with tomorrow?"

He studied her profile, preoccupied, drawn. He longed to dispel that tension with caresses. The doppelganger said, "You know that's not enough. It never *was* – not with her, not with *any* woman."

247

He ignored him, or thought he did.

He turned to her, words bursting out unplanned, "We need time to capture tenderness."

He wished he could cancel the word tenderness, but he had said it, and he must have meant it. Then he saw that he had confessed more than he thought – tenderness was what *he* needed!

She did not understand why his words disturbed her. She searched for an answer. At last she said, "I had not expected you to say those words, but you are right – they are the only ones to be said."

The three of them were silent for the rest of the drive to the hotel.

Gideon liked to eat quickly and crudely, crouched over the table, elbows spread out like outriggers, shovelling food from his plate while his cheeks bulged with the previous mouthful – his "Caliban act", Leo called it. In the seemly ambience of the hotel dining room Leo was tempted to reproach him as he did at home, "Come on old boy, sit up straight and put your knife and fork down while you're chewing!" – but he could not embarrass him in Chiara's presence. He reminded himself that such words seldom had more than a passing effect, sometimes limited to sulking or a snarl of discontent, provoking paternal wrath. Miriam, when the children were younger, had often threatened a "smack across the chops" for such behaviour. These days she protested that Leo's attempts to instil good manners were a waste of time and nervous energy. "They will grow out of it. It is the influence of peer group pressure at school!"

Her cant middlebrow jargon was irritating enough,

248

but her habit of opposing him in the children's presence was infuriating. In private he complained, "How can I have any authority over the children if you oppose me in front of them?"

"Don't worry, darling. You've got plenty of authority."

"Well, if I have, it won't last long if you go on like this!"

"Don't get angry, darling, it's bad for your blood pressure."

"I haven't *got* blood pressure but I *will* have if you don't stop shooting down what I say in front of them!"

Sometimes she made matters worse by pretending to support him, saying to the offending child with a conspiratorial wink, "Now then, Papa's getting angry so behave yourself" the wink saying, "Let's humour him shall we?"

This time the Caliban act was convenient. Gideon would race through his food and rush upstairs all the sooner.

In the long low dining room with dove grey wall panels picked out in thin gold lines, voices were muted. Sultry air drifted in through lattice windows open to the rear courtyard. The last yellow gleams of day cast shadows between the ranks of tables with stiff cloths hanging in regular folds almost to the polished wooden floor.

Leo and Chiara made polite conversation, while giving Gideon their main attention, concealing their impatience for him to go upstairs. Gideon was wondering whether he would get to the strawberries and ice cream in time for the Western film soon to begin on television.

Leo and Chiara had barely begun their main course when Gideon gave a grunt of victory and looked up. "Papa, could I please have my pudding now – there's a Western on in a few minutes?"

Leo raised a hand to summon the waiter.

"Papa, let *me* order! I want to practise my Italian."

The middle-aged waiter, a figure of patience with drooping shoulders and snow-white hair and fresh, smooth face, looked as though he was familiar with this schoolboy phenomenon; he stood with hands clasped before him while Gideon mouthed each word with care: "*Io voglio* – er – *fragole con gelato* – er I mean – *gelato vanilla*. Was that all right Papa?"

The waiter intervened, in English only slightly accented: "Bravo, young man, you will soon speak like a true Roman!"

Gideon, put out at not receiving the recognition of a reply in Italian, felt he must show his mettle again: "Er – *per favore* – er – " the words for "I want it quickly" eluded him and he struck out wildly: "er – *voglio rapido*," and finished with a relieved, "yes – *grazie!*"

This was not the moment, Leo decided, to tell the boy that "*rapido*" could also mean an express train. The waiter struck him as a man given to irony – he would leave it to him. The waiter clicked his heels. "At your command, young sir! I will bring it to you by fast train!"

Gideon was only momentarily puzzled about the "fast train"; he would ask Papa about it later. He held his spoon at the ready. The waiter returned in less than a minute and placed the bowl before him, great blunt cones of glistening scarlet with a ball of ice cream balanced among them. Gideon raised his spoon but remembered his manners and lifted his head, said "*Grazie!*" to the waiter and fell to. The spoon flashed between bowl and mouth, clicking in two-time on the bowl and his teeth, with intermittent indrawn breaths to counter the ice cream's chill. His lightly bronzed cheeks shone as he sighed, crumpled the stiff napkin, and murmured gravely, "Please excuse me."

Chiara smile fondly and touched his hand. "Go my son, go and enjoy yourself. We will meet again tomorrow I hope. Good night."

Leo prayed that the boy did not guess his relief. "Off you go."

Gideon, on his feet before the words were quite uttered, turned and sped out of the room, the torn denim at his knee flapping. They heard him bound up the stairs.

Chiara said, "He is a sweet, fine boy. You have reason to be proud of him."

Before he knew what he was going to say the words were out. "I envy him. I know I shouldn't but I do." He bit his lip.

How often had she heard that sentiment in the milieu? How sad it was. If only she had a son! She said, "I know you do."

"How do you know that!"

"Do not be concerned. I will not betray you!" She paused and added, her voice softened in a kind of caress, "A woman knows many things."

"*Some* women do!" He had not meant to say that either and was shaken even more.

"You mean your wife does *not*?"

"That's not the point at all." He was furious at having been caught so neatly. He could not remember her having talked with such probing precision years before. Well, he was certainly not going to be led into that classic plea for sympathy, "My wife does not understand me."

Thinking to find safer ground, but doing the opposite before he knew it, he said, "Besides, who understands *anybody*?" Then added quickly, "That is not the point either." He laughed to hide his confusion, "I am not sure what *is* the point!" He reached for the bottle of Barolo. "Let me fill your glass."

The uncertain exchanges must have cancelled doubt, for they moved closer, lowering defences.

Was he losing his reason? He did not care; let everything be said! He longed to see the mirage of perfection dancing before him once more, confirming important truths – his strength, his certainty reborn. The doppelganger was right again – he desperately needed to see himself truly, for it seemed he had not done so for a life-time. But how could he say that he needed to see himself in *her*? What a confession that would be!

She saw the way ahead plain. She had lived through a divine *entr'acte* that seemed to have lasted for ever. The play could not be resumed completely, but *something* could be redeemed. She would move the world to achieve it.

In saying, "A woman knows many things." she had

voiced a piece of traditional family cant often uttered by women of her mother's generation – a woman "knew" life with her insides! Her womanly power could help him find what he had come to Rome to discover. She must find another way of saying it; instinct told her he needed that pledge.

Trying to cancel her gaffe about his wife, she whispered, "I could say the same about Franco! But as you say, it is not the point. Do not think badly of me for talking freely. There *is* sweetness to be found – not the whole world and all the stars! – but something to nourish our hearts. I *know* it is so. I think you know it too."

He dared not look at her. He did not want her to see into him further. He bent his head, looking into his glass, hiding his face.

She wanted to touch his hair, its scattered grey filaments marking the lost years. How much more dare I say? I feel I am holding the world in balance. Again she murmured, "You have a fine boy in Gideon." This time the words were uttered with a passion that startled her. He *must* understand – he must!

Torpor descended on him again and hid the glimmer of comprehension trying to break through. At last he spoke, flatly, awkwardly, and the words surprised them both, for different reasons. He answered something he thought she had just said – in truth she had said it much earlier, but the words still sounded in his mind, softly, compellingly, "He could have been mine – *ours*." He answered, "Yes, I suppose he could have been."

The words had indeed been on her lips again, and she had longed to say them, and when he now spoke in seeming reply she really thought she *had* said them again, and hope lifted.

His "reply" sounded banal to him. The next moment the words he had *imagined* he had heard, taken with his reply, conjured a grotesque possibility, yet unaccountably familiar, like a thought remembered from a dream. The doppelganger said, "You are imagining too many things. You are in a frenzy of delusion about recapturing lost opportunity and lost time. And so you toy with the fantasies of youth – and of older men too – including that classic one, planting a 'cuckoo in the nest' – a love-child growing in a woman, with no responsibility on your part. I have warned you against that – for it is *she* in her desperation who is tempting you along that road. There is nothing exalted or noble in it, simply guilt and remorse blinding you to reality. You must turn away."

He ignored him. The "cuckoo in the nest" gibe was brutal, and went deep. In the old furious days one had certainly toyed with such fantasies – more than toyed. He recalled a wild night changing partners on the river bank near Lady Margaret Hall; and afterwards punting away, heads spinning in victory and spent lust, chanting, "Oh oh oh, which little girl will know . . .!" So that demonic desire had surfaced again, to place the spark where that lost image of himself now beckoned again, in her beside him. For her to stir that desire in him was natural too – *her* mirage crying out in her womb.

No, it was absurd, a late, tantalising trick of the gonads! Yet the thought was there, poised between them! No, there was nothing exalted about it, simply a sordid fancy.

Chiara felt that she had shouted it out loud, and now there was a wonderful clarity in her, a surge of freedom and resolve. He was moving towards her, but he had so many scruples. Her thoughts leapt ahead. Thank God she had money. She could do whatever she wanted. There need not be any outward upset in the marriage – but who could foretell the future! It would mean telling some lies, mainly to protect the child. In any case the world was changing fast, and people were beginning to live in a fashion that would not have been countenanced all those years ago. As for Leo's marriage she would do nothing to endanger it; but there again, who could tell what time might bring? In the coming years she could share the same roof with him in whatever snatches of time they could steal from their other lives – in a "side-life" dedicated to them alone. As for the boy – in her imagination "it" was a boy – yes, there would be difficulties, dimly glimpsed, his upbringing, his identity in every sense. It would not be ideal, but what upbringing was! She would find a way. Above all the child would have love. That prefigured life whirled in golden sunbeams in her head.

If Franco had given her a child would she have felt like this? He *could* have done; they had both been tested. She did not want to answer the question. God worked His will inscrutably. He had brought Leo back to her and made his heart open to her again, slowly, cautiously – but how could it be otherwise? Another miracle *must* happen! Blessed Mary I beseech your pity and your mercy! Grant this prayer and let Leo give me the child we should have had if I had not sent him away. I am strong in my certainty

255

now. I can face anything. I am strong enough for us both.

"Her state is tragic," the doppelganger said. "She hardly knows what she asks of you. You cannot do this, even from pity, or the hope of finding yourself again through her. Be kind. Be gentle. But you must not even hint that what she asks is remotely possible. Do not give her false hope."

You have no charity. I want to do one decent thing! Reason doesn't exist any more. I want to pay a debt, a debt to myself. I can't explain it. Some sense of rightness draws me to do what she asks.

There was no answer. In the sultry air he felt cold.

She picked up her glass. Leo was looking straight through her with an expression reminiscent of Gideon's when they rescued him, the shock of seeing more than he wanted to see. Why does he say nothing? He is waiting for me to say it all! Yes, he is right. It must all be said. The wine will help me.

She seldom took alcohol, the occasional few mouthfuls of wine with a meal, but her throat was tight with sudden fear. She gulped the wine as if it were water, and spoke in a hypnotic whisper, as in the confessional, more and more explicitly, till at last something checked her. She needed his help to say the words, "I want you to give me a child." Only when the words were spoken could she tell him that she would take all the responsibility, rearrange her life as it must be from the moment the child was on the way, create a separate "side-life" to include *him*, but only as far as he wished it. Again she told herself, "Who can say what the future might bring?" He must help her say it all.

He still held her her with that look of awed fascina-tion, and she could not continue. A little desperate now, she held her glass out to he filled again, and drank most of it and took heart and spoke her thoughts plainly.

The doppelganger whispered urgently, "When she says, 'Who knows what the future may bring,' she means the future with *you* At this moment she genuinely believes that she will make no claims on you, but she will not be able to keep that promise. I can see you are going to pretend to agree, make excuses to gain time, and then reject her again. If you do that it will kill her."

Leo wanted to say to her, "I have dreamed of this – a true love child. Not one born of duty." But something else forced its way out instead – weak, unsure, cowardly. "We must see everything crystal clear first, the consequences for us both. We must be sure of everything." He did not know what he meant by "everything".

Her full lips parted in a hesitant smile and she leaned close, waiting for his next words.

He tried again. "Yes, we must be absolutely certain – for the sake of the . . ." He could not bring himself to say. "the child."

It was not the secure acceptance she had hoped, but that would come, she was sure. He needed time to take the thought fully into himself. She saw him lose his seeming detachment, but misinterpreted the look of wonder that replaced it. She said, "You must not worry about me. I will manage everything – everything. I will take all responsibility. I swear it. I will do nothing to endanger your marriage – not a whisper, not a sign! You can trust me. But you are right. We must talk everything through like . . ." She laughed shakily. "Like responsible people! Which is what we are after all. Are we not?" She took his hand, and he saw in her eyes the possession he remembered on the plane as she stood at her post waiting for him to take her in his arms.

Stolidly he said, "We have two days left. We will talk everything through so that we know each other's mind completely. And I will be back in a couple of weeks."

Something prompted them to look round. The diners had gone. There was a resonance in the air as in a place where an oracle had spoken. The world would never be the same again. Chiara had spoken of the deed as a kind of purification. How could her certainty move him so?

There was a sudden break in the silence as if a thread snapped. He heard running feet and Gideon appeared in the doorway, breathless, eyes wide, his words falling over each other: "Something terrible's happened. I think I got the meaning right. They have attacked Israel! An Israeli general came on speaking English. He had a black patch over one eye. He said, 'It's going to be the hardest battle we've ever fought.' What did he mean? Could Israel be wiped out and the Jews massacred like they were in Germany? If I say I'm older could I get into the Israeli army? After all I'm big enough! I could be older? I want to go and save Israel."

Leo hoped the boy did not read his thoughts. Reality had broken through with its customary savagery. The nightmare scenario was upon them. As his father would have said, "It is written!" Please God let it not happen! What was the use of saying that? God *had* let it happen before – many times.

Chiara stood with her face in her hands. All perspectives were gone. Did *he* remember her words in bed, "I see you are Jewish!" What did they mean to her now? She stopped trembling. A new clarity appeared. Those words belonged to a world far away, but they had been purified, and were potent in the present with a different meaning, beyond logic, beyond all questioning – and now bound her to Leo, and to Gideon, with a protective passion never known before.

Gideon stood stiffly to attention, arms stretched at his sides, thumbs at the seams of his trousers, the soft light gleaming on ruffled hair and flushed cheeks, girding himself, like his namesake the son of Joash the Manassite, to deliver Israel. Infected by that passion, Leo wished he could go with him and take his chance too. He would attain, if only for a moment, a triumph of a kind – the prospect of death a good reason for having lived, as he had known it in Hitler's war. And as for this stripling standing ready before him, in the days of Gideon ben Joash he would not have been too young to buckle a sword at his hip! Now, thank God, there was little chance of that – though if the boy set his heart on going could he stop him? Would he want to?

Gideon's face was damp with sweat. "Papa, tell me. What can we do? And me? Will you let me go?"

Chiara's shoulders shook. She raised her head from her hands, tears on her cheeks. "No, my son – you see I call you my son for I feel close to you and I cannot help speaking to you from the heart. The world will not allow such evil to happen again to the Jewish people. We have learnt our lesson . . ." She faltered, asking herself, What am I saying? Why we?

Why *our* lesson? What lesson? She forced herself to continue. "I will pray for Israel and every single Jewish person. The Holy Father has spoken of his love for the Jews. Believe me, what you fear will not happen. I am sure of it."

Chapter 18

"Go back upstairs," he told Gideon, "and watch for any more news about Israel. I'll join you soon and we'll talk about it."

"Right, Papa." In his excitement Gideon had almost said, "sir", in a recall of school cadet discipline. Turning on his right heel, with a stamp of the left foot he did a smart about-turn and shot out of the room.

Chiara saw that the news struck Leo with a force that was ancient. She tried to feel its strength in her own body, and it seemed that she succeeded, but for an instant only. She felt it only as imagined emotion, not in her bones, as he must feel it in his. Perhaps she never would. No, she would not accept that. She would *make* herself share it. She would remind herself at every moment that Leo was a Jew and teach herself to feel as he did – and as Gideon did. Being a Jew linked you inescapably with a tragedy of incalculable dimensions. She must try to understand that. Awareness of all things Jewish must now be part of her, a change far from comprehended now, but it *would* be, in time – she was certain of that. Was she better prepared now than she had been before? She thought she was. Unlike her friends whose children kept them joined to the Catholic faith, her links had weakened over the years, transmuted in solitude to a wholly personal communion with the divine. She could not remember when she had last seen Father Umberto.

How was she to ask Leo – not now but soon – what to be aware of, how to respond to whatever affected Jews? The questions that raced through her mind sounded so naive! But she must ask them, and she would learn.

As for his child, would he be Jew or Christian? The future swam in her mind, and all was indistinct. When the child was on the way, that question, and many others, would fall into place and she would know. That single event in the future outshone all other thoughts.

The familiar world, absent in the last hours, had not yet fully returned. She was alone in an emptiness between the past and a prefigured future. She needed him so! Yet she must let him go to Gideon and give him comfort. Had Gideon not been here – another "if only"! – how much further would they have travelled on this apocalyptic day? Well, their time would come. She counted her blessings. Leo was past military age, and Gideon was too young.

In silence they went out into the piazza. He was impatient to go to Gideon. Present and future were in flux. Chiara's tenderness towards Gideon had moved him powerfully, one more element in this catalytic minuet, which must now be halted – no, not halted, postponed.

Even at this late hour the piazza was full of figures in restless movement, faces fleetingly illuminated by the night-time lights – middle-aged couples strolling in plump ease, young ones hand in hand or swaying

262

along entwined, exuberant tourists with cameras on their chests. Above the accumulated rattle of talk and laughter sounded the buzz of Vespas on which youths weaved through the crowd and circled groups of budding girls in tight linen skirts of yellow or white and clinging black sleeveless blouses, dark bobbed hair curling inwards against high cheek-bones, knowing, provocative faces.

He took her hand and they went through the shifting throng to her car parked in the shadow of the *II Tempo* building on the far side. She leaned against him in the obscurity and he held her to him, and the past was reborn in the response of her taut body. At that moment the demon touched his shoulder with a new urgency; he must get Gideon back to London as soon as possible. The boy had taken the news hard, and to insist on staying on in Rome at this crisis time would upset him even more – apart from anything else, Gideon would guess that Chiara was the reason. As for Chiara, he knew what he would do. God alone knew what was going to happen in Israel now. If all went well he would come back. If not there would be a new darkness as in Hitler's war, with all tomorrows uncertain, and how trivial everything else would seem. He held her tighter. The answer to that question – and this one – must wait.

He said, "This war changes one thing only for us, *time*! Only time. First of all I must take Gideon back to London tomorrow; it is too late to get a plane tonight. As for us, I want it to happen – I am certain now. But this war! Even with a miracle it may mean delay. But that is all. We must plan now – how and when I can get you on the telephone discreetly. I will speak to you as soon as possible, and tell you how soon I can get back here. I will ring the airport in a few minutes and see if there's a plane . . ."

She did not let him finish. Sick at heart she said, "You are right. The boy feels everything deeply. It is right that you should take him back as soon as you can, even though it means . . ." She must not say more, but she could not stop. "*Mio caro*, a miracle has happened and I have been lifted up. But I do not know how to bear it until – until – I cannot say more. I am afraid."

He said bitterly, "God knows what will happen if things go badly in Israel – massacres, atrocities as bad as in Hitler's war, survivors fleeing wherever they can. Why does God continue to punish us. He has done it countless times through the centuries. Sometimes I feel He is playing some mad game with us, with the whole world. Sometimes . . ."

In fear she put her hand to his lips, "You must not say these things! We understand so little. We must suffer. I feel I must suffer *with* you, with you and Gideon, in this hour of sadness. But do not call down the wrath of God. I am afraid for you. I am afraid for *us*!"

He held her full against him. "Sometimes it is hard to have any trust in what we have been taught to believe."

"I understand." She did not know what she understood, only that she must give love and trust.

"I hope you do." He glanced round warily and released her. The contrary pull of desire and circumstance recalled wartime partings on railway platforms, future conditional. She still leaned her head on his shoulder.

"Listen," he said. "Before this news hit us I had made up my mind to come back to Rome in two weeks' time to be with you. I should have been going to the Middle East on business then, and I would have stopped off here on the way out, and on the way back too, but this war changes all that. Give me a phone number and a time of day when it is safe to phone you. I will phone as soon as I can and tell you when I am coming. I will book myself in here at the Nazionale. But I *will* come to you. That is certain."

Trusting again to the deep shadows and the indifference of the shifting crowd he kissed her. She moved against him, and whispered, "It is like the madness on the plane, remember?"

He remembered Death at their side, driving them on. Now, with this new war, he felt his presence again. Had they sensed his approach in the distant air? He said, "I remember everything."

"Yes," she breathed. "we need time – time, and peace – ah yes peace! I will pray for you, and for Gideon – " She wanted to add, "and for your return to me," but did not dare offer a hostage to fortune. Instead she said, "and I will pray for Israel."

Blessed Mary, let it be true! I cannot help myself. She pressed his hand to her breast.

She found a card bearing the boutique telephone number, and wrote the apartment number on the back. He should call the boutique at a certain hour, her apartment only in emergency, but in either case he must identify himself as "Grischa from Zurich" -- a *nom de guerre* invented on the spur of the moment; some of her suppliers were Swiss. He should use the simple code,

265

"Goods arriving . . .; postponed till . . .". She did not ask him for a London number; he had not volunteered one and that was warning enough. As for dealing with Franco, her lips tightened. Franco needed the marriage to mask that other life of his; she would know what to do if necessary. She would strike a bargain of confidence with him. That was in the old tradition, where it was in each party's interests to turn a blind eye. Meanwhile the cover name Grischa from Zurich would serve. Looking further ahead, more settled arrangements could be made. She could take a second apartment, perhaps across the river in Trastevere, where she and Leo could have their discreet "side-life".

He made to take her in his arms again, wanting to delay her going for a fraction of time longer. With fervour, but with gentleness, she said, "No – *mio caro*, no – you must go to Gideon. He needs you. When it is time to go, delay hurts the heart even more." Then she could not help adding in a whisper, "You know what I need – what we both need – time, much time, to be together, in peace?"

"I know."

She told him she would take a sleeping tablet when she got home; being so strung up.

"You shouldn't do that after the wine."

Warmed by his concern she laughed. "Oh, I am used to taking tablets. Besides I did not have so much wine." She could no longer resist giving a hostage to fortune. "Come back soon! Then I will need no more tablets."

"I will. I promise."

She got into the car and wound down the window. In the car's interior light her cheeks glistened wet; she brushed away the tears and held out her hand and he kissed it, and she touched his face fleetingly, saying, "Believe in us – believe in *us*." She started the engine and drove off.

He watched the car move slowly round the fringe of the crowd and turn down a narrow side street opposite, where strollers pressed themselves against the confining buildings to let it pass. Its rear lights mingled with the lights of bars and shops and were gone.

He remained in the shadows, suddenly short of breath. He questioned his decision to leave the next day. Was he using Gideon as an excuse to escape? There was no need to escape. He simply needed a breathing space – time to get used to this rediscovery of himself, this return to attachment.

He crossed the piazza and went into the hotel bar, deserted now, sombre in dove grey despite the pink neon strip lights illuminating coloured bottles on the shelves behind the barman. He leaned on the bar, grateful for the silence and the shadows among the empty tables. The dapper barman in short white jacket and black trousers must have sensed his mood, for he left him to his thoughts and continued his mysterious ordering of his domain, now and then stealing a glance to see if he was needed. At last Leo ordered a Grappa and gulped it down and went to the telephone in a dim corner. At the airport a tired voice at a reservation desk said he could get them away to London the next morning at eight – all later flights were full. Leo booked two seats and felt the consolation of action. He returned to the bar and ordered another Grappa and drank it slowly. He was not accustomed to solitary drinking, but he needed this isolation. He would go upstairs soon and phone Miriam from the room and tell her they were coming back earlier. Would she think his decision strange? In her secular outlook – more English than the English he sometimes teased her – she might not have given much thought to Israel's danger, regretted of course, but not as if it touched her personally. Yes, she might think his action strange. He doubted if she would think any further than that; in recent months she had started calling him a "fuss-pot". So be it.

He thought about the war. Faced with the apocalypse what did individuals matter – what did *he* matter! No, that was not the way to think. Whatever happened you owed something to yourself. But *what* – how much, how far?

He noticed that his glass was empty and did not know how long he had been leaning on the bar looking at it. Absently he signalled for a fresh Grappa. He saw besieged Masada, its defenders watching at the ramparts as the Roman attackers built their assault ramp higher and higher, each increase measuring the survivors' remaining days fewer. He saw on their faces the awareness that the Almighty was not going to save them, and they must find their agreed escape in death at each other's hands. Something not very different could happen in Israel now. Compared with that, what price *his* concerns! He had trimmed and shifted all his life, not daring to take the prize he longed for, shackled by doubt – till the prize was out of reach. His doubt was different now, not about the wisdom of resuming the quest, but whether he could stay the course if he did.

The doppelganger said, more sympathetic now,

"Doubting one's worth is nothing to be ashamed of – it happens to everybody at times. But doing something about it takes courage. So get on with it."

He did not answer. He recalled Moorlock talking of spiritual exhaustion, when all choices appeared flawed, all values blurred, all effort vain. He had tried, long ago, to shut away the things of the spirit. Since then he had looked facts in the face – and facts only – risen to the business opportunities offered by the changing world, played the heady game of venture capital and the markets. That had been safe, a world where only the mind was engaged. What he now felt was an awakening in the furthest depths of him, a longing to turn away from facts and let the spirit breathe once more whatever the cost. Now, if the spirit *had* broken free at last, where did one start!

He was angry with himself. He was used to being in control, and now he was not. He swallowed yet another large Grappa and made his way upstairs, somewhat unsteadily. Gideon, intent on the television screen, did not look round when he entered the room and put a call through to London. Miriam answered breathlessly; she had just returned from a Law Society dinner and the phone had rung as she unlatched the front door. Frances, she told him quickly, had been baby-sitting with Judith. There was no reason for her to convey this trivial news, but something about his unexpected call had jolted her out of her usual self-possession; his speech was slurred and his voice betrayed an unexpected excitement. She asked, a trifle brusquely, "Why are you coming back earlier? You needed the change of scene

269

– to get away from everything? Has anything happened?"

There was something she could not put her finger on,
and that always upset her.

"I've just told you why! This new war in Israel, and
that means . . ."

She cut him short. She was angry now, and puzzled
because there was no obvious reason, and that upset
her the more. "I *know* you've told me, but I still don't
see what that has got to do with it."

He said testily, unwilling to humour her though he
knew he should, "It's the right thing to do for Gideon's
sake. He's upset by the news – and would you believe
it, he wants to go there and fight, at his age! I thought
you would understand."

He was at last aware that the Grappa had taken his
temper to pieces as well as his speech, and he was angry
with her, and with himself. He cut the call short, and
only then realised that he had forgotten to put Gideon
on the line to her, which she had probably expected.
He had not forgotten. The last thing he needed was for
Gideon to chatter to his mother about Chiara.

Chapter 19

When she opened the front door and heard the shrill phone bell, Miriam still felt the euphoria that always lingered after a professional junketing. Even after so many of them over the years, each was still an affirmation of her success in that man's world. Hearing Leo's voice shaky with unfathomable excitement, she was aware of a shadow at the back of her mind, inexplicable too; and when she put the phone down a few moments later she realised that the shadow had been there since Leo and Gideon had left for Rome. Looking down at the mute telephone on the little shelf of the hallstand she asked herself why she was downcast. There was no answer. She tried to dismiss the shadow and let the euphoria sweep through her again, but Leo's slurred voice and the fugitive signals of hidden significance would not go away. As always she cast about for a logical explanation. The news from Israel was worrying, but he had never sounded so out of control. Of course Israel made him feel guilty, and at such a moment the guilt must be especially heavy. If you really cared about Israel, he often said, you must live there and share its fortunes, and if you could not abandon a comfortable Diaspora existence to do so, you did not care enough. Well, that sentiment might explain part of his disquiet now, but not the excitement. There must be something else.

She looked in the mirror set into the centre panel of the oak hallstand and questioned the figure she saw there, in black dress with a short loop of pearls at the squared-off neckline, loose black jacket with silk facings, image of the woman in full command, dreamed of since schooldays. No, she was not in command. Here were questions to which she had no answer; she was used to having ready answers, and having none upset her. An unidentifiable fear upset her more. Leo had always been predictable, which had suited her perfectly. Here was an unsuspected quality of mystery in him, reviving girlhood self-examination that had always found her wanting, days of doubt she had thought never to confront again, at odds with that confident image in the mirror. What had happened to Leo of late? What had happened to *her*! The silence of the house at this hour, which at other times confirmed her in her feeling of being in control, was suddenly equivocal, yet all seemed normal. The centre light with its crystal pendants threw warm rainbow gleams through the long hall. A light shone in the sitting room, the door ajar. Frances must be curled up reading. Judith must be asleep upstairs. All was in order. Yet not in order. Something was wrong; something, she told herself with a shiver, that was not new.

She realised that she was looking into the mirror unseeingly. She drew back and came close again, raised a hand to her rounded forehead and ran fingertips down her cheeks to the emergent lines at the side of the mouth, then with a sigh drew back but could not move away. She stared down at the phone again, wishing it would speak. So much of Leo was unknown to her. The thought had never struck her before.

Frances had been lying on the chaise longue in her flame-coloured silk *peignoir*, hair loose, furry mules neatly side by side on the floor beside her, cocooned in soft yellow light from a standard lamp, turning the pages of *Harper Queen*. Hearing the front door open and close and Miriam's distinctive flourish of keys, she had waited for her usual breezy entrance, after which they would adjourn to the kitchen for a "girls together nightcap" and a cosy bedroom talk. During the telephone call – it was obviously Leo – there had been an unusual tremor of unease in Miriam's voice. The clatter of the phone being put down hard was followed by a silence whose completeness made her catch her breath. She sat up and swung her feet to the floor and tiptoed to the door and peeped round, and saw Miriam standing before the hallstand staring down at something there – but there was nothing there except the telephone! She flung herself to her, and took her in her arms. "Darling, what is the matter! You look so – so –! Tell me!" She hugged her and Miriam gave a sigh that was partly a sob and quickly draw breath to cancel it.

In a flat voice Miriam retailed the call from Rome more or less verbatim; reiterating her puzzlement at Leo's excitement and tension, especially the excitement. Frances told herself that this sudden change in Miriam could not have come from the telephone call – that had been a fortuitous trigger, nothing more. Leo's words, and his decision to cut short the trip, had by chance unlocked a secret sanctuary in Miriam,

273

storehouse of unfulfilled emotion. It had been Miriam's way, all her life, to put emotion far away from herself. Her legal work must have given her many examples of settled married men going suddenly off the rails! Or not suddenly but secretly, and accidentally discovered. Frances had good reason to know the married man astray! But Leo was not one of those. No, the demon was in Miriam herself, prompting doubt, insecurity, a secret sense of inadequacy long hidden away.

"Darling, you are not yourself! Now don't take on so. I'm here. Don't be upset over nothing. It's this Israel war – the shock of it. Come now – I'll make a nightcap and we'll go upstairs and talk. Everything's all right. I'm sure of it."

As they went to the kitchen, Frances was aware of her own rising excitement. Frances worked by intuition and instinct. She had often thought Miriam's marriage too perfect to be real, too ordered to have had much true passion in it. For such as Miriam the slow, subterranean movement of emotion must one day throw up a stumbling stone, and now it had happened. Miriam, always under tight control, was frightened by the demon within, unaccountably awakened. There had to be a reason, and so she found it in Leo.

It had never occurred to Frances that she might one day be jealous of Miriam. Her love for Miriam would not allow that. Still, though Miriam's ordered, almost businesslike marriage was not for her, she had sometimes perversely envied her possession of it. Now life had brought Miriam down to *her* level – well, not exactly, but the untroubled pattern was gone, perhaps for ever. She felt a guilty thrill. As for unfulfilled emotion, that must be true of Leo too, a thought that had occurred to her, she now remembered, on the day of the heart to heart with him in the park, when "something", a reaching out between them, had almost happened. Or had she imagined it? No, she had not. It could happen still. It could happen, as they used to say at school, "one day when you were not looking!"

In the kitchen she felt his presence. Incongruously she thought of his occasional clashes with Miriam over its character, for it was of her choosing – the reproduction Welsh farmhouse furniture, the long table of uneven planks with the artificial "scrubbed look" – which to Miriam's annoyance he dubbed "cult bogus". Miriam had said he had no soul. In such small ways had they declared detachment. Frances had sympathised with them both.

She busied herself making the nightcap, which she had decided could not be the bland school dormitory brew they usually had but a good-sized mug of "hot toddy", strong milky tea powerfully laced with whisky.

Miriam sat hunched over the table as if her body could no longer support itself. She talked obsessively, conjuring theories and dismissing them and coming round to them again. Frances thought, Oh these brainy, disciplined souls when disorder strikes!

She reasoned with Miriam. "Darling this isn't like you. You're always so sensible! Nothing has *happened*. Tomorrow you'll ask yourself what could have got into you. It's all imagination. I can't think where you've got this upset from! Everything's all right. I'm sure of it."

Miriam shook her head and Frances understood and

275

was saddened even more. The demonic upheaval had created its own self-justifying scenario. All that was left, while the shock lasted, was to retreat into this warm, womanly intimacy, trusted of old.

Frances held her in her arms. Miriam took meditative sips of the hot, heady drink, then mouthfuls, and soon finished it. "You're probably right. I don't know what has got into me. Maybe it's been there a long time and I – and I didn't want to think about it . . ." She held out the empty mug and Frances went and made another hot toddy, stronger this time. Miriam seldom drank spirits, and never this amount. They fell silent. Presently they went up to Frances's room and curled up on her bed in the soft pink light and talked and whispered, retraced old secure ground, old perspectives, now and then drawn back to the present.

Frances said, "Maybe he feels more deeply about Israel – about being a Jew in fact – than he has ever admitted to himself?" She felt sure this was not the reason, but said it to comfort her.

Miriam nodded in half-acceptance.

Frances thought: "Suppose this *is* another example of what I have suffered from so many times – The Indian summer of a frightened man? If so, Miriam has nothing to fear. Leo will swing back to her. They always do!" That reflection brought bitterness. What hope could she herself have if love deceived her, time and again, into helping a married man pretend to recapture his youth? Leo had said as much in their talk at the fountain. Sometimes she even found herself sympathising with the man in his illusion, and that made the bitterness worse. Where were the simple truths of long ago? There

276

remained, it seemed, only the bitter-sweet fulfilment of moments like this, giving and sharing, poignant residue of past certainty.

What did Leo settle for in marrying Miriam? She had asked that question, perhaps unwisely, of her married lovers, and the truth beneath the vague, evasive replies was repugnant – it had been a detached, pragmatic act, a kind of retreat from life, to quell a restlessness of the flesh that had ceased to bring glory, if indeed it ever had! Could that have been true for Leo?

The second hot toddy had made Miriam drowsy. By and by their whispered talk faded. Frances supported her across the landing to the main bedroom and undressed her, and held her in her arms till she slept.

They were approaching the high frontier of the Alps. The pilot's crisp tones had told them to expect "some turbulence that might be uncomfortable". The Trident shuddered more and more violently. Through the square window beside him Leo watched the wing thrash up and down as if giant hands tried to wrench it off. The mountains floated beneath, dazzling white in the morning sun, sculptured ridges, precipitous gullies, fields of glistening sugar icing pierced by crevasses lined with sapphire shadows. The wing held his attention – how could it be forced so far out of the horizontal and not break off at its faired root in the fuselage? He tried to imagine it. The crash might be soft, in one of those snow fields that seemed near enough to lean out and touch. Even if one survived, it would be pointless to think of rescue at that great height. He was thinking of it calmly. Come off it – you have responsibilities as a family man! No, there must surely be other, better reasons for not wanting to be killed? He could not think of any. All he cared about was that it should happen suddenly, without warning. It was unusual for him to think of death, hardly a good portent. If only there was a sure route to fulfilment? The doppelganger was right again; he was not at all sure that Rome held any answers, no permanent ones at any rate. Rome would be a small, occasional crumb, not a continuous feast. Life's accumulated baggage impeded one at every step. He wished he were free, alone and yet not alone as he pleased. He must be in a bad way! Nothing was worth the effort – was this simply an obstinate reaction to the shock of Chiara, the trauma of the dutiful husband breaking out at last!

He thought he had spoken out loud and looked round to see if Gideon had heard. The seat was empty. He remembered that Gideon had asked the stewardess if the pilot would let him visit the flight deck; that had been before the warning of turbulence. Permission received, he had darted forward along the aisle to the flight cabin.

He could do with a drink. Drinking at breakfast time? That certainly would show Gideon how far gone he was! Gideon would report it to Miriam, and it would make a bad impression after last night. Had she guessed he had been drinking? Probably not. She was not observant, so she might well have attributed his slurred speech to a bad telephone line. Whatever he did from now on must appear normal. If she *had* noticed, she might put two and two together, especially when Gideon told her, as he surely would sooner or later, that they had met a lady who knew him well! Her suspicions once aroused, there could be awkwardness when it came to fulfilling his debt to Chiara – tensions, telling lies, watching every step.

The doppelganger said acidly, "It will not mean awkwardness, for you have no intention of keeping your promise to that woman. I can tell you this – you will find another way. Your gloom is a reaction to what you have seen in yourself in Rome, the years of drift, the accumulated baggage that prevents you doing what you want to do."

He tried to be acid in return. You mean that's why I don't care if the plane crashes?

The other did not answer at once. At last he said, "I will talk your language. Your life is your capital – as a businessman you know that capital should be invested to get the highest return. You have invested your life with far too little return! That's over and done with. Make up your mind what you want and go for it and don't look back any more."

You have changed your tune?

"You have at last begun to see who you are and what you want. Not completely yet – but you cannot stop the process now. Of course it is painful to have to admit to so much self-delusion. But you can no longer stand still."

Gideon strode along the aisle towards him, face flushed, glory in his eyes – he was a fighter pilot returning from a combat mission. He sat down and said, "Papa, I want to apply for an RAF flying scholarship. The commanding officer of the Cadet Force says I have a good chance. When I've got my wings I will go and

279

join the Israeli Air Force. That's the way I want to help them. What do you say?"

Leo glanced round. The seats in front and behind were empty. Even so, from long habit of confidentiality in business he put a warning finger to his lips.

Gideon opened his eyes wide. "Why?"

Leo said in his ear, "The country you are talking about has many enemies. You never know when one of them will overhear. One day, who knows in this frightful world, your life might depend on that *not* happening. About the flying scholarship – by the time you finish school and go through all the training you are speaking of a good many years – about seven or eight I should think. If this war lasts any time at all, there won't be anything of that country left to fight for."

Gideon stared glumly out of the window at the peaks and snowfields floating by below the wing and the hard blue sky beyond. Standing in the flight cabin he had taken to himself the nonchalant certainty of those two men at the controls, and felt titanic power at his finger tips, master of the sky. Papa was saying, "You can't do what you like, *when* you like. Something always gets in the way." Where was the sudden glory to be found?

Wistfully he said, "Frances says it's wrong to postpone things you want to do, for you might never get the chance again. She talks about living life to the full whatever the cost. But when I ask her what she means by 'cost' I can't understand what she says."

How cruel it would be – to them both – to reveal the poignancy of her words, knowing as he did what lay behind them? In any case, whatever explanation he gave would be beyond the boy's reach. Gideon's attitude to life was still Pavlovian, responding to the promptings of crude desire alone. Dimly he saw what values were, but the idea of good or bad desire would come to him slowly, painfully. How could he be expected to see, at this stage along the road, that desire would always leap far ahead of understanding? In Rome he had tried to tell him that you must bridle desire, be in control. Had he himself followed that rule? No. He had let desire drive him, towards the sublime vision waiting for him just beyond the horizon. Then tomorrow had come and the vision had leapt far away. Gideon might well ask why God had decided that understanding should always come too late, or desire too early, why one was always out of step with life, why wisdom must be bought with pain. Gideon was right. Life was not fair. God was not fair.

He thought of Frances and her apparently earthy exchanges with the boy. Was her frustration seeking relief in this reckless talk? How could one tell what damage had been done? To be angry with her, upset the household in the process, even send her away, might incise the damage deeper. To strengthen Gideon was the only way.

Gideon wondered why, whenever he mentioned Frances's talks, he saw a questioning alertness in Leo's face. Frances had uncovered for him a world where danger and glory lurked, inspiring in him feelings of power and challenge in prospect, not unlike those that had surged through him in the flight cabin. Papa had conveyed, not in words but in some indefinable fashion, that Frances should not have talked to him in that way, that there were meanings in what she said that might be dangerous for him to know

– or know too soon. How could you know things too soon?

Leo needed time to think, and asked a delaying question. "What did she say when you asked her what she meant?"

Gideon rambled like someone hypnotised, speaking in dream language.

Leo gleaned a crucial statement from Frances, its meaning obviously lost on the boy, not unlike something he himself had said, "Life often forces you to make do with substitutes for what you really want." What substitutes did Frances make do with, in retreat from her former fury of desire?

Gideon knew he was floundering and was angry with himself. How could he have thought the apprenticeship was complete? He was as much in the dark as ever, and the life of grown-ups continued to retreat as he reached out to it. Now, trying to understand the experience of the previous day, he still could not decode any of it. In some fashion Frances had failed him. He could hardly ask her when they got home, for he had no idea what questions to ask! Would it be all right to ask Mama? Frances had warned him that "people might misunderstand what we talk about". He had known what she meant – well, he supposed he did; he thought of the boys at school being secretive about measuring each other in the shower room, with a boy posted to cry "cavey" when a master was in the offing. And Papa? Papa was safe – he was sure of that. He did not know how to ask him either, but was beginning to think he could, after their talks these last days. Papa had been more at ease since they had come to Rome, closer to him than he had ever felt him to be, and there was something wonderful about that.

He could not have said why so much of the experience with Frances had chosen this moment to tumble from his lips. There were so many things he desperately needed to know, yet he could not put words to them, and this awareness now made him feel hollow inside, vulnerable as he had never felt before. Papa said that life taught you about yourself as you went along but that its lessons could hurt you. He wished he could tell him how puzzling that statement was. For instance the woman Chiara was linked in some hidden way with Papa, and the link seemed to hurt them both. What was that link, and why did it hurt? She was gentle and warm and something about her had stirred him and made him want to be close to her. He knew, and did not know, that she brought echoes of experience awaiting him in the future, dark, exciting, drawing him onwards. Yesterday's happenings had sent him signals about life whose meaning he "knew" but could not fathom, except that they seemed to confirm Frances's gnomic words, "you must fulfil the body's commands *one way or the other*". How could you fulfil them if you were not sure what they were? And what did "one way or another" mean?

Something else she had said brought panic when he thought about it – all certainties betrayed you sooner or later. It had come to mind when Papa said that the Israel war would be over long before he could get his wings and go there to defeat its enemies. Time would change each dream, cancel or postpone its fulfilment, perhaps for ever, for postponement was a kind of cancellation.

Something told him that that cruel truth would burden him for ever. It wasn't fair.

Gently, Leo stopped the boy's stumbling account of Frances's lesson. It had been interesting to hear how a woman covered the ground, her emphasis on delight, gentleness, sympathy and, strangely, obedience! Presumably obedience to the woman's rhythms and moods? Not very different, except in emphasis, from his own lesson. The combination of the two might have raised more devils of doubt than it had banished! He said, "Be patient. You will learn to see many things differently from how you see them now. You will learn to be sure of yourself and of what you know."

Gideon nodded doubtfully. Leo added, "We'll talk a lot more. You can trust me!"

Why mention trust? He was trying to say that he was on his side, especially to hint, delicately so that Gideon would not be alarmed, that he was not disturbed by Frances's talks with him. The boy needed to lean on him at this time.

They were both exhausted. They had sat up till two in the morning talking – Gideon had been insatiable – about Israel and the war and being a Jew, the identity that could never be shed, the meaning of faith; and that other burden through the ages, Divine wrath. That had been the most difficult to discuss, for Gideon, so recently Barmitzvah, was more learned than *he* was in the traditional explanations, nimble in argument and delighting in it. Late in the night Gideon had exclaimed, "So this war is the latest blow from God! Why is there so much punishment? Maybe people are worse than they think they are? Maybe God is tired of it all?"

Leo marvelled at the verdict of an innocent – God is tired! "You may be right. God may well be tired. Looking at the world, it's not surprising."

Gideon, sitting on the edge of his bed, put his head in his hands, and was silent for a long time, then looked up dreamily, with smoothed out face. "God must know what is right for us. After all He created us. God is all mighty, all powerful. He can do whatever he wants. So there *must* be hope. We can't live without hope."

They had risen at six to catch the plane. The renewed discussion had sharpened Leo's thoughts to an unbearably fine edge. He said, "I can't keep awake. We'll talk again, lots of talk! I want to listen to you a lot more. But I really must get some sleep. We've got another hour."

Gideon was half-disappointed at the talk being cut short, but felt a surge of happiness – Papa had listened to him so carefully, and there would be more talk – there was so much more he wanted to say. "All right Papa. I want to talk more too – but you have a sleep. I'll wake you when we're over London."

Chapter 20

Gideon considered Leo as he slept, lanky form in crumpled blue seersucker jacket and grey trousers folded in on itself in the cramped space, broad-knuckled hands resting in his lap. The long sallow features with high bulging brow remained aware as if their talk continued and at any moment the pallid lips would make a pointed comment. Papa was tired and troubled. He was glad he slept. Why was Papa troubled? Another puzzle of the adult world. He wanted to raise him up and support him with his youth and strength. He did not know how to support him, not in the ways that mattered, but he would learn. Why did grown-ups see every word as significant, to be tested for hidden meanings? The world of Papa and Mama and Frances, and of that mysterious woman Chiara, was not like his own with transitory imaginings, fleeting, exhilarating, with no before or after. For them every word, every thought was incised in stone. But that world had begun to beckon him more strongly with every moment, and there was no going back. Suddenly he was happy. Papa had sensed so much that had been bottled up inside him, things he had dearly wanted to say and did not know how to – and made it easy for him to say them. Papa had spoken to him as someone who "counted"; and so had that woman Chiara who understood him so well. After all he was a man now, since Barmitzvah, so why should that not be so? Yes, Papa had opened the gates for him. He would talk to Papa about many things from now on, without fear.

Leo woke to Gideon's fingertips gently caressing his face. It seemed that no time at all had passed. "Papa, wake up! We're going in to land."

The plane tilted and all he saw through the window was a pale blue sky with a scattering of cirrus. They levelled out over the reservoirs and made a wide turn and entered the glide path. That sighting of the rectangular patches of still water with neat patterns of suburban settlement round them always brought a pang of regret, renewing the pull of the ordinary world.

When they entered the house Gideon leapt away like a dog slipping the leash and darted up the stairs two at a time to his room. Leo paused in the shadowed hall. Sunbeams filtered through open doors and threw patches of gold on reddish carpet and darkly gleaming wood. All was still. Estrella must be out shopping, Judith "parked" with Miriam's parents. He felt the touch of undeviating order without horizon. He wished he could turn about and leave the house and walk away. He put his suitcase down beside the dark hallstand and paced through sun-drenched rooms where thin summer curtains hung limp in the still air. Here was neither serenity nor emotion, only containment. The windows on to the back lawn were slightly open under the security locks, admitting pungent scents of dusty foliage and acrid smell of petrol, breath of Primrose Hill on a hot summer's day. He conjured the heavy humid heat and domestic smells of Rome, and saw Chiara's wistful features again in the shadowed Piazza. He turned on his heel and went to the telephone in the hall and rang Moorlock.

He said, "I'm back early. Can we meet for dinner soon? I need to . . ." He had been about to say, "I need to talk badly, as soon as possible," but he heard a door swing to upstairs, the small thud of a latch hitting the jamb but not clicking home. He listened but there was no further sound.

Moorlock sensed the shadow. "Old boy, I understand perfectly. I could manage tomorrow night. Will that do? At my club?"

"That would be fine, but what makes you think . . .?" Leo began, but decided he had said enough. Gideon might be listening after all, though he thought it unlikely.

Moorlock did not want to say he had read the desolation in his voice, so he answered cheerfully, "You're back some days early aren't you? That's all I need know! Till tomorrow then."

Leo put the phone down and felt the weight of the house upon him, its stillness, its detachment – especially the detachment. Outside all was stilled too, except for the distant metropolitan hum, a dead time in the dusty London summer. He felt taut as if held together by nerves alone. From now on nothing would be as it had been, although all would have to appear unchanged. He was trying to imagine what it would be like to live another life side by side with this one. He had never been unfaithful to Miriam – perhaps passing desire had not moved him as strongly as in the old days? For some reason he could not fathom, that other life now on offer – the "side-life" Chiara had called it – did not give him the feeling of infidelity.

He telephoned his secretary at the Cannon Street offices and asked her to send his car to collect him, and also to send his desk diary to him in a sealed envelope with the driver. He needed that diary at once. It contained his coded notes of deals in commodity futures; some of them, for critical materials, must now assume high importance because of this war. He took his suitcase upstairs. Thumping noises came from Gideon's room above. He took a shower and let the water run quite cold, then put on a dark grey suit with a fine chalk stripe, crisp white shirt and college tie. He went up to tell Gideon he was going out and found his door ajar. Gideon stood in the middle of the room surrounded by cardboard boxes evidently flung down from the shelves, some with toys and games and construction sets spilling out. The boy stared down at the chaos in obvious perplexity. Hearing Leo's voice he looked up blankly. Leo left him to his thoughts.

On his way downstairs it struck him that Gideon might indeed have left his door ajar on purpose. If he *had* overheard, what could he have learned? He would have known who he was speaking to, for he had given Moorlock's name to the secretary at the consulting rooms. Had he let slip a tell-tale word? That was perhaps irrelevant. Moorlock's name might have been enough for Gideon's imagination to feed on. Why had his father phoned his doctor the moment he returned? Gideon might not know what to make of the question but Frances would! And perhaps Miriam too. What *had* he been up to in Rome? They might alarm the boy with questions about his father's movements in Rome; had he ever gone out and left the boy on his own? He cursed his thoughtlessness; it showed how unnerved he must be, or rather how inexperienced he was in domestic intrigue. He could have made the call on his private line at the office. Long fidelity made one careless.

In the car, the leather-bound volume open on the foldaway desk before him, the cutting edge of business thinking returned. He contemplated the contracts to be brokered on the international markets, their political importance promising high premiums because of this new war. In such dealings his instinct had always been good, and his nerve too. He stood to make a killing. For the rest of that day his dealings on the markets were inspired, and he made a lot of money.

Gideon had not thought of eavesdropping. He swung round and round on tiptoe in the middle of the room till he was dizzy. Then he unpacked the presents he had bought in Rome and carried with him on the plane in his cadet haversack, phials of *eau de toilette* and little porcelain figures of rustic nymphs for Mama and Frances, and for Judith a huge slab of dark Ferrero chocolate and a headscarf that was not silk but looked like it. He arranged them in a mystic pattern on his desk at the broad window that looked out on the back garden. He considered their Art Deco gift wrappings and resolved to rescue them in due course and keep them for ever in the box in his wardrobe containing important relics, picture postcards, bits of rock gleaned on holidays, travel labels and writing paper from hotels, landmarks along the road. He looked up from them and contemplated the garden.

It was about fifty yards long and twenty wide, with an apple tree and a pear tree, fruit bushes spreading wild, and climbers on the timber fencing at the sides and at the bottom. Long ago he had seen it as a vast wilderness of secret groves, a world of magic, of heroes and wizards. Everything in it, trees and flowers and bushes, even the shed at the bottom, had been a real person with a name and a voice and a story to tell, and in the shadowy undergrowth had dwelt sprites, furtive creatures of the wild who spoke to him in magic whispers. At some time in recent years – he did not know when – the "people" had from time to time gone away and returned and gone away again, and at last had not returned at all, leaving in their places substantial shapes that never spoke. Now, as he looked out and tried to see that vanished world, melancholy swept over him, not so much because those days were gone but because he too – or some part of him – had moved away from *them*. That world still gleamed and whispered in his heart, but he knew it was lost for ever. With an effort of the imagination he conjured the voices again, but they were faint, far away, and told him in their simple way a truth that had come to him in Rome, that the things one loved were mutable, and would pass out of one's life one day for ever.

He turned away from the window and without con-scious decision went to a corner of the room beside some shelves and drew out a tall box whose contents, long untouched, he had once loved with passion, a train set. He assembled it on the floor on the hinged base board, stretched the cable to the power socket near the desk, then sat on his heels and ran the trains for a few minutes – but inexplicably he was annoyed with himself. He packed the set into its box and stood it on end beside the door. He would take it up to the loft later on. He knew he would never open it again.

On the shelves were other boxes he had not opened for a long time, board games, construction sets, a chemistry set, building blocks. With sudden passion he pulled them all down and threw them on the floor at his feet and stood staring at them with resentment and a sense of betrayal. Papa looked in and went away. He kicked one of the boxes away, then another and another, till they were scattered to the corners of the room, under the bunk bed, behind the desk, under the wash basin. He considered the result. This was childish behaviour he told himself with distaste. It was the first time he had ever used "childish" about anything he had done. He gathered up the boxes and piled them beside the door next to the train set. All at once the air was heavy and he gasped for breath, and he felt he must escape. He ran down the stairs and out of the back door into the garden and down to the shed, and took out the talisman that in recent months he had turned to for a different kind of magic, a potent communion with himself – the croquet set.

In the hard sunlight he dug the hoops into the grass. Then with each stroke of the mallet, intent on the mystical line traced by the ball across tufts and molehills, the lawn became a chart of his inner world; each threadlike line marked a new exploration of himself, awesome, challenging – and as they crossed and re-crossed and formed patterns, some of the Rome experience was translated into his own secret language. He had not been ready for the demons that had been let loose in Rome. He could not know that the full meaning of those days in Rome was a vast distance ahead in emotional time, and that he would only come close to it slowly; and years later would go there and try to understand the person he had once been, and the one he had become, as his father had done before him – and return again and again to renew the understanding and re-fashion it. All he could see now was a sequence of faint images of himself, some hard to recognise, the detail diffused as in photographs taken in too strong a light.

A whisper insisted that he had understood more of what he had experienced than he thought, and that his father had intended it all to be a mirror held up to life not as it was but as it *would* be – the light and the dark; and that it was hard, sometimes, to tell the one from the other. He could not have put words to the feelings that made him want to shrink away from the future as he believed he had seen it. That in itself was frightening, but he knew that he did not really want to shrink away, and that in any case it was impossible. He sensed also, dimly and without understanding, that he had been shown the bleakness that might await him on the far side of desire. He did not really understand what desire was, except that it was something vague but immensely powerful, and at that thought, as happened so often these days, his flesh rose, and amid the heat and turbulence he did not want to believe that there could be a dark side to it. Surely God would not have created you like this and then punished you for it? Frances, when he had voiced that question, had never had a satisfactory answer. All she could say was, "Desire is a precious gift. Accept it with love and trust, as a blessing!" That must mean, though she did not say it, that the shadow that awaited you really *was* the natural order of things. It wasn't fair of God to do that.

It was going to be difficult to be grown-up. But Papa said that something inside you insisted that life could be better than it was, if only you tried hard enough. So there was hope after all? He wished he knew what "trying hard enough" was – and how it could cancel that shadow.

Chapter 21

When Miriam awoke that morning at her usual time of six o'clock, the sun streaming in through flowered net curtains, a sky of vivid blue enamel promising another hot day, she did not immediately remember Leo's call from Rome the previous night. As she surfaced from sleep, the memory returned, and it seemed that she had put the phone down that very moment, with Leo's unusually tremulous voice conveying inexplicable excitement, and was upset again, but less so. She must look at it in cool logic, as if it were a "worry" brought in by a troubled woman client. What uncertainties had burst out of the shadows? What doubts? She had not been aware of any till last night, and still could think of none. Yet the thought was there – and there must be an answer.

She swung her legs out of bed and stood up and stretched her arms up high before the long mirror and felt little clicks in the hips that unaccountably excited her, the body releasing itself, and nodded to her naked reflection. It had been a mischievous fancy – it had to be! How sensible Frances had been, tender as always! She thought about Frances with a surge of concern. What was going to happen to her – life was narrowing before her;

she ought to settle down. The thought brought a shiver – how would she manage without Frances near her? They needed each other so. No, it would be all right; even if Frances did get married they would always need to be close. They would find a way.

She dimly remembered going to sleep in Frances's arms. Their tender communion resumed its magical comfort as it always did. She swung round the bedroom in a euphoria she could never express when Leo was here. Halting in a shaft of sunlight, she turned her mind to the new day. She went to the dressing table and took the appointments book from her leather portfolio. She had a busy day ahead – two client meetings before lunch and preparation for a conference with counsel in the afternoon on a complicated matrimonial issue. She snapped the book shut, then took a pad from the bedside table and made notes of what she must do before she left for the office. Estrella's shopping and cooking must be amended; presumably Leo would be in for dinner. She should have asked him last night but in her upset it had slipped her mind.

She returned to her reflection in the looking glass, and her thoughts went to the unthinkable. *Had* the earth shifted under her feet? Could Leo have moved away from her! No, it was absurd – solid Leo, utterly dependable Leo! All the same, what if he *had*? She thought of divorce clients who let slip that it was hurt sexual pride that was unbearable; for the rest they were not sure. If it hurt me *here* – in girlhood simplicity she laid her hand on her heart – I don't think I could bear it. But down there – involuntarily she pressed her thighs together – I don't know. I don't want to have to answer these questions. I know what I *ought* to think, being sensible about it; if I was sure he cared for me, and he had done nothing that couldn't be swept under the carpet like getting someone pregnant, I ought to turn a blind eye to it. But could I? I don't know. I don't want anything to destroy this life I have made. I don't want anything to change.

She addressed her naked reflection under her breath. My figure is slim and firm. I am sure everything's all right. Why shouldn't I be calm? I've seen so much nastiness in matrimonial cases, diabolical things lurking beneath a "nice" surface. Leave well alone if you can! I've said it so often to clients. Have I become hard? No, I am not hard. Just anxious suddenly, and I know I shouldn't be. Am I happy – or *was* I till last night? Funny, I have never asked myself that, which must mean that I am! But *he* isn't. I never thought of that either till last night. Ought I to feel guilty? How *can* I be? I took it for granted he wanted the things I did – God, how often clients tell me that? Was he ever happy? I don't know and that's a terrible thing to admit! I have been too busy working hard, building a career and a home. I have nothing to feel guilty about.

She realised she had been standing before the mirror a long time. She had looked into herself deeply, and some burden had gone – unnamed, unknowable, but real. She shook herself. One thing I am sure of now. However painful it is going to be, I must be patient with him. Whatever it is, however long it takes, let him get it out of his system. I want life to go on undisturbed.

She did not know what she meant by undisturbed – except to express the conviction, also learnt from clients, that revolutions in marriage solved nothing – there was too much invested in the past ever to set you free – and life had a nasty habit of having its way with you whatever you did.

That's enough, she said to herself. Life is really not too bad. It could be worse – much, much worse. I'm a lucky woman. I have Leo, a good, decent man. And Frances, tender, loving Frances. I have a great career. I can put up with a lot to save all that. She turned her back on the looking glass and went to run her bath.

That evening at dinner Gideon talked exultantly about Rome, of his easy movement between its past glories and surviving grandeur, dream and reality, magic, and the long talks with Papa that had taken him further than he had ever dreamed possible. But he gave no details of the talks, only hints of new vision, understanding, confidence. And then the Israel war had come, and that was a terrible thing to happen, and they had to come back. Leo wondered how he would treat the subject of Chiara and the attack by the young men at Ostia. Gideon said not a word about either! Leo had not asked the boy to say nothing, nor how to speak of them if he did. Gideon must have been inspired by a sure intuition. If he did not mention Chiara now, when it was all so fresh, he probably never would. Gideon was already learning to weigh the importance of things, and keep his own counsel. It was unbelievable, yet it was true.

Miriam, uplifted by Gideon's headlong narrative, his happiness, his certainty, was content. The boy had been so explicit in his talk of their movements in Rome that in his innocence he would have mentioned anything "significant" if it had happened.

Judith said, "Papa, take *me* with you next time – soon, Papa soon? And talk to me like you talked to Gideon?" Leo answered absently, "Yes I will. When you're old enough to get the full benefit." He was still marvelling at Gideon playing the discreet accomplice. The excitement of the night before returned. He must be careful not to let it show.

Frances wondered why Gideon had not shared his experience with her first, as he did after other adventures, school field trips, cadet camps, initiative courses. Something – or somebody! – had replaced her. She felt a tug at her heart. Perhaps Miriam's instinct had been right after all?

Judith shone her great dark eyes at Leo, and broke through the talk across the table. "Papa, there's something different about you. What is it?"

After the heat of the day the air was breathless with electric tension presaging thunder. Leo thought of his telephone call to Moorlock on arrival, and his friend's instant awareness of a change in him, simply from his voice. He smiled and shook his head. With any luck Judith would forget the fancy and turn to something else. Was this a foretaste of his life in the house from now on, constantly on guard?

Miriam, from force of habit, intervened in her usual humouring manner, which Judith, already showing signs of being "on the turn" as Frances put it, had begun to resent; "What *are* you imagining this time. darling? There's nothing different about Papa."

Judith tossed her head. "Mama, can't you see? Papa

looks as if . . ." She had been about to say, "as if he's not here at all." Instinct told her not to, and she finished lamely, "I just can't explain it."

Miriam did see. Leo was at ease, as he had not been for months. No, she would stick to her resolve – leave well alone! Lightly but firmly she said, "Darling Judith, it's always like this when someone comes back from a journey – they only *seem* different. Papa's the same today as when he went, not different at all."

The electricity in the air held them. All were aware of change but none dared speak of it.

Judith was sure the grown-ups understood what she had tried to say but pretended not to. It wasn't fair. She turned to Gideon in silent appeal. "Make them take notice of me! I *know* it is so. Tell them you can see it too."

Gideon made a minute movement of the head, a signal they both knew from their private plots to outwit the adults. "Wait – not now." Judith turned away. Gideon must have a good reason. She saved her hurt for another day.

Gideon knew what she had seen, and knew also that this was not the time to draw attention to it – but he could not have said why this was so. He only knew that he owed it to Papa. In what way had Papa changed? When? As with the sunflower whose tropism you did not see happening, so this change had given no sign. Was it linked with the woman Chiara? He supposed it could be. He must be solid with Papa. That much he was sure of. The electric air stiffened the hair on his neck. Everything was in movement. He and Papa and Chiara had worked on each other in ways he did not understand. He feared to pursue this thought further. He was not ready.

With lowered eyes he considered Frances. She had greeted him with her usual close embrace when she came in from the office, enveloped him in a swirl of summer cotton that made him heady with the odour of her, then moved slightly away and held him with outstretched arms and studied him and smiled knowingly, with a kind of qualified happiness, but with a shadow of sadness too. Then he had gone on his way. A small distance had opened between them, and he knew it was irrevocable. He had been glad and sorry. So much was now happening too fast. Had *he* changed, or she? Looking at her now, it seemed that she was in some indefinable way diminished, and then he saw, what he had begun to guess in Rome, that no one changed by themselves. You responded one to the other, and the change happened in spite of you. He felt a dejection that he would later know as mourning, for a time when life's riddles had never troubled him as inescapably as they did now.

He looked across to his mother. She had changed too. Ineffably she was behaving differently to Papa. She too must be responding, indirectly, to what had happened in Rome; how could it be otherwise? How did people intuit changes in each other and respond with such immediacy, and with such potency for the future! Perhaps, as Papa had said, the spirit did have power to command you after all, and through you, others – and you could not silence its voice however hard you tried? Like the thunder now awaiting its time in the sky but sending its accumulating tremors on before, all of

301

them were speaking eloquently without words, or rather *beneath the words*, affirming new seasons of the heart not yet understood but demanding responses none the less. But what if you did not understand the signals others sent you? Perhaps there were some shifts of the spirit, in you or in others, you never would fathom? Who would help you then?

Frances studied Judith and tried to imagine the future woman whose essence was even now beginning to show itself – already formidable, a fitting image of Miriam. Something about the girl made her envious and she was ashamed. She herself had had something of that power at that age – but what was her life worth now! She tried to dismiss that line of thought, as she always did, seldom successfully. Judith's darting awareness of change in Leo now spoke to her too – but not his alone; new tropisms of the spirit were at work in all of them, that was plain. Leo, sitting in seeming detachment at her elbow, *had* indefinably changed. Could this be the movement in him she had often dreamed of? And now? What did she want to happen? She was not sure, and was miserable to have to admit it. In any case, was it not too late? Miriam's intuition the previous night had been right of course – there *was* something new about him, even in the way he held himself, the way he looked and spoke, especially the detachment – oh yes she knew the signs! – revealing another woman's influence. Was it really too late?

She glanced across at Gideon steadfastly looking down at his plate. He seemed to have grown taller and broader even in those few days away. Greeting him earlier, she had been discomfited by a new wariness in him, a new sovereignty, and had said to herself bitterly,

"Even in the child that he still is, there is such power to wound!"

She caught Leo's eye, and he seemed to smile at her in secret complicity, as if he wanted to draw the two of them apart from the tensions among the others. That potent sympathy of his, discovered in that heart to heart in the park, reached out to her, and she was uplifted.

She was only partly right. His smile had not been of intentional complicity; he had been reminding himself how careful he would have to be in the house from now on, with all of them on the move, all of them watchful. Seeing her turn to him blinking away a tear, he had been touched and was moved to comfort her.

Suddenly he was very much aware of her, glowing there beside him in a crisp white blouse that gaped deeply, pensive one moment, caught up in the chatter the next, now and then giving him a searching glance. Yes the temptation was there, and she must know it. To take his mind off it, he thought of her place among them, inexplicably essential.

He thought of the times when he had been powerfully tempted, as on that day in the park – yes, but never quite enough. Perhaps "never quite enough" summarised her life? Had she chosen, unawares, to absorb the unfulfilled passions of others, always extending emotion that would never be returned in equal measure? How cruel that was? What would happen to her – it did not bear thinking about. Strange that he had never thought in this fashion before.

Back and forth across the table went the tumultuous talk. No one seemed to notice his silence. That pleased him.

303

Chapter 22

The next evening Leo stayed on at the Cannon Street offices till it was time for the car to take him to Moorlock's club. He was considerably richer from the repercussions of the Israel war. Dealings had been hectic again, and all else had been forgotten. As the car neared St James's the tensions returned.

The dining room at Moorlock's club, its linenfold oak panelling surmounted by a line of enamelled shields, recalled the atmosphere of a dining club where Moorlock had belonged in Oxford. The white-haired steward might have been translated from it. He could even serve an especially strong brew not unlike Audit Ale. The place usually conjured elegiac moods, recalling a time of freedom before life got out of hand. This time they were disinclined to think of those days. They sat at their usual table in the long narrow room beside a broad sash window open to the airless evening, overlooking a walled garden. Moorlock gasped weightily for breath.

"I feel old today? The heat gets me sometimes." Brows lowered, he looked round at the room. "This place is fine when the young chaps are not around to remind you how things used to be with us – only just down, still too young to give a damn! Thank Heavens there are none of them here this evening." At the far end of the long room two heavily built men, perhaps the right side of fifty, talked quietly. The rest of the building was subdued too. He took a long pull from his initialled silver tankard and shook his heavy head. "Summer is a bad time. Those old days return to mock you. That's how I feel today. Or maybe your trip to Rome has affected me too? Come on, let's have it." He leaned his elbows on the table edge and waited.

Despite the thin cover of facetiousness, his tone was so sombre that Leo wanted to ask what was wrong. Instinct told him not to.

He began by admitting that he had taken Gideon with him to Rome, then wondered aloud why Moorlock showed no surprise.

The other laughed, a little grimly. "Odd hints you dropped in the last few months cast their shadows before. Many things were on your mind and that boy was one of them. Interesting, isn't it, how we can't throw off the bugbear of duty! However, it looks as though the trip has shifted you in spite of having him with you, or perhaps because of it?"

Moorlock looked at him with such affliction that Leo could not resist asking, "What's the matter? We'll talk about something else if you'd rather?"

Moorlock took another pull from the tankard, and did not meet his eye at once, "I ought to have foreseen that this trip of yours would bring a few things home to roost in me too. You and I have gone through many things, by separate routes it's true, but deep down, not very different. Besides, we share a difficulty of another kind, we can't speak freely with anyone else. Thank

God we understand each other! Sometimes life's ironies get too close for comfort, that's all. We can talk about me later if you like.'

The confession seemed to refresh him. The ruddy cheeks lifted a little. "Let's get back to you. Something tells me it wasn't a casual bit of the other that's stirred you up? An old flame perhaps? Ah yes, I see it in your face! All right then, let's have the whole story."

As Leo talked, Moorlock studied him with increasing concern, the dark eyes hooded. When he finished, Moorlock looked down the room, his jaw tightening, and when he turned to him again Leo could not quite believe the distress he saw. Moorlock pulled the dark blue silk handkerchief from his breast pocket and mopped his brow, which was indeed glistening with sweat, but dabbed his eyes too. He said, "It *is* a nuisance having a soul that won't leave you in peace. I know the feeling well – 'nuff said! This freak meeting has shaken you up and that's on the credit side, but it has brought so much guilt to the surface that you are ready to do almost anything to dispel it. I gather you don't intend it to be a long-running affair?"

Leo wanted to answer "No" without hesitation, but the madness of the last night in Rome returned and so did uncertainty – and he hedged. "I don't see it as an affair, but as an act of propitiation, paying off a debt. I want to do the decent thing. But it won't continue afterwards. It can't give me . . ." He had been about to say, "what I want," then saw that he did not know what he wanted, though he half-glimpsed it – to do something because his whole heart was in it, for the very first time. He looked down at his plate and toyed with his steak.

Moorlock was angry with himself. He ought not to resent Leo's assumption that certain choices were still open when they should have been put to rest long ago. Yet Leo was seeing them as still available – and half-persuading *him* to think so too, and that was bitter. And so he was sad for his friend, and for himself. He said softly, "You are not sure what you want – not yet. As for her, it's damned hard, now that you have wakened hope in her, but life won't be easier for her even if you give her what she *says* she wants. It seems an easy thing to do – and she might really mean that she won't make claims on you, but she won't be able to help herself! It won't stop there – believe me it never does. And if you think you have no peace of mind now, take it from me, the doors of hell will fly open and never close again. I know what I'm talking about."

Moorlock shaded his eyes as if the light was unbearably bright, though the declining sunlight coming in from the garden was diffused by overhanging foliage. He said, "This sort of thing happens oftener than you think, not often as premeditated as in her case, but even that is not uncommon." His next words came out with sudden passion, "Life makes no sense! I spend most of my time trying to make people see that, including . . ." He halted and looked down the room again, The two other diners, heads together in quiet conversation, did not appear to have noticed. Leo wondered whether Moorlock had been about to say "including myself".

Moorlock lowered his voice, "I suppose you loved her, really loved her?"

Leo chewed over the question. At last he said, "I suppose I did. But it wouldn't have worked. Jew and

307

non-Jew, the inescapable perspectives diverging! When you're young and idealistic you believe that love can make *anything* fit, though you've no idea what 'fit' means. Desire can sweep differences aside – or rather hide them for a time – we know that. But what happens after? In those days with her years ago, I must have seen that I couldn't answer that question. So I ran away. Any excuse would do. Which meant I didn't love her, or love her enough. Of course I'm guilty – I can't make any bones about that! I want to cancel *something* of the past – in different ways for her and for me. That's all I know."

Moorlock said gently, "This was her idea, wasn't it?"

Leo nodded, and was ashamed. He saw why Moorlock asked the question. Because *she* wanted a child, he felt free of responsibility, and that, and that alone, was why he had agreed.

Moorlock continued, "There are no fresh starts in life, only compromises piled one on top of the other. With each, in spite of what seems an immediate gain – love, pleasure, freedom from old guilt – we give up something of ourselves, till in the end we have nothing left, only emptiness. It happens all the time. Believe me, I know what it feels like."

Leo had not been prepared for the intensity of emotion in the other's words. In all their confidences over the years nothing had conveyed such anguish. Something had been hidden, and there must have been a painful reason for hiding it, which now strove to be heard. Moorlock wanted to save him from such suffering. Perversely he did not want to be saved.

Moorlock gathered himself together. "And afterwards? What then? There will be pressure to keep an affair going. Of course there will. And not least from the child – believe me, blood pulls at you! I ought to know." His face flushed a darker red and he pressed his lips tight.

Leo ignored the slip. "I have thought of that, but it's not *on*! And I think she knows it."

Moorlock persisted. "She seems to think differently. Tell me, has she talked of a life with you 'on the side'?"

"How could you know that? I couldn't take it seriously!"

Moorlock laughed without humour. "My dear chap – they all do! They really believe it can be done – or at least they say so, but secretly hope for a miracle to join you together completely. People try it all the time. But never with any success – that is, with any contentment! All it does is make the guilt worse. You think you have little peace of mind now? By God you will have none at all *then*!"

Their tankards were empty, and the attentive steward took them away to be charged again. Moorlock looked out of the window till the brimming tankards were once more before them. Each took a long pull of the heavy ale. Moorlock glanced down the room. The two middle-aged diners had gone. He leaned close. "I have been along that road. I'll fill you in about it another time. I was under similar pressure – sweet and loving pressure but all the more potent for that. Sentimental fool that I was I gave way. I have cursed that day ever since. Women know how

309

to play on our weaknesses. By God they do! And I am torn still. Shall I tell you what I think, bluntly?"

"Go on."

"Keeping it all going will tear you apart. You will be at peace nowhere. In desperation you will cut yourself off from both home and the 'side-life'. And then you will be totally alone. And I think part of you wants to be alone. Yes, loneliness *is* a kind of purity! The purity of death. Sorry! There is no other way of putting it."

They sat in silence. Leo wondered why he was not upset by Moorlock's verdict. Then he saw that he knew it already, and had lived with it a long time.

What an ironic contrast with his confident dealing on the world markets! Here he was, a man of the world in his middle years, floundering in the emotional tides like a youngster, having seen so much and learned so little. Rome had been all fancy. Once more he had been cruel. Not intentionally, but that was no excuse. Moorlock was right. One could not join blood to blood and simply walk away. There could be only one answer. He must break his promise to Chiara. How could he have blundered into this sentimental trap? He said, half to himself, looking out of the window at the still foliage, "I thought of it only from her point of view – or fancied I did – and I felt a kind of youthful pride, doing something noble at last. Just another delusion."

Suddenly there was too much to say. They raised their tankards in stoic sympathy and sat for some time in silence, gazing out at the sombre brilliance in the evening sky.

Without turning his head, Moorlock murmured, "Have you given any thought to the other prescription? A woman separate from the rest of your life, who needs a special relationship – with affection, but no burdensome demands – who drains the concupiscence from you, lifts away the chagrin of marriage, a good friend. And by the way, it's not for money. The one or two I have in mind need what I suggest for much the same reasons as you do – a discreet, warm relationship.'

Leo felt mists dropping away. He needed to say it out loud before he answered. "In Rome I met myself as I once was, and that was painful, and yet for a moment refreshing, feeling the old innocence again. And then Chiara appeared out of nowhere and offered the chance of redemption, one pure thing I could do. I owed it to myself to do it. Now even that crumb of certainty has gone."

He finished his steak and placed knife and fork side by side. The steward silently appeared and removed the plates. Moorlock ordered golden syrup pudding, a favourite in the Oxford days at Saturday lunch, when he consumed several helpings "for ballast" before the afternoon rugger game. For old times' sake Leo ordered it too. He said, "I wanted to make her life happier. From guilt, yes – shame for how I had behaved before. Of course it might not make her happier, who knows? but I can't do it."

"Are you sure?"

"I will take your other prescription, with love if I can

find it, try to upset nothing, and soldier on at home. That is as far as I can see ahead. Or as far as I want to see."

When the steward brought coffee, Leo, rather to his surprise, asked Moorlock, "How old is . . ." He could not say the words but Moorlock knew; and knew what had prompted the question. The promise to Chiara had not quite slipped away; and Leo wanted to imagine what his feelings would be if she had his child.

"He's ten," Moorlock said stonily. "But I never see him. I couldn't bear it." He put his hand over his eyes and murmured, "I'd hate to see you going through all that."

Saddened, for Moorlock, for them both, Leo said, "I'm sorry. Shall we stop? I'd no idea . . ."

"Not a bit of it!" Moorlock interrupted. "You had to know sooner or later I suppose. I am simply soldiering on." He suddenly grinned, lifting his heavy shoulders, and took another pull of the ale. "So don't let this revelation get you down. I just want you to watch your step."

A tension had gone. He said, "Anyhow, you were going to say something else? I want to hear it. But listen – don't hold anything back because of – well, because of *my* sensibilities! Say what you want to."

"All right." Leo had been about to say, "I don't want to believe everything's too late," but suppressed it. He said, "You are right about being alone, there *is* a kind of purity in it, but it's the wrong kind. My father in his uncompromising way achieved purity of a sort but at a terrible price, to himself and those

312

around him. Perhaps, unawares, I have wanted to follow him. But I won't. I know I won't. So what's left?"

It seemed to Moorlock that Leo was emerging with eyes dazzled from a long dark journey, and he was glad. He said, "What are you going to do?"

"Rome was a mirage. I have behaved atrociously to her again, but I cannot do it."

"There was no redemption to be found there, for you at any rate."

Leo said, "Why do we make other people victims?"

Moorlock nodded agreement. After a silence he said, "There's always *something* left – pleasure! As long as you don't hope for anything more from it, you can play that game out to the end."

Leo tried to smile at this echo from the wild past. He glanced up at the shields on the wall and saw his own college crest, and heard Domville's precise, resonant voice. "Desire or lust? The name hardly matters – but this is sure, *neither* has any lasting power." How far had he travelled since that day? Not far – hardly at all.

Moorlock spoke in a distant, contemplative voice, "When I talked about the 'other prescription' I didn't mean the 'side-life' she mentioned in Rome – but a relationship with no claims and no commitment. You destroy nothing, keep the marriage going, your outward life unchanged. But I am afraid for you, because you insist on hoping for the complete answer – which, even if it ever *was* possible, isn't any more. If we think we can behave like young heroes again,

313

chasing miracles, there's only one possible result – disaster. I don't want that to happen to you. This prescription will give you a hermetic equilibrium, a wonderful release from tension, an unexpected freedom – provided you act decently and sensibly. But don't hope for a miracle."

"That sounds wonderful to be going on with. So I agree. The fact is I need to feel emotion again – and seeing Chiara made me think it was possible after all. How strange at our age to be talking of miracles! But, you know something, if a miracle does come, I don't want to hurt Miriam. That's a desperate contradiction I know, but it's how I feel."

Moorlock wanted to say, "You are asking the impossible. In any case the miracle is never real! It's only a miracle because you want to *think* it is." He decided not to. Leo's instinct to keep the marriage intact might protect him from losing his head completely.

Leo felt a burden lift. "I came a long way in talking to Gideon in Rome. Trying to explain what love was, for instance, I realised I was asking myself for the purpose of living – the things that love should nourish if it really was love. The test, which I don't think I succeeded in explaining, was whether the woman speaks to your condition as the mystics say – hears the cry in your heart and answers it. Why did I not recognise that truth before? I didn't want to admit that all the fury and wildness of the old days had been a waste of time and hope. Now I *can* admit it – whenever I found a woman who spoke to my condition I ran for my life, as I ran from Chiara.

Why? I was afraid to face a searching attachment until I knew who I myself was! And now? Do I know now – really know? Yes, but not completely – but at least I *want* to know at last, even though it's late in the day. Is it too late? I suspect it is. I probably don't deserve to find what I want. You see the guilt is still there! Anyway I'm going to go on hoping – I've *got* to."

Moorlock shook his head in wonder, asking himself how this clarity of vision had suddenly been released, the harshness too – Leo's verdict was more severe because it was his own. Much of it applied to himself too, but that had to be digested, painful as it was, in this moment of extreme candour they might never venture upon again.

Leo went on, "How am I going to do it? There's your prescription, for a start – a possibility, who knows, of finding that answering voice, but in any case some peace of mind away from everything, a hermetic equilibrium as you put it. For the rest I shall go on hoping – there is nothing else."

There was something Moorlock felt he must say, though it went against the grain. He looked out at the darkened garden now stirring with a slight breeze, and turned back and said carefully, "You know, I'd hate to see you stumble into the classic syndrome of the mid-life man and the young woman, a fine explosive mixture of desire and dreams, which often ends savagely. But if it did by a miracle go well – whatever 'well' means – what will you do? Smash up everything, tear your life in shreds? I'm putting it in the worst light deliberately."

Leo smiled with great patience. He had thought of this one too. "I am not looking for young thighs and the flattery of young blood. I can have that any time I want – with money it's easy, as you know. Of course I am in one hell of a jam – a colourless marriage, an emptiness of the spirit, perplexity about being a Jew, and no clear road through any of it. These last months – I suppose since Gideon's Barmitzvah come to think of it – I have been searching for a man I did not know well, or at all – myself! I have found him, puzzled still, with a little less guilt than before, but with an empty heart! How can I let him continue in that state? Yet in spite of everything I have a strong sense of loyalty to Miriam, to Gideon, to Judith. Perhaps that says it all? If the miracle happened, I would be in terrible torment – I can see that already. But time is against me. Time might put paid to hope, I know that too, But I am going to go on hoping as long as I can."

Moorlock studied him now with his physician's eye. Leo looked in better condition than when he had last seen him. The signs of stress were receding. Leo was taking possession of himself. Moorlock was comforted. He had feared Leo might go under. Now it was unlikely. Would he have a better life from now on? That was a different matter. The odds were against it. That was par for the course. He felt a surge of envy and was ashamed. He envied Leo his determination, so late in the day, to revive hope. It wasn't fair! But that was par for the course too.